Billionaire's Sons

Julie L. Spencer

Spencer Publishing, LLC

Click or scan here to request a complimentary book when you join my newsletter.

ISBN: 978-1-954666-07-8

www.AuthorJulieSpencer.com

Contents

Note to Readers:

The entire Royal Family Saga is written in the Contemporary genre. That means they all have cell phones and private jets and superyachts. Even though the saga spans multiple generations, each story is designed to take place in modern day. None of the stories are historical fiction or futuristic. For any similarities to historical events, I have taken extreme artistic liberty. Send me an email when you figure it out! -Julie

Another Note to Readers:

Falling in love is the greatest feeling in the world. That's why I write romance and love stories. The day I met my husband I looked across the room at him and knew I was going to marry him. I didn't know his name (it's Clayton), I didn't know how old he was (nine months older than me), or if he was dating anyone (he was). All I knew was I was going to marry him. Almost twenty-five years later we're still on our honeymoon. Because that is my experience with falling in love, my characters tend to fall in love just as quickly. Love grows over time, but sometimes you look at someone and just *know* they are your person. You can call it Instalove, Love-at-First Sight, whatever you want. I pray that everyone in the world experiences the kind of love I feel every time I look into the eyes of my eternal companion.
God bless you, my friends. Stay safe! -Julie

Part One: Following the Billionaire

Nicholas Cohen

As told by Nicholas Cohen, son of Levi and Sarah Cohen, at the time when King Sayid was in his forty-second year as the story begins...

Chapter One

Skydiving

"Y ou're seriously going skydiving?" Nick asked.

"Yes, and *you* are coming with us, little brother." Liam laid his hand on Nick's shoulder, with a smirk. At six foot one and twenty-two years old, Nick was hardly little. But his older brothers were similar in height and bossed him around as if they were still in their teens.

"Have you forgotten that we all have jobs? We have responsibilities. We can't just take off a whole day to do something reckless and dangerous."

"When your daddy is your boss, you can get away with just about anything," Liam said. His job was more public relations anyway. Liam was little more than a figurehead at their father's business. The oldest son in the Cohen Empire, he was the guy who attended the black-tie social events, writing checks to whatever charitable organizations their father, Levi, believed in that month.

They were the richest family in the greater Jerusalem area, controlled a dozen of the finest resort hotels in Israel—holdings in every natural resource in the Arab region—and owned more land than God. Everyone either loved the Cohens or hated them, depending on whether their father had bought out their company at a fair price or held out as his toughest competition.

Nothing seemed to faze Levi Cohen. He expected great things from his sons but left them on too long a leash. Nick's older brothers often took advantage of their father's generosity and trust.

"Besides, you're not going to rat us out, are you?" Lyle, the second oldest brother, stepped just a bit closer, almost towering over him. The effect was mildly threatening, but Nick held his chin high. Always in their oldest brother's shadow, Lyle wasn't good for much in the way of business and usually just schmoozed the daughters and wives of whatever dignitary Liam needed distracted.

"There's nothing you can do to talk us out of it," Sam said. As the third oldest brother, he usually sided with Liam and Lyle. More responsible than the other two, he was actually quite intelligent with regards to their natural resource holdings, like petroleum and potash.

"I could encourage Father to disown you and cut you out of his will," Nick replied. They all started laughing at his matter-of-fact statement, which was an empty threat. Nick had very little control over what their father did, even though increasing responsibility seemed to fall on his shoulders as far as the acquisitions side of the business.

Nick was usually the responsible son. Why he was letting his brothers talk him into this was beyond him. Skydiving. The thought sent a little thrill up his spine. This was so unlike him.

The speed Liam drove down Route 6 was almost as dangerous as jumping out of the plane. He thought he was invincible and lived his life as such. They weaved in and out of traffic in Liam's custom-built Mercedes G63.

In this beast, Nick didn't fear for his own life, more for the innocent drivers all around them. He ground his teeth and clung to the grab handle as his brothers whooped out the open windows.

Liam slammed on the brakes and cranked the wheel before they could fly past SkyDef and slid into his own self-proclaimed parking spot in a cloud of dust.

Nick wanted to kiss the ground after he stumbled from the backseat but then realized the air around the vehicle was so full of sand he needn't bother. He reached back inside for his water bottle and rinsed his mouth, spitting into the dirt beside the car.

"Liam, I'm pretty sure this is not an actual parking lot," Nick said.

"I tip well," Liam said. "They won't care. Here, keep track of these." He tossed Nick the keys to the car.

"Gladly." Nick caught the little key fob and tucked it into his pocket. Maybe Liam would let him drive home. He watched as Liam slipped a silver flask from his jacket pocket and took a long pull and then handed it to Lyle. Nick grumbled under his breath. "Yep, I'm definitely driving home."

"Let's do this!" Lyle called into the air and then took another swig and blew a misty fountain of Bourbon that rained down, drenching them in alcohol.

"Cut it out," Sam said, brushing off his arms and face. He'd gotten the brunt of mist because he stood beside Lyle. "They're not gonna let us get on that plane if we reek of alcohol."

"I told you, little brother"—Liam leaned closer to Sam—"I tip well. They let me do pretty much anything I want."

The owner of SkyDef, a guy not much older than Liam, met them in the makeshift parking lot and welcomed them.

"Aharon, my man." Liam clasped the guy's hand and gave him a half hug, patting him on the back.

"You finally made it down to my fine establishment," Aharon said.

"I promised I would take my little brothers skydiving." Liam wrapped his arm around his friend's shoulder and turned him to face them. "This is Lyle, Sam, and Nick."

"I thought you had four brothers." Aharon crinkled his brow.

"Jacob's only seventeen, we'll bring him in a few years, if we still live around here."

Huh? What did he mean by that?

"Planning a move anytime soon?" Aharon asked.

"Oh, ya know, nothing set in stone or anything."

"What's he talking about?" Nick asked Sam.

"No idea, bro," Sam said.

"Lyle, do you know?" Nick pulled on his brother's sleeve.

"Not really." Lyle shrugged. "Dad's talking about some industry down in Dubai that he's trying to take over."

"Take over?" Nick raised his eyebrows. "You mean swoop in when the guy is at rock bottom and about to file bankruptcy so dad can buy the business below market?"

"Is there any other way to do business, little brother?" Lyle smirked and patted Nick on the shoulder. "Relax, Dad knows what he's doing."

Nick stopped short, and his two oldest brothers kept walking. "Yeah, but I usually know what Dad's doing also."

Sam paused and turned around. "I'm sure he'll tell you about it when he's ready."

"This makes me nervous." Nick resumed walking toward the building.

"What makes you nervous?" Sam asked, falling into step. "Skydiving? Or Dad not keeping you in the loop?"

"Both," Nick admitted.

"Relax," Sam said. "Dad's a visionary man. He always seems to know where the market is heading."

"True." Nick paused to open the door to the comfortably air-conditioned building. "He knows I'll go where he wants me to go and do what he wants me to do."

"Your blind faith is noble, my little brother," Sam said. "Now, let's strap you onto a tandem instructor and hurl you out of a moving airplane and see if you come out unscathed."

"Who in their right mind wants to jump out of a perfectly good airplane?" Nick grumbled.

"Let's go find out." Sam hurried ahead to join their brothers.

"What have I gotten myself into?"

Chapter Two

Can I Get Your Number?

"I can't believe I let them talk me into that," Nick mumbled to himself while he sat on the raised bed in the partitioned emergency room. Blood dripped from the gash on his left arm as he waited to find out if he'd need stitches or an amputation. He chuckled at his own joke and waited for someone to come check on his arm.

"Well, look who dropped by to mingle with us commoners." A beautiful, freckled nurse with long, strawberry blonde curls walked up, with a clipboard in her hands and a barely contained smirk on her lips.

"Adele?" Nick gaped. "What are you doing here?"

"I'll be your nurse this afternoon." She chuckled and then leaned closer and stage-whispered, "I get to be the one to torture you."

"You've been torturing me since we were in diapers." Nick cringed as she lifted his arm to assess the damage.

"Does that hurt?"

"Do you seriously have to ask?" Nick raised his eyebrows.

"Let's get you a shot of painkiller and get that wound cleared of gravel," Adele said in a cheerful voice.

After multiple pokes and prods and blood draws and papers to be signed, they were finally alone again, with a basin of some sort of foul-smelling liquid antiseptic and a variety of tools designed to frighten patients.

"So... whatchu been up to, Nick?" Adele asked as she more closely evaluated the gash he'd received while landing with his tandem instructor.

The last time Nick had seen Adele in person was when they graduated from prep school—number one and number two in their class—sitting side by side, always competing for the top spot. He still resented her giving that valedictorian speech even though his college entrance exams had only been five points lower than hers.

"I went skydiving. You?"

"I got accepted in the master's program here at Hadassah University Hospital."

"Wow, in what?"

"Nurse practitioner." She included an underlying duh with her declaration.

"Congratulations," Nick said, in awe of her accomplishments.

"What about you?" She dipped his whole elbow and wrist into the basin of foul smelling liquid. The shot of painkiller they'd injected into him was finally working. He barely felt a thing.

"Still helping run my dad's companies," Nick answered.

"You a billionaire yet?"

"Not yet, but I'm working on it." He was vaguely aware of her picking little pieces of gravel from his arm.

"You'll get there."

"I'm glad you have faith in me." Did his voice get husky? How embarrassing.

"How are your mom and dad?" she asked, pausing her work.

"Fine, I guess. I see my dad more than my mom, since we work together."

"You need to spend more time with your mother, Nick." She looked sternly into his eyes.

"How about if you come with me," he asked.

"If I did that, she'd get the wrong idea and think we'd gotten back together." Her voice was lowered, and she resumed picking gravel out of his arm.

"Would that be such a bad thing?" Nick boldly raised his free hand and lifted her chin gently.

"You don't even know me anymore," Adele said, not distracted by his gesture. "How do you know I'm not dating someone else?"

"Are you?" Nick asked. She didn't answer, just kept her tweezers moving. "That's what I thought."

"I follow your blog." Interesting change of subject.

"You do?" He couldn't hide his smile.

"You have interesting philosophical insights into the world."

"Thank you," he said. "I'm flattered."

"You should quit working for your dad and be a writer," she said.

"I was thinking about writing a novel, actually."

"Really?" Adele's smile lit her face.

"Ah, dang, you keep smiling at me like that and I'm for sure going to write a novel."

"You know how much I love your stories." She set down the tweezers and reached for some other torture instrument. He decided not to watch. "Which one are you going to write first? The dystopian one? Or the spiritual one?"

"Probably dystopian," he said. Was he really considering his youthful dreams? This was crazy. He runs into his childhood sweetheart and he's suddenly contemplating a career change? "Spiritual crap doesn't sell all that well."

"You'd be surprised." She finished by taping some gauze in place with sterile strips. "Do you promise to keep that clean and dry?"

"If you'll promise to come check on me in a day or two, like, say, at dinnertime tomorrow." Nick raised his eyebrows.

"I don't date my patients." The gleam in her eyes told him he wasn't her usual patient. He'd held her in his arms on the dance floor under twinkling lights in the gymnasium. He'd been her first kiss, and she'd been his only kiss.

"Do you ever wonder what might have happened if we'd stayed together?"

"We've moved on, Nick." Adele stepped over to the nearby counter and jotted something on the paperwork there. "The nursing assistant will bring you some discharge papers. Here are some additional instructions."

As she handed Nick the sheet of paper she'd removed from her clipboard, she finally looked him in the eye.

"It was really nice to see you again, Nick." She quickly walked away. He looked down at the slip of paper.

Clean and wrap your arm daily, no more skydiving, and call me if you need anything. She'd included her personal cell phone number.

Chapter Three

Peacock

"We're coming, and you're going to insist she bring her older sisters." Liam's statement was so matter-of-fact Nick couldn't help but chuckle.

"You probably don't even remember their names." Nick cautiously climbed into the backseat, trying not to jostle his arm too much.

"Miriam," Lyle said.

"Leanne," Sam added.

"I don't remember what the older girl's name is, but the one who's my age is Rachel, and she's smokin' hot, so you're inviting her." Liam shifted the SUV into reverse and backed out of the relatively normal parking spot he'd chosen in the hospital parking lot.

"They're probably all married by now," Nick said.

"No way. We would have received invitations. Our dads have been best friends since before any of us were born," Liam said.

"Besides, you owe us for having to sit in that horrible waiting room for an hour while you were flirting with Adele," Lyle added.

"Whose idea was it to go skydiving again?" Nick sighed and rested his head against the window and closed his eyes.

"It was your idea, Nick. Don't you remember?" Liam asked.

"No, definitely not my idea." Why could he be so confident and mature in front of Adele and then let his brothers walk all over him. He'd have to think about that. For now, he had a date to plan. And a throbbing arm. He moaned. He wasn't sure if the words he murmured were loud enough for anyone to hear. "How about a pool party? Would it be too forward to invite them out to the estate?"

"See, you do come up with good ideas." Lyle reached behind and smacked Nick on his leg.

They were quiet for most of the ride home, and his brothers scattered to their various suites when they got into the compound.

Nick trudged up the grand staircase toward his suite, wishing he'd taken the elevator, when the weight of the day's events hit him. Barreling through the open sky strapped to an instructor, crashing to the ground and having his arm torn up, and then being tortured by the most beautiful nurse in the greater Jerusalem area.

After he kicked off his shoes and slid into the middle of his king-sized bed, Nick pulled out his phone and sent Adele a quick text.

Meds wore off. What did you do to me? I'm dizzy and throbbing in pain.

Her text came back right away. *Sorry about that. It was just a few stitches.*

Stitches?? He looked down at his arm that was still wrapped in gauze. *When did you give me stitches?*

While you were bragging about how you'd soon be a billionaire and best-selling novelist. It's amazing what a girl can get away with when she's distracting a hot guy by making him feel like a peacock.

My brothers want you and your sisters to come over for a pool party this weekend...

You're not supposed to be getting your arm wet.

I'll sit on a lounge chair and watch the rest of you play in the pool.

I'd rather sit with you if that's okay, her text read.

I would love that. Would he ever.

Then it's a date.

My arm hurts, he typed. *Can you come nurse me back to health?*

Goodnight, Nick.

Goodnight, Adele.

Chapter Four

What's in Dubai?

"**C**ome to Dubai with me, son!" Levi swept into Nick's office, with an air of excitement. Nick couldn't help laughing and smiling along with his dad.

"Good morning to you as well, Father," Nick said, sauntering around the side of his desk to give his dad a hug. Then he gestured to one of the executive leather chairs placed in front of his desk, where he could sit across from a guest or business partner and offer them a brandy or cup of coffee.

At only twenty-two years of age and having seen his older brothers make fools of themselves while drinking, Nick had no use for liquor. He knew his father never drank alcohol either, and he certainly didn't need any caffeine this morning.

"What is all this talk about going to Dubai?" Nick asked, lowering himself into the chair beside his father. He purposely leaned forward so that his head and gaze were lower than his dad's. He was sure his father wouldn't understand the gesture but might feel just a little more in control of the situation than he would feel otherwise if Nick were even in height. "What's in Dubai?"

"Possibility," Levi drawled.

"Whose failing business are you snatching up for pennies on the dollar?"

"Natan Netanel." He spoke low, as if saying the name loud would enable someone else to swoop in and purchase the property before they had the chance.

"Aw man, Dad." Nick sat back and crossed his leg. "I know Nathan, he's a great guy." He also knew that Nathan preferred the more westernized version of his given name.

"But a terrible businessman," Levi said. "His yacht manufacturing company is failing."

"You're a real estate developer. What on earth are you going to do with a yacht manufacturing company?"

"I plan to put *your* design skills to good use, my son." Levi patted Nick on the knee.

"M-my design skills?" Nick pulled back from his father. "I've never built a ship."

"You don't need to know how to build a ship. You just need to have an eye for detail. And *you* have that. You can work together with Natan and pull his company out of bankruptcy. All he needs is a mentor."

"Dad, he's like, ten years older than me," Nick said. "And he prefers to be called Nathan."

"Perfect," Levi said. "You're already on a first-name basis."

Nick sighed. "I'm not going to be able to talk you out of this, am I?"

"Not likely." Levi stood and patted Nick on the shoulder. "Wheels up in an hour. I have Gregory preparing our private jet as we speak."

"Wait, you want to leave today?" Nick sprang to his feet. "I have a date tomorrow afternoon."

"We should be home by then." Levi shrugged. "If all goes well."

"Fine, have Pierre pack me an overnight bag. I know how you get when you attend these mergers and acquisitions meetings."

"Glad to have you on board, son. You'll be just what we need to soften up this Nathan kid."

"He's hardly a kid," Nick grumbled.

"When you get to be as old as me, you'll understand." Levi headed toward the door but turned back around as if just remembering one more thing he needed to tell his son. "Oh, and your mother's pregnant again."

"What?" Nick's jaw dropped. "She's, what? Forty-five years old?"

"Forty-six, actually," Levi said, then stepped back to pat Nick on the shoulder. "You forget we married very young. Your old man's still got it."

"Oh my gosh, Dad, that's gross."

"Nah, being as old as you are and not married yet, *that's* gross."

"I'm twenty-two!"

"Exactly," Levi said, opening the door to Nick's office. "Get on it, son."

"Hard to accomplish when my date is in Jerusalem and I am in Dubai," Nick grumbled.

"You'll work it out," Levi called from down the hall. "I have faith in you, my son."

"Glad one of us does," Nick said under his breath. He pulled out his cell phone and sent a quick text to Adele.

Might be a little late for our pool party tomorrow afternoon. I'm flying to Dubai.

Chapter Five

Pool Party

"**I** see you started partying without me," Nick said, setting down his overnight bag just inside the sliding glass door and sauntering over to the patio. Adele's sisters were in or near the pool with Nick's brothers. Adele and her oldest sister, Ruth, were lying facedown on lounge chairs, wearing skimpy bikini swimsuits.

Nick did a double take and quickly averted his eyes. Ruth's bikini top was untied, presumably to avoid tan lines. She was at least thirty by now, not exactly a temptation for a twenty-two-year-old guy, but still. Awkward.

Thankfully, Adele was mostly covered when she raised her head and glanced at him through her dark sunglasses. "Hey there, handsome."

He pulled up a lounge chair and kicked off his dress shoes. Before leaning back to be closer to Adele, Nick pulled his socks off and rolled up his slacks.

"Feeling better?" Adele asked in a playful tone.

"Not exactly," Nick admitted. "I may have to go change."

"How was your flight?" Adele asked.

"Not long enough for the nap I need."

"Wow, you're in a great mood this afternoon." Adele sat up and swung her legs over the side of her lounge chair to face him.

"Oh... my... gosh." Nick turned completely away from Adele, overwhelmed by the lack of fabric covering the woman who had replaced the girl he once loved.

"What's the matter?" She reached her hand out and touched his arm. "Are you okay?"

"Nope." He kept his eyes squeezed shut and shook his head. "Not even a little bit."

"Did something go wrong with your business deal in Dubai?" Her voice was laced with concern.

"Dubai was fine. We destroyed my friend's life with the stroke of a pen."

"Destroyed? How?"

"Babe, I'm gonna need you to put on a cover-up or sweatshirt or something in order for me to concentrate."

"You're such a prude, Nick." Adele chuckled but rummaged through her bag. He sensed rather than saw her wrap a chemise around her shoulders. "Better?"

He peeked open one eye and breathed a sigh of relief to see her fully covered. "Much better."

"Now, what were we talking about?" Adele asked. "Something happened in Dubai?"

"We're just a little bit wealthier than we were yesterday, that's all."

"Oh, is that all?" She leaned her head back and laughed playfully.

"Will you marry me?" Nick asked.

"What?"

"My dad wants me to get married, and you're the only girl I've ever loved, so I figured, why not you?"

"Why not me?" Adele's jaw dropped, and she lowered her sunglasses. "You run into me out of the blue after not calling me for four years and suddenly think we should get married?"

"It's only logical," Nick said.

"Logical? You think marriage is logical? Is this just because you saw me in a swimsuit?"

"I've seen you in a swimsuit," he said. "Not quite as filled out as you are now."

"How dare you!" Adele stood suddenly. All conversation stopped around them. "Four years, Nick. You haven't spoken to me in four years!"

"You're the one who ran off to college, not me." Nick rose to meet her heated gaze. "The phone works both ways, darling."

"You're still jealous that I got to go to college, aren't you?" She balled her hands into fists.

"Why would I be jealous? You were crammed into a dormitory the size of my walk-in closet while I flew around the world in my private jet, getting real-world experience that can't be duplicated in your ivory towers."

"You pompous, self-righteous jerk!" Adele pushed him backward, and he waved his arms in a circle to right himself. "This is about my graduation speech still, isn't it?"

"I don't know what you're talking about," Nick lied.

Adele laughed heartily. "You're jealous that my college entrance exams were higher—"

"Barely," he coughed into his hand.

"—and I got to give the graduation commencement address."

"Five points, Adele. Five. That's it. Yours were five points higher than mine."

"And you couldn't have just been proud of me?" She pushed him again.

"I was proud of you." Nick scrambled to maintain balance. "I'm still proud of you."

"Proud?" She stepped closer.

"Yes." He relaxed his shoulders,

"And jealous?" she asked.

"That's right."

"You're an idiot, Nick." With one little nudge, Adele pushed Nick backward into the pool.

Chapter Six

Pity Party

Nick sat on the balcony overlooking the pool party, which had shifted gradually into his brothers and Adele's sisters getting plastered drunk together. Most of them anyway.

While Nick excused himself to remove his soaked business suit, Ruth had driven Adele home, leaving Rachel, Miriam, and Leanne with Liam, Lyle, and Sam.

Hmm... well, Lyle and Miriam seemed to be missing, Liam and Rachel were making out on one of the lounge chairs, and Leanne was drinking a wine cooler way too fast and laughing at everything Sam said.

Nick didn't want to watch anymore. He stepped through the sliding glass door and flopped onto the leather sofa in his spacious office. There was nothing he wanted to work on, nothing he wanted to watch on television, no business or political websites he wanted to peruse.

He missed Adele immensely. This had been his one chance to reunite with her, and he'd blown it. How could he miss someone he hadn't seen in four years anyway?

Maybe he'd been so excited to see her this morning that the letdown of having her leave so suddenly was a jolt to his system.

She'd seen right through him, seen his jealousy and root of his anger. He was the jerk in the equation. What was he thinking, asking her to marry him? As if she'd ever agree to that. What an idiot he was.

"We need a designated driver, little brother," Liam said, barging into Nick's office.

"Where are you going?" Nick mumbled without looking at his brother.

"We," Liam corrected. "We are going underground, and we need *you* to drive."

"Pergamon?"

"Rachel wants good vegetarian food." Liam turned to Rachel. "Right?"

"Pergamon's the best place in town for vegetarian food," Rachel said.

"You heard the lady," Liam said. "Pergamon it is."

Sam stood beside Liam, holding Leanne in a standing position, barely. They all seemed to be holding in laughter.

"Where are Lyle and Miriam?" Nick wanted to refuse Liam's demand but didn't want any of his brothers driving themselves in their condition, so he hoisted himself off the sofa and reached for his wallet, which was still soaking wet from taking a dip in the pool.

"My keys are... somewhere." Liam reached for Rachel's hand and headed down the hall to the grand staircase, laughing at some private joke. They didn't even look back to see if everyone else was following them.

Sam helped Leanne stumble down the hallway, where she sat on the top step and leaned against the railing.

"Don't you have an elevator somewhere in this mansion?" Leanne slurred.

"Somewhere, I think," Sam said. "Come downstairs, and I'll show you our library."

"I like libraries." Leanne allowed Sam to help her to a somewhat standing position.

Nick didn't wait to see if she got down the stairs safely. He traipsed over to Liam's immaculate bedroom suite and reached above the vanity in his bathroom where he knew the housekeepers kept a spare key to Liam's Mercedes. On nights like this, his key could be anywhere on the grounds of the estate.

As he passed by Lyle's suite, he heard voices inside the closed door. Typical that Lyle had a woman in his suite. Frustrated that the woman was Adele's sister, Nick rapped his knuckles on the mahogany and called through the door. "Let's go, guys. We're heading downtown to Pergamon."

"Excellent," Lyle said as he opened the door. He tucked in his shirt with one hand and slipped his wallet into his designer jeans with the other. "I'm starving."

"Me too," Miriam called from where she sat on the settee, buckling a pair of strappy heels. Nick had to turn away to avoid seeing up her short skirt.

"What is it with Daniel's daughters not wearing enough clothing," Nick mumbled as he turned away.

"It's a beautiful thing, little brother," Lyle whispered as he draped his arm around Nick's shoulders. "Embrace the beauty of a woman's body."

"The perfume you're wearing tells me you've embraced a little too much of a woman's body this evening." Nick ducked out from under his brother's arm. "Let's go. Everyone else is in the car already."

"Sorry we kept you waiting." Miriam giggled as she snuck out the door to Lyle's suite.

"Not sorry," Lyle said, then pressed her up against the wall and captured her mouth in a passionate kiss.

"Gross," Nick mumbled, quickly excusing himself. "I'll meet you downstairs."

Chapter Seven

Shut Up and Drive

"I think I'm gonna be sick," Leanne groaned from the middle seat of the luxury SUV. Nick slammed on the brakes so she could let herself out of the car.

Sam climbed down from the passenger seat to help her. Liam and Rachel barely paused making out, and Nick didn't even want to think about what Lyle and Miriam were doing in the third-row seat.

Getting roped into being the designated driver made Nick wish he'd taken just a sip of something that involved alcohol so they'd have an excuse to pay a driver to get them downtown and back.

There was always the likelihood that his brothers would ignore the need for a driver and get behind the wheel themselves. That alone was motivation to maintain his sobriety in hopes of keeping his brothers out of jail, or worse. Not that their dad didn't have enough money to bail them out of whatever scrape necessary. Still, better to avoid the need.

"Can we take a detour and drop Leanne off at home?" Sam poked his head in the open window of the car.

"Uh... yeah. I think that was decided about the time she puked on the side of the road," Nick said.

"I'm feeling a little better now," Leanne said, taking a water bottle and swishing out her mouth.

"Too bad," Nick grumbled. "I'm taking you home."

Nick pulled out his cell phone and composed a text to Adele. *Your sisters are drunk. I'm bringing them home.*

You let my sisters get drunk?!? Adele's text came back almost immediately.

I was upstairs nursing a broken heart. You're the one who left them here.

Whatever. Just bring them home, and I'll deal with it. I'm better at nursing drunk people than nursing broken hearts.

Both scenarios are unfortunate. I'll see you in a few minutes.

Whatever.

Nick tucked his phone into his jacket pocket and waited while Sam and Leanne got situated. He handed her a trash can just in case.

Daniel's estate was only ten minutes farther and none too soon. Leanne threw up again as soon as she stumbled away from the vehicle.

Liam and Rachel helped Leanne up to the house and handed her off to Adele.

"Why are we stopping again?" Miriam asked from the backseat, her voice slurred and sleepy.

"We're home," Nick said. "Time to come up for air."

"When will I see you again?" Miriam whispered to Lyle.

"Dunno," Lyle said. "I'll call you."

"What a load of crap," Nick mumbled low enough so they wouldn't hear from the backseat. Never had Lyle called a woman. It would be against his modus operandi.

Nick kept his eyes trained away from the rearview mirror to avoid seeing any body parts as clothing was returned to the proper positions.

Miriam gave Lyle one last, lingering kiss before slipping out of the backseat. Lyle pulled himself over the seatback into the middle seat just as Liam returned to the car.

Liam opened the passenger door and demanded that Sam let him have the front. Sam reluctantly moved to the middle seat to sit next to Lyle.

"All right," Liam said with a grin. "Let's get downtown."

"We're still going to Pergamon?" Nick asked as he shifted into drive. "I thought we were only going there because Rachel wanted vegetarian food."

"They also have the best beer selection," Liam said.

"I am not interested in drinking beer."

"You're the designated driver, so it doesn't matter what you want." Liam punched Nick's arm. "Now drive."

Chapter Eight

Landon

They walked toward the door of the nightclub.

"Well, if it isn't Jerusalem's royal family," a booming voice slurred from the shadows near where they parked the SUV. No one was around to hear their arch nemesis hurl the mocking salutation. "Whatchu doin' slummin' it with us common folk?"

"Greetings to you as well, Landon," Liam said, sauntering toward him. "How's the upgrade to your resort?"

"You mean yer daddy's resort?" Landon stepped right up to Liam, toe to toe.

"He bought you out fair and square," Liam said, not flinching.

"For pennies." Landon spit the words at Liam, who wiped his face with his sleeve.

"He saved you from financial ruin, and you know it," Liam said. "How about I buy you a conciliatory drink?" Liam reached out to drape his arm around Landon's shoulder, but Landon sucker punched Liam in the ribs.

While Liam doubled over in pain, Lyle caught Landon's jaw with a right hook.

Nick watched from a distance as Landon returned Lyle's punch before shoving Sam out of the way. Nick was determined not to get involved.

"I'm tired of you spoiled kids getting whatever you want," Landon growled.

"We're hardly kids," Sam said.

"Dude, what's going on?" Zach, Landon's friend and business partner stepped over to the group, with two beers in his hands. "Well... if it isn't the golden boys."

"We are *not* boys," Sam insisted again. "We're grown men."

"Shut up, kid," Landon said. "You don't know nothin' about bein' a grown man. Grown men don't let their daddy take care of them."

"He took care of *you*," Liam said, still holding his side.

"I'll show you who takes care of me," Landon grabbed Liam from behind and wrapped his arm around his neck. Suddenly everyone was involved. Zach tried to reason with Landon. Sam clawed at Landon's arms, trying to free Liam. Lyle punched Landon, to get him to let go, and Liam gagged and choked as he worked at freeing himself.

Nick didn't think. He grabbed one of the beer bottles from Zach's hand and broke the bottle over Landon's head. He dropped to the pavement, releasing Liam, who gasped for air and stepped away. Everyone gathered around Landon, who wasn't moving.

"Nick, what did you do?" Zach asked.

"I had to do something." Nick took a step back and grasped his hands into his thick hair, pulling in frustration. "He was trying to kill my brother!"

"Well, I think *you* killed him."

"I doubt it," Sam said, poking Landon with the toe of his loafer. "He's probably just knocked out."

Zach crouched beside his business partner, held up his wrist, and then shook his head. "He's got no pulse."

"Are you sure you're doin' it right?" Sam said, pushing Zach out of the way. Sam poked around at the large man. "He's not breathin'."

"We've got to get out of here." Lyle looked around frantically, his inebriated state exasperating his panic.

"No one saw what happened," Liam said, still breathing heavy. "There's no way anyone could pin this on one of us."

"All anyone else knows is that there's a man on the ground and five of his friends are standing over him," Sam said.

"None of us are his friends," Nick said, shuddering at the thought. Then he looked up at Zach. "Except you."

"I'd hardly call him my friend." Zach snorted. "More like partners in crime, I mean, business."

"You have to come with us," Liam insisted. "At least until we learn whether or not anyone saw what happened."

"Shouldn't we be calling an ambulance?" Zach asked, his words slurring almost as much as Nick's brothers'.

"Someone else can call an ambulance," Lyle said. "We gotta get out of here."

"I feel bad just leaving him here," Sam said. "Does he have any family?"

"Nope," Zach said. "As his business partner, I'm pretty much all he's got."

All four brothers stared at Zach, and Nick gulped.

"That's motive..." Liam let his statement hang in the air.

"I didn't kill him!" Zach cried and then pointed. "Nick did!"

"I didn't kill him. It was an accident." Nick was shaking.

"It's your word against ours," Liam said.

"And there are four of us." Lyle raised his eyebrows.

Liam repeated his earlier statement. "You have to come with us."

"Maybe Father can give us some advice on what to do," Nick said. He held up the keys to Liam's Mercedes. "Let's go."

"You just gonna let Daddy take care of everything?" Zach asked.

"You got a better idea?" Nick asked.

"Fine, I'll come with you." Zach started to set his unopened beer bottle on the ground next to Landon's body.

"Dude, that's got your fingerprints all over it," Sam said. "Don't leave it here."

"Here, I'll take care of that for you," Liam said, reaching for the bottle and twisting off the cap.

"You're such a class act, Liam." Lyle teased. "Takin' beer from a dead guy."

"You know, this could have all been avoided if we'd have just stayed home and hung out at the pool."

"Shut up, Nick," all three of his brothers said at once. It was a somber drive back to the estate.

Chapter Nine

The Snap of His Fingers

"Nick killed Landon," Lyle blurted as soon as he stumbled into their father's home office.

"As in... *killed*, killed?" Levi sat back in his fine leather chair and folded his arms across his middle.

"Knocked him over the head with a beer bottle," Sam confirmed. His eyes had cleared; a testament that he hadn't drunk nearly as much as the other two.

"He was trying to kill Liam," Nick said, his heart in panic mode. "What was I supposed to do?"

"Why were you drinking beer, Nick?" Levi asked. He creased his brow.

"Dad, you know me better than that. Do you honestly think I would drink beer?"

"It was my beer." Zach stepped forward.

"Zach"—Levi nodded regally—"How's the resort?"

"Much better now that we're not in bankruptcy, sir. Thank you again for the bailout."

"I'm not sure that's how Landon saw the *buy*out," Levi said.

"Yeah... he still pretty much hates you."

"Not anymore." Lyle snickered, and Liam joined him. "Because he's dead."

"They're going to regret this conversation when they've sobered up," Nick said.

"They probably won't remember this conversation when they've sobered up." Levi shook his head.

"Dad, what do I do?" Nick lowered his voice and pleaded with his eyes. Somehow asking his dad to help with this made him feel like a little boy. "I don't want to go to jail."

"How about you go back to Dubai?" Levi rubbed his chin in contemplation. "I need you there anyway. I'll see what I can do to make this incident disappear. After all, you were only defending your brother."

"Yeah," Liam said, wrapping his arm around Nick's shoulders and breathing stale beer in his face. "It's better that one horrible man should perish than your loving brother."

"How about if you go sleep it off, Liam?" Nick ducked out from under Liam's arm.

"You can sleep on the plane." Levi stood and picked up his cell phone. "I'll have Petrus bring the helicopter around and tell Gregory to have the jet ready within the hour."

"Just like that?" Zach asked. "You just snap your fingers and a helicopter and private jet appear out of thin air?"

"No." Levi held up his cell phone. "It requires my fingers to *text*, not snap."

All three of Nick's brothers snickered and even Zach chuckled. Nick just shook his head and started to walk from the room. "I'm going to pack an overnight bag."

"You might want to pack for more than just overnight," Levi called after him. "You're going to be there awhile."

"This is what I get for saving someone's life." Nick dragged his feet up the stairs, planning to head back to Dubai for the second time that day.

As he was walking up the stairs, Nick sent a quick text to Adele. *I'm flying back to Dubai tonight.*

She never returned his text.

Chapter Ten

Which Daughter?

"You shouldn't be taking a phone call at the dinner table," Sarah mumbled under her breath. Not that their father could hear her since he was already having an animated conversation with whoever was on the phone.

"Mom, maybe this is an important call." Nick gulped and awaited his fate. After eight weeks of hiding in Dubai, they still had not heard anything. The threat of a murder accusation loomed over everything he did. From his dad's angry expression, he was sure this was the call.

"How am I supposed to raise my boys up right when their father isn't setting a good example?" Sarah asked

"We're all adults, Mother." Liam lifted his glass of wine in a solemn toast. No one else returned the sentiment.

"Not Jacob," Sarah said, turning to their younger brother. At seventeen, he definitely looked like a boy. "And not little Joseph." She rested her hand on top of her growing belly. At five months gestation, she was just starting to pop out.

"And how is this *my* problem?" Levi asked into the phone, anger creeping into his voice. "I see."

Levi raised his head and narrowed his eyes, glancing around at each of his sons.

"What do you suggest we do about this?" Levi paused with a scowl as he listened to whomever was on the other end of the phone. Everyone at the dinner table waited silently, and Nick felt his heart pound. "I agree. Uh huh. Yep. I'll get right on that. You'll be hearing from me s oon."

Levi tapped the screen of his phone to end the call and took a long, calculated breath before raising his gaze and looking around at each of his sons in turn.

"Which one of you got Daniel's daughter pregnant?"

Chapter Eleven

Not What We Had in Mind

"Which daughter?" Liam asked. He gulped and glanced at Lyle.

"How many of them are you concerned about... Liam?" Levi's menacing whisper was fiercer than his shout.

"Uh... well, uh."

"I'll put you out of your misery, son," Levi said. "Miriam's eight weeks pregnant."

Lyle whimpered and lowered his head into his hands. All eyes shifted to the second oldest.

Nick couldn't fathom how his brother must be feeling right now. He would never put himself in that position. He would never put a lady in that position. He would never put his mother and father in that position.

He glanced at his mother, whose head was held high despite the tears gathering at the corners of her eyes. Her hand rested on her baby, due to be born in four months.

"I guess we'll go tomorrow to get you fitted for a tux." Levi glared at Lyle as he stabbed his fork into the filet on the plate in front of him. He picked up his steak knife and calmly sliced a thin piece and lifted the fork to his mouth. He hesitated as Lyle spoke.

"A tux?" Lyle sounded as if he was choking or fighting tears maybe.

"Daniel and I always hoped one of my sons would marry one of his daughters. Kinda thought it would be Nick and Adele for a while there." Levi glanced at Nick, with a pointed expression. "This wasn't exactly what we had envisioned, but Daniel and his family will be here by the end of the w eek."

"The end of the week?" Lyle's voice squeaked.

"Do you have a problem with that, son?" They didn't exactly live in a society of arranged marriages, but sometimes when two patriarchs insisted on certain standards, their adult children were expected to follow them.

"No, sir." Lyle stood and pushed back his chair. "If you'll excuse me. I need a moment." Before leaving the room, Lyle stopped at the beverage cart and lifted a decanter of bourbon. He didn't bother with a glass.

Nick didn't see him again for two days.

Chapter Twelve

Prince Marcos

Planning a wedding, even on short notice, wasn't difficult when funds were unlimited. Dubai was an elegant location, and Levi spared no expense. He lavished gifts and praise and affection on Daniel's daughters as if they were his own.

Miriam was elegant, and Lyle was the perfect gentleman, and everyone pretended there wasn't a proverbial shotgun to his head.

To Nick, the fortunate benefit of having his brother marry Adele's sister was that they were forced to spend time together. There were formal brunches, photo shoots, and receptions as Levi's newly acquired resort welcomed dignitaries from across the globe. Nick was surprised how quickly Daniel and Levi were able to gather friends.

The person Nick was most excited to see was the young Prince Marcos from the tiny kingdom of Madain Saleh. He arrived amid much fanfare, in place of the Crown Prince, Jared, whose absence was as much a snub to Daniel's family as it was a recognition of Ruth's refusal from the previous year.

Nick confidently approached the third prince in line for the throne in his tiny kingdom, with whom he'd spent many days causing trouble during prep school in their early teens.

"Your Highness," Nick acknowledged Prince Marcos with a slight bow of his head and a smirk.

"Don't insult me by throwing around my title, Nick. We've known each other since we were in primary school."

"Only in public, Marcos." Nick kept his voice low. "I love how you're trying to disguise your accent."

"I'm planning a holiday to the States in a few months and desire to assimilate."

"Good luck with that." Nick chuckled. "You are royalty, through and through."

"For now," Marcos grumbled under his breath.

"What do you mean by that?" Nick was genuinely concerned.

"My country is in turmoil," Marcos said. "A civil war is brewing. My brother and I are concerned."

"I'm truly sorry to hear that," Nick said. "If there's anything I can do to help, allow me to offer my service."

"Possibly asylum," Marcos murmured.

"Looking for that myself," Nick replied just as discreetly as Marcos had. "I may or may not be running from the law because I may or may not have murdered someone, but you didn't hear that from me."

Marcos stopped short when Adele and Ruth came around the corner to the lobby. Adele narrowed her eyes at Nick, and Ruth halted and folded her arms across her chest.

Nick lifted his hand as if presenting a prize on a game show. "Adele, Ruth, may I present Prince Marcos Sayid of Madain Saleh."

"We've met," Ruth said, not releasing her arms from their closed position.

"Your Highness." Adele offered a slight bow of her head and hint of a smile. Was she flirting with him? Great. Just what Nick needed.

"A pleasure to finally make your acquaintance, Adele." Marcos extended his hand, inviting Adele to offer hers.

"Likewise, Your Highness." Adele slipped her hand into his, and Marcos leaned down to place a kiss on the back of her hand.

Marcos turned to Ruth. "Lovely to see you again, Ruth."

"Whatever." Ruth turned on her heel and walked back the way she'd come.

"What did your brother do to offend her so thoroughly?" Nick asked.

"Assumed a betrothal without proper courtship," Marcos said.

"Gee, I can't imagine anyone doing such a thing," Adele said, turning to Nick. "Can you, Nick?"

"Thank you, Adele, for pointing out my errors in judgement," Nick said.

"Were you intended?" Marcos glanced sidelong at Nick but kept Adele's hand in his.

"No," Adele said. At the same time, Nick mumbled, "I wish."

"I'm famished from my journey," Marcos said, speaking directly to Adele. "Would you kindly show me the way to the dining quarters?" He lifted his arm in invitation to Adele.

"I'd be honored, Your Highness."

"Please, Adele, call me Marcos." He took her arm in his. "Tell me, how does a beautiful woman such as yourself occupy her time?"

"I'm an ER nurse and working my way through graduate school," she said as they started down the hall. "How about you?"

"Well, since I'm third in line to the throne, I basically have zero purpose in this life."

"You're so funny, Marcos." Adele tucked her hand more firmly into the crook of Marcos's arm as they walked toward the private dining room.

Nick followed quickly behind, not willing to let the two of them out of his sight.

Chapter Thirteen

Never Anyone Else

Nick attended more parties that week than ever in his life. Each time more dignitaries arrived, the champagne flowed, and Nick relished the opportunity to have Adele by his side. He was almost distracted enough to forget about Landon's murder. Almost.

Thankfully, Prince Marcos was often pulled away for diplomatic appearances and side meetings. That meant he didn't have time to flirt with Adele. At the moment, he was surrounded by two businessmen and one of the Saudi princes. Neither of them wore any adornments setting them apart as royalty, and yet even at a party as large as this gathering, they stood out.

"I don't envy him." Adele spoke so casually that Nick was taken aback. They'd been standing together all week, and she'd barely acknowledged him, yet she now commented on Nick's old friend as if Nick were her confidant.

He hadn't realized they'd both been observing the young prince from across the room until that moment. Nick didn't want to question her sudden change, so he just as casually responded. "Why's that?"

"His life is not his own. He doesn't get to choose who to talk to, where to stand, what to do. He goes and does what he's told."

"What? Not interested in accompanying him?" Nick shifted his gaze to the beautiful woman by his side. "I'm sure you could liven up the party for him if he had you on his arm."

"Please." Adele rolled her eyes. "I was only flirting with him to make you jealous."

"Really?" Hope swelled in Nick's chest.

"Did it work?"

Nick guffawed. "Uh, yeah."

"Don't you know?" Adele asked in a low voice. "There's never been anyone but you."

"There's never been anyone but you either," Nick whispered.

"I wish we could go back in time and pretend the past four years never happened." Adele met Nick's gaze, with longing.

"We could start over." Nick turned to face her and tucked a lock of hair behind her ear.

"No, I'm afraid we can't," Adele said. "You ignored me for four years, then insulted and offended me. I'm only here because my parents forced me to come."

"I'm truly sorry about everything. Please, let me make it up to you."

"It's too late, Nick. But thank you." She turned but stopped before walking away. "I'll see you at the wedding tomorrow."

Chapter Fourteen

Same Thing

Nick stood in the dark near the garden's entrance at the back of the resort. Filled with winding stone paths, flowers, shrubs, trees, and little settees, the garden was meant to be a haven from the stress of life in the busy city of Dubai.

There was no haven from the stress of losing Adele, again. Why did he keep offending her? She slipped through his fingers like the sand of the desert.

Nick was drawn forward, down the stone path, holding on to the railing that served as a barrier between the garden and the brackish river flowing beside the path. He contemplated where his life was heading.

Three months ago, he'd been happily working for his father's empire, helping build their family's fortune. Now he was pining after his high school sweetheart, who was barely speaking to him. His brother was getting married and having a baby. His mother was having another baby and he'd be gaining another little brother. He'd been uprooted from his home in Jerusalem and was hiding in Dubai.

Oh, and he'd committed murder.

Nick collapsed onto one of the little stone benches near a beautiful tree at the back of the garden and put his head in his hands.

Normally when he needed to vent, he just wrote a blog post and sent it out into the world. He couldn't write about this. The only people he could talk to were his family, and they were no help. They all wanted him to wait and see if anyone came after him.

He considered going back to Jerusalem and turning himself in, but that wouldn't help anything either. No one seemed to have missed Landon. No one seemed to be searching for his killer. His death never even made the news. Maybe people just thought he drank himself into a stupor and fell down to die in the streets.

Landon was an arrogant jerk, and no one liked him. But he didn't deserve to die. Self-defense. Nick couldn't wrap his brain around that. That wasn't really *self*-defense. It was defending his brother. Was that a good enough reason to kill someone?

"Is that a good enough reason to kill someone?" Nick called into the night sky.

"Nick?" Adelle spoke from ten feet down the path. Nick jumped.

"You startled me," he said, breathing hard. He moved over to make room on the bench. "You can't just sneak up on a guy like that."

"Sorry, you walk faster than me, so I couldn't keep up."

"You followed me all the way out here?"

"I felt bad about the way I ended things earlier, and I wanted to apologize. But now I'm a little bit worried about you." Nick suspected she was no longer talking about following him to the back of the garden.

He knew why she was worried, and he turned away, not wanting her to see the guilt in his eyes.

"So... was that a rhetorical question?" Adele asked, her brow creased. "About killing someone?"

Nick leaned forward and rested his elbows on his knees, clasping his hands together as if in prayer and lowering his forehead. He took a deep breath and let it out slowly. Adele's hand rested on his back and rubbed circles there. An hour ago, that would have been his undoing. Now, he was too consumed with his own guilt to get distracted by a pretty girl.

"Do you want to talk about it?"

"I killed Landon Phillips." There, he'd said it. He'd admitted out loud to someone outside his immediate family. Her hand stilled for a moment, and then she resumed rubbing circles on his back.

"And you want to know if that was justified?" She didn't wait for him to answer before she added. "If I know you as well as I think I do, I can't imagine you doing anything to hurt another human unless there was a darn good reason."

"He was trying to kill my brother, Liam. Is that a good enough reason?"

"Maybe. Maybe not. Did you have another choice?"

"I hit him over the head with a beer bottle. I just needed him to stop choking my brother. I didn't mean to kill him."

"Is that why you left home?"

Nick nodded, without looking up.

"No one's searching for you, Nick," Adele said.

"You don't know that."

"Why didn't you tell me?"

"You weren't exactly taking my phone calls."

"I'm sorry," she whispered, her voice trembling.

"Me too," Nick answered. He didn't know what else to say.

"Could I ask what Liam did to anger Landon so much that he was choking him?"

"Liam was spouting off at the mouth like he always does. Landon was drunk. They got into a fight. It ended in me hitting Landon over the head with a beer bottle."

"Wait... does this have any correlation to Zach hanging around your father?" Adele asked. "Weren't he and Landon business partners?"

"Zach came with us when we left Jerusalem," Nick said. "If the police determined Landon had been murdered, Zach would have been implicated. He had the most to gain from Landon's death."

"I guess it's better this way," Adele said. "Keep your enemies close."

"Zach isn't our enemy. He's a shrewd businessman, but he's a decent guy. He sees our vision."

"What vision?" Adele asked.

"Our path forward, our principles, our company's mission and business plan. He understands that it's better to grasp on to the success we've proven than to dwindle with Landon and all his darkness. Staying with us will lead him to the life he's always wanted."

"You really are full of yourself, aren't you?" Adele asked.

"What do you mean by that?" Nick lifted his chin, offended by her words.

"You think your father's company is the best in the world and others will only succeed if they follow your example."

"I think our success proves the validity."

"Your pride is going to be your undoing, Nick." Adele stood and started down the path back toward the resort.

"Wait, don't go." Nick reached for her hand, and she stopped.

"Nick, look around you. We live in separate worlds. I'm just a simple girl from Jerusalem and you're a world-traveled billionaire."

"Son of a billionaire," Nick corrected her.

"Same thing." Adele stepped closer and raised onto her toes, kissing Nick's cheek softly. "I love you, Nick. But it would never work."

Adele walked away, and Nick once again sat on the stone bench alone.

Chapter Fifteen

A Fool and His Brother

M iriam floated down the aisle, a vision of elegance, and not a sign to indicate there was any reason to question the sanctity of her white dress. Lyle stood beside his brothers, with a gleam in his eye. He was either a very good actor or was truly excited to have Miriam for his wife.

Nick hoped it was the latter.

He glanced across at where Adele stood beside her older sisters. Ruth, the maid of honor, had walked alone ahead of Miriam. Liam had escorted Rachel, Sam had escorted Leanne, and Nick had the good fortune to escort his former sweetheart and the woman he wished could become his bride.

As if sensing his gaze, Adele lifted her eyes, and a tiny smile pulled at her mouth before she forced it away and looked back to her sister.

Warmth spread in Nick's heart, together with hope. He would be patient. There was no one else but her, and she had admitted there was no one else but him.

Lyle and Miriam committed their life to one another and seemed genuinely happy to have been forced into this union. They exchanged rings, and vows, and a kiss that made the old ladies in the room blush crimson.

Nick had to look away and chuckled to meet Adele's gaze across the aisle again. He raised his eyebrows at her provocatively and smirked.

Adele's jaw dropped, and she looked away but not before she bit her lower lip to force away a smile.

After a million photographs, the wedding party was led into a grand reception hall where they were welcomed with applause as the DJ introduced Mr. and Mrs. Lyle and Miriam Cohen.

They were expected to interact with the guests as they made their way across the large room full of tables before reaching the wedding party's table where they would be seated and treated to a dinner befitting a king, or a billionaire in this case.

Liam managed to find champagne, within seconds of walking into the hall, but dinner wasn't for another forty-five minutes. By the time they reached their table, he was stumbling and hanging on his date. Rachel didn't seem to mind and had already drunk a few too many as well.

"They need food," Nick said to Adele. "Now."

"Follow me." Adele didn't wait for Nick to answer, just held his hand as she led him over to a man in a suit who seemed in charge. She didn't bother with pleasantries. "Get the bridal party plates of food immediately."

"Yes, ma'am." The man turned and stepped through a door. By the time Nick and Adele had corralled their brothers and sisters into the waiting chairs, servers were delivering elegant platters to their table.

Thankfully, Liam dug in with gusto, and Nick breathed a sigh of relief. The last thing he needed was for Liam to make a fool of himself at their brother's wedding.

Chapter Sixteen

Lucky In Love

The great thing about being in a wedding party was that a guy didn't have to worry about asking a girl to dance. It was expected.

After the bride and groom had their obligatory first dance, Nick led Adele onto the floor and confidently pulled her into his arms. She didn't resist.

This was the first time Nick had ever held her that firmly. While in their youth, they held hands and kissed a few times, but never with any passion. Theirs had been an innocent, young love affair, complete with constant chaperones and strict warnings about right and wrong.

Nick had never been the kind of man to covet a woman's body or be motivated by physical attraction, but the magnetic force holding Adele's body close to his was powerful.

The people and tables and elegance around them faded into a distant space beyond his mind. The music was the pulsing beat of his heart.

Adele's strawberry blonde hair fell in wisps from the clips and flowers that had hours ago failed to hold it in place. Her crystal blue eyes held his as if he were the only person in the room. The only person in the world.

He released his hands from her waist and reached to caress her face, allowing one hand to follow the line of her jaw, the other to brush his thumb across her lips, which she parted with a sigh of invitation.

Nick raised Adele's chin gently and lowered his face to hers. She lifted onto her toes to meet him halfway, closing the distance and sealing the kiss he'd longed for since the day he'd chanced to meet her in the hospital emergency room a few months before.

How lucky that his brothers had dragged him to go skydiving.

How unfortunate that Liam and Rachel stumbled onto the dance floor, waking Nick and Adele from their trance.

The couples on the dance floor stopped and took a step back as Liam pulled Rachel close, dancing provocatively. His bowtie was hanging around his neck and his shirt was untucked. Rachel's dress was askew, and her hair had been completely pulled from the clips that had once held it in place.

Within thirty seconds of them entering the dance floor, Nick had Liam by one arm and Sam held the other in an attempt to escort him from the room.

"Let go of me," Liam slurred, trying to twist his way out of his brothers' captivity. "I was dancing with my date."

"I think you've had enough for one night," Nick growled.

"Come on, man," Sam said. "This is not cool. You need to sober up."

"I am plenty sober," Liam said, finally breaking free. "I am going to dance with my Rachel."

Suddenly, Levi stood in his way and demanded that Liam leave immediately and stop disrupting his brother's wedding reception. Liam could fight with his brothers, but he would not directly disobey his father, at least not to his face.

Nick and Sam took the advantage of the distraction to escort their oldest brother from the grand hall. Liam cursed and argued and stumbled all the way up the elevator to his suite, insisting he was fine. It took them hours to get him calmed, and he finally passed out.

By the time Nick made his way back down to the grand hall, the reception had ended and only an empty dance floor remained of the magic he'd shared with Adele.

Chapter Seventeen

Name Dropping

"I still can't find my cell phone." Nick was ready to pull his hair out. He hadn't seen it since the day before when they were getting into their tuxes.

The day had not started well. He awoke to discover Daniel had left with his daughters, claiming he didn't want any more of Levi's sons to corrupt them. Nick was devastated. Until he found his phone, he wouldn't be able to call or text Adele. He couldn't remember her phone number. He had relied too much on the technology with his contacts list.

As brother of the groom, his job was far from over. He was expected to greet the guests as they were leaving the resort, thanking them for coming and wishing them well on their travels.

Prince Marcos was the first person to razz Nick about making out with Adele on the dance floor. "I knew when I met her that she was smitten with you."

"That's all fine and good if I could get in touch with her," Nick said.

"Let me ask my brother, Jared." Marcos patted Nick on the shoulder. "It's a long shot, but maybe in all his conversations with Ruth, he obtained her sister's number."

"I'm not holding out any hope," Nick said.

The young prince pulled his cell phone from his jacket pocket and called Jared. Nick hung on his every word. Marcos explained the situation, waited impatiently while Marcos explained to his brother that, no, Ruth was not interested in dating again. Marcos thanked him as he wrote down a phone number then said goodbye to his brother. He handed the piece of paper like a lifeline.

"Don't get too excited," Marcos said. "It's Ruth's phone number. Jared assumes she would be able to get in touch with her own sister."

"Thank you, Your Highness," Nick said with complete sincerity. "I owe you my gratitude."

"Now there you go again, throwing around my title like name dropping is going to get you anywhere."

"It got me a phone number." Nick shrugged and chuckled.

"Eh, it's been so good to see you again, my friend." Marcos reached and wrapped Nick in a hug.

"You as well, Marcos." Nick pulled away from their hug. "Now I just gotta go buy myself a new phone."

"Good luck to you," Marcos said, turning to walk away.

"Let me know if you need anything," Nick called after him. "Like a new kingdom, or something."

"You're one to talk." Marcos turned but kept walking backward. "An exiled murderer running from the law."

"And a prince without a throne. We're quite the pair."

"Goodbye, Nick," Marcos called.

"Fare thee well, my prince!" Nick turned and walked the other direction toward the front desk of the resort lobby. "Where can I buy a new phone?"

Chapter Eighteen

Wrong Number

"Ruth, this is Nick," he spoke into a recorded message. This was the fifth time he'd left a voicemail asking to speak to Adele. "Please, I'm desperate. Please help me get in touch with Adele. Call me."

He received a text within a few minutes.

Look, I don't know who you are or why you keep leaving me voicemails. I don't know who Ruth is, and I don't know who Adele is, and I don't know anyone who lives in Dubai. If you don't stop calling me, I'm going to block this number. I might just do that anyway. Goodbye, Nick. Good luck finding your girlfriend.

"It's the wrong number," Nick whispered, then turned and called out to his brother Sam. "He gave me the wrong phone number."

"What?" Sam trudged out of his suite with a towel around his neck as if he'd been working out.

"Prince Jared gave his brother the wrong number for Ruth and that's why I can't get a hold of Adele."

"I have no idea what you're talking about." Sam turned to head back into his suite.

"Wait," Nick called after him. "I need you to go with me to Jerusalem."

By nightfall their private jet had landed at a little airport outside Jerusalem within a few miles of Daniel's estate. They called for a limo, and Nick bit his fingernails all the way up their drive.

He ran up the porch steps to the elaborately carved front door, Sam trailing behind. A doorman let them in, and Daniel soon joined them in the grand foyer. Nick remembered Adele's comment about being a simple girl from Jerusalem and chuckled. Her family was almost as rich as his.

"What is it you want?" Daniel asked, folding his arms across his chest. His brawn was intimidating, but Nick didn't back down.

"I need to see Adele," Nick pleaded. "Please, sir."

"Your family has done quite enough, thank you very much," Daniel said, then turned to walk away. "You're not welcome here."

"Adele!" Nick called as loud as he could, hoping the sound would reverberate in this vast space and reach her in the far corners of the mansion. "Please, Adele, I just need to speak with you!"

"Nick," Daniel looked back at him. "Go home to whatever resort your vagabond family is living in these days. Leave my family alone."

Nick's shoulders slumped in defeat as Daniel turned and walked away, leaving him standing there by the entrance to the estate.

"She's not here." A small voice spoke from beside them. Leanne stood there, tucked into one of the alcoves in the foyer, her arms crossed and a sad smile on her face. "Hey, Sam."

"Hey," Sam answered, shuffling his feet and sticking his hands into his pockets.

"Do you know where she is?" Nick asked, grasping Leanne's shoulders.

"She's working second shift at the hospital this evening."

"Oh, thank goodness." Nick turned to the door. Sam didn't follow. "Come on, man."

"Gimme a minute," Sam said. "I'll meet you at the car."

"Come on—" Nick spoke through gritted teeth.

Sam pulled him aside and whispered harshly. "If this were Adele standing here, and I was rushing you out the door, how would you feel?"

"Take as long as you need," Nick mumbled and left the house, trudging down the stone stairs to the waiting limo.

True to his word, Sam was out the door in barely a minute, and traipsed down the stairs, looking down at his phone. He tucked himself into the car and pulled the door closed, then held up his screen for Nick to see. "Got *one* of Daniel's daughters' phone numbers anyway."

"Good for you, man." Nick patted his brother on the shoulder. "Now let's go find another one."

Chapter Nineteen

Son-of-a-Billionaire

"I need to see Adele," Nick told the receptionist at the emergency room entrance. He was breathless after rushing from the limo.

"Are you family?" the annoyed receptionist asked.

"I'm her fiancé," Nick said.

"I wasn't aware Adele was engaged." The woman crossed her arms and sat back in her chair.

"I'm not sure she's aware either." Nick chuckled.

The woman didn't look amused and didn't make a move to let him in the door.

"Could you please just call back there and let her know I'm here?" Nick asked. "Please, I'm desperate."

She picked up the phone to make the call and then raised her eyebrow. "Whom should I say is here to see her?"

"Tell her a cocky, prideful, son-of-a-billionaire is here to see her. She'll know exactly who you're talking about." He was certain his playful grin was a bit smug, but he didn't care. He was going to see Adele in less than a m inute.

"Hi, it's Judith at the triage desk. Could you tell Adele that her fiancé is here to see her?" She paused while listening to whoever was on the other end of the call. "Yeah, I didn't know either. Mm hm, okay, I'll tell him to wait awhile. Thank you." Judith hung up the phone.

"Well?" Nick raised his eyebrows.

"She'll be out after she gets done inserting an IV into the arm of some guy who has such a bad migraine that he won't stop puking."

"Sounds lovely." Nick wrinkled his nose and walked over to have a seat beside his brother but kept eagle eyes on the door to the emergency room.

After what seemed like hours, Adele exited the ER, her curls slipping from her hair clip and her shoulders slumped. Nick rushed up to her but stopped short of pulling her into his arms. She crossed her arms over her chest.

Nick pulled out his brand-new cell phone and held it up for her to see. "Do you know what this is?"

"Next year's model of the iPhone, which won't be available to us commoners for another eight months?" She sneered.

"The make and model are not important," Nick said, not denying her observation. "What's important is that it's replacing my old phone. The phone I've had for years. The one with all my contacts inside."

Adele's facial expressions softened, but her eyes remained hard.

"I have been trying to figure out how to get in touch with you for weeks. I finally just hopped on a jet and flew up here. But then your dad wouldn't let you see me, so I figured the hospital would be the next most likely place to find you."

"So that's why you didn't call?" she asked, lowering her gaze. "I thought you wanted nothing to do with me."

"I want everything to do with you. I love everything about you," Nick said, leaning closer. "I can't think, I can't work, I can't breathe without you."

"I miss you too." Her whisper was barely a squeak. "But Nick, I'm not sure you can change. You're too perfect. You think everyone should follow your example and live their lives the way you do."

"But I *have* changed," Nick said, pleading with his eyes. "I took to heart what you said about my pride, and I think I understand. I'm not as smart as my father is and when I try to emulate him, I become cocky and prideful. I'm trying to be more humble... and I could learn a lot from you."

"We come from separate worlds, Nick." Adele was grasping, still fighting to find a reason to push him away.

"We're not so different, Adele." Nick chuckled and shook his head. "We're both rich kids trying to make a positive difference in the world. You're so intelligent that you intimidate me. But... I'm almost as smart."

"Five points less smart." She tried to hide a grin but failed miserably. That gave Nick the little bit of confidence he needed to finish his passionate apology.

Nick knelt on one knee, right there in the waiting room of the emergency department and held out a small black box containing a simple diamond engagement ring. "Adele, I'm sorry to ask you to give up your life in order to follow the fugitive son of a billionaire, but would you do me the honor of becoming my wife?"

"Yes," she said without hesitation. "Nick, I will follow you anywhere. I would be honored to be your wife."

Nick hopped to his feet, forgetting he was supposed to put the ring on her finger first, and wrapped his arms around her. He whispered over and over. "Thank you, thank you, thank you."

"You have a lifetime to keep apologizing." She laughed.

"I'll never stop," he said, then pressed his lips to hers, sealing his promise.

Chapter Twenty

You Have My Heart

They planned the wedding in Dubai, at the Cohen's largest newly acquired resort so Adele's friends and family members could come down to attend the wedding. After months of hiding, there was no hint that anyone was searching for the person or persons who had been responsible for Landon's death.

While in Jerusalem, Nick helped his father quietly sell most of his land holdings and business ventures. They made preparations to leave Israel, presumably forever. Nick knew his father was working on other business ventures in Dubai, but he was unwilling to even ask until after returning from his honeymoon.

Nick had one thing on his mind; planning a wedding so he could be with Adele forever. His older brothers teased him mercilessly about his unwillingness to be alone with his bride until after the wedding. He wasn't taking any chances. He was already tempted nearly beyond restraint by the woman he'd loved since they were teenagers.

Adele planned a simple wedding that got out of hand. A girl could not marry the son of a billionaire and avoid having dignitaries from all over the world invited. The guest list was beyond their control, but she insisted on simplicity in her dress and flowers and pageantry, and a meal without drinking and partying. Nick was completely fine with that. He didn't want anything—or anyone—ruining her special day.

The wedding party was nearly identical to that of his brother and Adele's sister. The biggest change was the order of the lineup, and one additional brother: Nick's best friend, Prince Marcos Sayid of Madain Saleh. The simple crown he wore was tucked within purposely shaggy hair, grown out just a little for the occasion. In his sorry attempt to conceal his royalty,

Prince Marcos instead took on the appearance of a rock star in a tux with a crown. Every eligible woman in the room batted her eyelashes.

The large garden to the back of the resort, where Adele had first told Nick she loved him on the night before their siblings' wedding, was the perfect location for her to walk down the cobblestone path to meet her groom.

Nick waited in anticipation—his brothers by his side, his father and very pregnant Mother sitting in the first row of seats, and his friends and family nearby—for his bride to descend the path and come join her life to his.

The music shifted and Ruth began her descent, followed by Rachel, then Miriam, her dress altered to beautifully showcase her growing belly, and last was Leanne.

Again, there was a change in the tune emanating from the grand piano that had been carefully transported and placed in the garden, and the members of the audience stood. Nick wished they hadn't. His view was impeded. He broke from his place of honor and stepped to his right, standing instead directly before the aisle where Adele would appear at the head of the path. He wanted to be the first to view the elegant woman who would descend to him.

Tears ran unabashedly down his cheeks as Adele appeared on the arm of her father, Daniel Ashish. He held back his desire to run to her, sweep her into his arms and carry her the rest of the way, demanding the officiator hurry with their vows so he could be forevermore her husband.

Painstakingly slow she walked forward, cobblestone step by step by step, until she stood by his side and Daniel handed over his daughter for safekeeping to the man he had forbidden to enter his home a few short months prior.

Nick broke his gaze from his bride for a few brief seconds to look his new father-in-law in the eye, man to man, conveying with every fiber of his being that he would protect and cherish this woman whom they both loved.

With no further fanfare, Daniel released Adele's hand and placed it into Nick's, then ducked away to sit beside his wife in the front row.

"Can I kiss you now?" Nick whispered, gazing into Adele's eyes.

"Nope," she whispered and winked at him. "Marry me first."

He gently pulled her forward, never releasing her gaze and stood before the man who prompted their vows and rituals that would bind them together legally.

Nick barely registered the words he repeated, yet felt them to his core. He was promising everything to Adele and more. He was promising forever, if that existed.

As hurried as he'd been to get to this moment, when the officiator pronounced them husband and wife, time slowed. He closed the distance between them and lifted her face delicately, lowering his while maintaining eye contact until the last possible second. He hesitated and hovered inches from a kiss and waited for her to lift onto her toes and meet his lips, sealing their love for one another.

This was only their second real kiss as adults and might as well have been their first with how sacred this felt.

When they pulled apart an inch or two, Nick pressed his forehead to Adele's and whispered, "Thank you."

Adele threw her arms around Nick's neck and kissed him again, a combination of humor and passion, then pulled away and laughed lightly. "I love you!"

"I love you too." Nick laughed along with her, lifting her off her feet playfully. Setting her down, he whispered for her ears only, "Am I allowed to admit I'm terrified right now?"

"Good, I'm not the only one." She giggled. "How about this? Let's go eat a little food, dance the obligatory number of dances, then go upstairs."

"Sounds good to me," Nick said a little louder than he should have.

Adele grabbed Nick's hand and held it up triumphantly, calling out to the crowd, "Finally!"

Everyone laughed as Adele playfully tugged her groom up the cobblestone steps to the grand ballroom inside. Nick allowed himself to be pulled along, unable to deny his new wife one moment of this new excitement.

Nick had no idea how long it took the rest of the wedding party to ascend the path from the garden, but by the time anyone else arrived in the ballroom, where the tables were situated around a small dance floor, and were awaiting the meal, he and Adele were alone on the dance floor, holding one another close, swaying to dinner music played softly by the string quartet in the corner.

They eventually allowed others to pull them apart just far enough so they could sit at the head table and eat a little food. They were dragged around the room, greeting the myriad of guests, dancing and dancing and dancing, cutting cake, posing for a million photographs, and hugging many friends and family.

"Look at Sam and Leanne," Adele said from where they stood on the other side of the ballroom. Nick glanced over to the dance floor where she pointed, and his heart warmed. They were dancing together, cheek to cheek, both of their eyes closed in a bliss he understood all too well.

"Reminds me of a few months ago when you and I held each other the same way at Lyle and Miriam's wedding," Nick said, pulling Adele closer. "Maybe a few months from now we'll be celebrating another wedding."

"If he can get her out of the library long enough to date," Adele said. "Maybe we should warn him about the uphill battle he'll fight."

"Nah, I don't want anything interrupting this moment. I remember what that was like." Nick kissed the top of her head. "Besides there are a few other things I'd like to do right this minute."

"Yeah?" Adele turned away from watching the dance, and Nick caught her in his arms, loving the silky fabric of her wedding dress beneath his hands. "Do any of those things involve you finally taking me up to your suite?"

"*Our* suite," Nick whispered. "From now until forever, what's mine is yours."

"All I've ever wanted from you was your heart." Adele gazed into his eyes, passion replacing humor.

"You have my heart." Nick pulled her closer and his breathing increased. "Would it be okay if I give you the rest of me too?"

"Only if I can give you the rest of me," Adele whispered.

The purr that emanated from somewhere inside him came out as a soft growl. "Mrs. Cohen, I would very much like to escort you upstairs to *our* suite."

"I'll follow you anywhere, Mr. Cohen."

With no other formal invitation or goodbye to friends and family, they ducked out the nearest door, and Nick swept Adele into his arms, carrying her up the stairs.

Part Two: Following the Billionaire's Son

Sam Cohen

As told by Sam Cohen, son of Levi and Sarah Cohen, brother of Nicholas Cohen at the time when King Sayid was in his forty-second year as the story begins...

Chapter Twenty-One

Presumptuous

"You're not going to lose your cell phone and run off and ignore me for weeks like your brother did to my sister, are you?" Leanne asked, her deep blue eyes vulnerable and haunting. The sparkling lights from the disco ball turning above the dance floor cast shadows and glitter across her face.

"I have my phone right here," Sam told her. He released her gently from his arms, immediately missing the feel of her silky bridesmaid dress. The music from the string quartet continued from the corner of the room. "And your phone number is at the top of my contacts list, see?" He swiped open his phone and showed her the screen.

"Leanne Cohen?" She raised her eyebrows. "You seriously paired my name with yours? Isn't that a bit presumptuous?"

"I'd call it 'hopeful' rather than presumptuous," Sam answered, slipping his cell phone back into his pocket and pulling her back into his arms. "I promise not to get down on one knee and hold a ring in front of you until we're both ready to take that step."

"What if I'm never ready?" she asked.

"I find that unlikely." Sam lifted his chin in mock superiority.

"Again," Leanne said. "Presumptuous."

"Just don't run off on me like Adele did to Nick," Sam said. "We saw how that turned out."

"Well, I'd say it turned out okay in the end, since they are now married." Leanne turned her wrist to view her nonexistent watch. "As of an hour a go."

"The road to the altar was bumpy to say the least," Sam said.

"Good things come to those who wait," Leanne said.

"And to those who are persistent." Sam twirled her around and then pulled her close again. "I know how to be patient."

"We'll see."

Chapter Twenty-Two

Prince Charming

Sam and his brothers had said goodnight to Leanne and her sisters after the wedding reception, then headed to the tiki bar by the pool at the resort, along with Prince Marcos. They lounged in chaises where they could kick back and loosen their ties and remove their sport coats. They had even gone so far as removing shoes and socks and rolling up the pant legs of their tuxes.

"Fantastic wedding." Prince Marcos Sayid of Madain Saleh held up his glass of Scotch in a toast.

Sam had already tossed back a couple of glasses, as had his two older brothers, Liam and Lyle. Their youngest brother, Jacob, was barely eighteen and was sipping a soda. He raised his glass as well.

"I'm glad it's over," Liam grumbled. "I haven't gone that many hours without a drink in years." He downed another large glass of Scotch and laid his head back on the lounge chair, eyes closed and probably not long from needing an escort to his suite for the night.

Nick and Adele had decided not to serve any alcohol at their wedding because Liam had made a complete fool of himself at Lyle's wedding. But when the bride and groom snuck away, presumably to head up to their hotel suite, they left the rest of the bridal party to fend for themselves. By eleven-thirty, the guys headed out back to the tiki bar near the pool.

Since Nick was upstairs doing what Sam wished he could be doing, Nick had better not fault the guys for having a little fun of their own.

Sam was eyeing the pool and its promise to wash away the oppressive heat that never seemed to dissipate in the City of Dubai. Rather than traipsing all the way up to his suite, Sam settled for the next glass of Scotch a waitress brought him.

She also handed a drink to Prince Marcos, who was completely oblivious to her flirting. He'd been ignoring women the whole evening and never seemed to dance with any of them more than once.

The young prince, who had been Nick's best friend for years, had nearly upstaged the groom, because he was required to wear his crown while attending formal social events. The way traditions had been explained to Sam was if the occasion warranted a tux, it required at least a simple band of gold around Marcos's head.

To his credit, Marcos had grown out his hair a little in an attempt to hide the crown. It hadn't worked. The effect just made him look like a rock star in a tux with a crown. He could probably have his pick of the single women in this outdoor bar.

If Sam hadn't already been in a relationship with Leanne, he might have been jealous of his younger brother's best friend. As it was, Sam couldn't care less how many girls fell at Marcos's feet.

Or into the pool.

A blonde in a little black dress had locked eyes with Prince Marcos and had become so distracted that she walked right into the pool and landed with a giant splash.

Sam fought the impulse to laugh and pretty much lost the fight, along with his brothers, when Marcos jumped in after her, fully clothed in his tux and crown, presumably to rescue her.

Although the pool was shallow enough for her to touch the bottom, Marcos wrapped his arms around her waist, and she wrapped her arms around his neck. Sam couldn't hear what they were saying from out on the pool deck, but they were obviously enamored with one another.

After flirting incessantly for several minutes, Marcos carried her out of the pool and set her on the patio right in front of Sam and his brothers. He heard Marcos call her Lyla, then he asked a pool attendant to jump in and fetch Lyla's shoes from the bottom of the pool.

They stood there dripping wet for a few moments, then made plans to meet back there after getting dried off and into something more comfortable.

Lucky prince. They'd been at the bar less than an hour, and he already had a date with a pretty girl.

Not that Sam couldn't spend the night in the arms of a pretty girl. If he wanted to push the issue, he could have Leanne join him at the pool as well.

She left with her sisters at the end of the reception, claiming her feet were sore. He'd complain also if forced to wear heels with two-inch spikes.

He was just fine right here with a glass of Scotch and his brothers. They wouldn't stay too much longer. Just long enough to get Liam inebriated so that he'd stay in his hotel room when they tucked him into bed. He'd caused enough trouble at Lyle's wedding that the guys were determined not to let that happen at Nick's wedding.

Before any of them could think of leaving the bar, a very frantic Prince Marcos hurried over to them, wearing jeans and a T-shirt. "My brother, Jared, was in a terrible motorcycle accident and I need to fly home." Marcos handed a folded sheet of paper to Jacob. "Please make sure Lyla gets this note. You're the only one sober enough who I can trust."

"I promise to get this to her," Jacob said, taking the note.

"Hope your brother's okay," Sam said.

"Thanks, man. They said he doesn't look good." Marcos reached out for a quick hand shake, then hurried out to the back of the resort where a helicopter was just landing.

"*Crown* Prince Jared?" Liam asked with a sneer. "The same guy who dated Ruth Ashish when he was already married to that princess from Tayma?"

"Yep, Jared is Marcos's older brother," Sam answered.

"Excuse me." The beautiful blonde named Lyla stood beside them in comfortable clothes that looked suspiciously like pajamas, with fluffy pink slippers. Her wet hair had been combed out and she'd washed off the smeared mascara. "Was that Marcos?" She pointed to where the helicopter was lifting off the back lawn of the resort.

"He asked me to give you this." Jacob rose from his lounge chair and handed Lyla the folded note.

Lyla read it with a crease in her brow, then glanced longingly in the direction of the retreating lights and fading whir of the helicopter blades. "I hope his brother will be okay."

"Me too," Sam said. "Or your prince charming is about to become the future king of Madain Saleh."

Chapter Twenty-Three

Family Meeting

"I have a family announcement to make." When Levi Cohen, Sam's father, called a family meeting, everyone listened. At least he had waited until brunch the day after the wedding. Sam and his brothers were still nursing hangovers from staying out at the tiki bar the night before.

"Gee, Dad, don't you want to wait until Nick and Adele are home from their honeymoon?" Liam asked with a sneer. As the oldest of Sam's brothers, Liam had a hard time accepting their father's doting attention to their younger brother. Historically used as a public relations figurehead in the Cohen dynasty, Liam had been less and less capable of handling any social events without embarrassing the family.

"Nicholas has known about this for months." Their father waved his hand dismissively. "I'm buying a yacht manufacturing company."

"A y-yacht company?" Sam asked. If someone had asked Sam five minutes prior what business venture his father would tackle next, he never would have come up with that answer. "But you know nothing about building yachts."

"Nicholas told me on our last acquisitions trip that he'd like to learn to create things rather than just acquire them," their father said.

"And we're back to Nick again," Lyle said, draping his arm around the chair of his wife, Miriam. His role in the family businesses had shifted since getting married. Where he used to schmooze the daughters and wives of dignitaries and royalty, he had calmed down and resigned himself to becoming a dad. "Sometimes I wonder if you remember that you have five sons, rather than one."

"Soon to be six," their mother said, resting her hand on her rounded belly. At forty-six years of age, Sam's mother, Sarah, had conceived again unexpectedly, and was due to have her baby just two months ahead of her first grandchild.

"Don't worry, gentlemen," their father said to all of them. "When I die, my fortune will be split equally among you and all will be well."

"I think we'd all rather have *you* than our inheritance," Jacob said. As the youngest brother, for a few more weeks anyway, he was still a spoiled teenager. Mostly a momma's boy growing up, Jacob had been spending more and more time with Nick and their father, learning the family businesses and earning their father's respect.

Sam wasn't exactly jealous, but he was quite literally stuck in between his younger brothers, Nick and Jacob, and his older brothers, Liam and Lyle. At twenty-five years of age, Sam was unsure where he fit into this family. He had embraced his role as one of the four vice-presidents in the family's conglomerate of businesses, but still preferred working with the natural resource holdings.

For most of their lives, Liam and Lyle hadn't done much to be proud of. Living like rich playboys, they had partied more than they worked and used their father's generosity to their advantage. Sam had hovered in their shadows, not quite encouraging their wild antics, but not stopping them either.

In recent years, Sam had gravitated more and more toward their younger brother, Nick. There was something about Nick that drew the world to him. His charisma, his communication skills, his natural leadership ability. Sam never felt inferior to Nick as he did with their older brothers. He just felt *good* in Nick's presence.

"Does Nick know he's going to be manufacturing yachts for you?" Sam asked.

"Somewhat."

"When were you planning to tell him?" Lyle asked.

"Or us, for that matter?" Liam sat back in his chair and crossed his arms. All eyes were on their father and open hostility rolled across the room.

"We needed to get through the wedding." Their father shrugged. "You all knew there were things in the works. Even Nicholas knew. I've been openly selling off all holdings in the greater Jerusalem area. We will be leaving everything behind. Israel will no longer be our home."

"Where does that leave my family?" Miriam asked, her eyes lowering. All focus seemed to shift briefly to her pregnant belly.

"Your father and I have come to the agreement that we will all leave together." Daniel Ashish had been their father's best friend all their lives. Relationships had been strained between the two families in recent months when Lyle had gotten Miriam pregnant and been forced to marry her.

"Daniel is very much a part of all my dealings in Dubai," their father explained to Miriam.

"So, you've just decided that we're all moving?" Sam asked, frustrated. "What if I don't want to move? What if I like the life we have in Jerusalem?"

"Son, I need you here in Dubai."

"I want to focus on our natural resource holdings, not yacht building."

"We are not selling off our holdings in petroleum and potash," their father explained. "You will still be in charge of those aspects, but our main business center will be in Dubai. Your offices will be in Dubai." Father looked around the table pointedly at each one of them and everyone backed down.

"We will go where you want us to go, Father," Jacob said, his youthful innocence in stark contrast to his older brothers' skepticism. Yet Jacob said what no one else was willing. It didn't matter what any of them wanted to do, they followed their father's lead.

Levi Cohen was a visionary man. He may be a hard-nosed businessman, but he had an instinct for knowing where the market would swing next. Sam suspected Dubai would be temporary as well although he had little evidence to support his gut feeling. Something about purchasing a yacht manufacturing company made him suspect their family would soon be boarding a yacht and setting off in whatever direction their father would lead them.

Sam took a deep breath of resignation and focused his attention back to the breakfast plate in front of him. No sense in arguing. Everything would fall into place somehow.

Then he remembered what his father had said about Daniel Ashish. His family would be joining them in Dubai. Which meant Leanne would be coming back to Dubai. Sam hid a smile behind a glass of juice, suddenly a little more optimistic.

Chapter Twenty-Four

Vanity Metric

"No, I'm not moving to Dubai," Leanne said, shoving another pair of shoes into her suitcase. "I'm halfway through my master's program at Jerusalem University. I'm not going to just move down here." She had been casually packing to leave the resort and was now angry.

"But *my* father said that he and *your* father had already decided." Sam sat on the sofa in her hotel suite and explained the conversation with his family at brunch. "Think of it. We wouldn't have to be apart and struggle with a long-distance relationship."

"So, being in a relationship with me is a struggle?" Leanne stopped packing and folded her arms across her chest.

"That's not what I meant." Sam rose from the sofa and hurried across the room. He tried to pull her arms apart and wrap them around him. "It's just that we could be together all the time and not have to fly back and forth to see each other."

"It's only a four-hour flight, and you have a private jet. I think you'll be okay." She softened a bit in his arms.

"True..." Sam couldn't argue with her logic.

"Look, I'm sure there will come a day when we can be together." Leanne rested her hands onto Sam's chest and pushed him slightly away. "But now is not a good time. I need to focus on my studies."

"You're not breaking up with me, are you?" Sam asked, clinging to her waist, wishing he could close the distance between them but not wanting to pressure her.

"No... not really." Her reply was not exactly the boost of confidence Sam hoped for. "I mean, I'm not actively looking for someone to replace you.

I just need to get through these last few years of school before I think any further in my life than that."

"Few years?" Sam's voice cracked. "I thought you were halfway through your master's degree. You've only got about a year left, correct?"

"I want to get a PhD." Her matter-of-fact statement came with an implied duh.

"Why do you need a degree at all?" Sam asked. "If you marry me, you'll be so wealthy you'll never have to work."

"You think I'm getting a degree so I can get a *job?*" She was no longer pacifying him and had shifted back to anger. What had he said wrong?

"I don't know, maybe? Why else would someone get a degree from a university?"

"To learn knowledge."

"You can learn without having to sit in a classroom. I mean, I'm designing advanced engineering schematics for natural resource mining, and I don't have a college education."

"I want that degree, okay?" She shrugged. "I want the diploma, the piece of parchment paper I can hang on my wall in a frame."

"I'll never understand that," Sam admitted. "The degree just seems like a vanity metric."

"Now you're calling me vain?" she asked, pushing him completely away.

"No, I'm not calling you vain." Sam tried to backpedal. "I'm just saying you don't need the piece of paper. All you really need is the knowledge."

"Get out of my hotel room." Leanne pointed toward the door. "Now." Her quiet firmness was more frightening than if she'd yelled at him.

"Leanne, don't do this." Sam reached to pull her back into his arms.

She pushed him away more forcefully. "I said, 'Get out of my hotel room. Now.'"

"Okay, okay." Sam held up his hands. "I'm going."

He walked to the door to her hotel suite but turned around before leaving.

"When can I see you again?"

"How about never?" She lifted her chin.

"That doesn't work for me," Sam said. "I need to see you sooner than never."

"Come to my graduation ceremony to watch me get my PhD and maybe I'll talk to you then."

"I'll take it." Sam brazenly crossed the room again, pulled Leanne into his arms, and kissed her soundly for several long moments, long enough for her to surrender to his embrace, then he released her and stepped away. "See you after graduation."

Chapter Twenty-Five

News Reports

"Crown Prince Jared Sayid of Madain Saleh passed away last week, following a tragic motorcycle accident," the news anchorman said.

"Turn that up," Sam told his brother Liam. The television was mostly background noise in his office, but that announcement caught Sam's attention. The newscast continued as Liam reached for the remote control.

Liam was lounging in Sam's fine leather executive chair as Sam unpacked supplies transported from his old office in Jerusalem to his new penthouse suite of offices in a high-rise downtown Dubai. Another newly acquired real estate venture their father had purchased the previous year.

"He is survived by his wife, Princess Tayma, and their son, Prince Omar."

"Yeah, right," Liam said. "Jared's lover is probably more upset about his death than the princess."

"You're probably right," Sam said.

"There are rumors that Prince Jared's younger brother, Prince Marcos Sayid, intends to challenge the throne from his nephew, claiming a five-year-old is too young to hold the title as Crown."

"Dude, seriously?" Sam's mind whirled through possibilities. A five-year-old crown prince? Yeah, that wouldn't work. Someone needs to be ready to take over the kingdom if King Sayid dies. But Prince Omar would be next in line for the throne. Sam wondered how they would make that work.

"The king has yet to release a statement regarding the matter." The background behind the reporter changed. "In other news, Wall Street stocks rallied after last week's announcement that Cohen Enterprises would be acquiring the struggling shipping company, Calwell Industries, following weeks of negotiations."

"Hey, we made the news," Sam said. Guess they couldn't keep things under wraps for long.

"A spokesman for Calwell Industries told the Associated Press they were honored to be working with the international conglomerate and expect an amicable transition."

"What?" Liam called out. "There was nothing amicable about that hostile takeover. They're such liars."

"I'm sure Nathan didn't want the world to find out what a terrible businessman he was." Sam chuckled.

"Not everyone was meant to run a business." Liam leaned back and kicked his feet onto the desk in front of him and laced his fingers behind his head.

"Present company included," Sam grumbled. "Why don't you get over here and help me unpack these schematics."

"Don't we have people for that?' Liam asked.

"I don't trust anyone with my engineering plans." Sam allowed the scent of the familiar ink and paper of his engineering drawings to replace the new carpet and fresh paint smell permeating his office.

"And yet you would trust me?" Liam chuckled.

"No, not really." Sam realized Liam had a valid point. He switched topics, knowing the only reason he hadn't kicked Liam out of his new office yet was because he was getting up the nerve to ask him the important questions. "Have you heard from Rachel?"

"Yeah, we text all day long, but she hasn't mentioned Leanne if that's what you're really asking." As if to confirm his statement, Liam's phone binged with an incoming text, and Liam grinned as he responded to the message.

"She won't return my calls," Sam admitted.

"That ship sailed before you climbed on board," Liam said. "Might as well find someone else. Leanne's way too boring anyway. She's such a geek."

"Watch it, that's my future wife you're talking about."

Liam threw his head back and laughed. "Yeah, right. She's gonna want to marry a professor or something. She needs someone with a little more intellectual stimulation than you, little brother."

"Hey, I'm smart. I can design a complete mining plan to refine potash and extract potassium salts without a stupid degree."

"That's the real issue, though. She'll want a guy with a degree."

"You think?" Sam's shoulders slunk, along with his hopes.

"Yep." Liam popped his p for emphasis.

"Well, that just sucks."

"If you really want to win Leanne's heart, get yourself a nice pair of glasses, an Oxford sweater vest, and a pocket protector, and meet her at the library at her university."

"Very funny."

"Come here, little brother." Liam stood from the chair and stepped to the floor to ceiling windows of Sam's office. He draped his arm around Sam's shoulders and gestured out the window. "See that city? Dubai is filled with thousands of beautiful women. Take your pick."

Sam shrugged out from under his brother's arm. "I don't want thousands of women. I want Leanne."

Chapter Twenty-Six

Because She's Leanne

"Sam, I need your help," Prince Marcos said, breathless with urgency.

"How can I be of assistance, Your Highness?" Sam shifted his phone to his other ear. "Oh, and sorry to hear about your brother."

"Thank you, he will be missed." His answer was a little too dismissive for a relative in mourning. Marcos hurried on with the reason for his call. "I need you to locate Lyla Donovan. She's a guest at your resort."

"Is she the woman who fell in the pool after Nick's wedding?" Sam didn't immediately hop up from where he was having dinner with his older brother, Liam, in the Sushi restaurant at the resort. With Nick on his honeymoon and Lyle dealing with his wife on bed rest because of a difficult pregnancy, Sam found himself often stuck alone with Liam.

"Yes, I'm going to marry her," Marcos answered.

"Really? Does she know of your plans?" Sam pushed a little piece of salmon around with his chopsticks, dipping it in soy sauce and a tiny pile of wasabi.

"I told her, but she hung up on me."

Sam couldn't help laughing loudly. "Just hung up on you for no reason?"

"Well, I may have offended her," Marcos said. "But I'm coming to beg her forgiveness."

"Oh, this I gotta see. What do you need my help for?" Sam lifted the perfectly garnished raw fish into his mouth, along with a clump of basmati rice.

"I don't want to have to search the whole resort for her. I don't have time."

"What's the urgency?" Sam asked, setting aside his chopsticks and dabbing at his mouth with a cloth napkin. He rose from his seat and pulled a money clip from his pocket. He tossed a hundred dirham note onto the table, glancing over at his server to make sure she saw him pay for their meal along with a generous tip. He kicked his brother, who was completely distracted by his phone, probably texting Rachel again.

"My father's making me get married and produce an heir as soon as possible."

"And you're going to ask Lyla to marry you?" Sam asked. "Couldn't you snap your fingers and find a princess somewhere to be the lucky egg donor?"

"I want Lyla," Marcos said so matter-of-factly.

"Well, I want Leanne, but a guy doesn't always get what he wants," Sam said. "I suppose if you're a prince you can get anything you want."

"You'd think," Marcos said. "But it's not that simple. Lyla hates me."

"If she hates you, why do you want her so badly?" Sam wondered if he was asking himself or Prince Marcos.

"Because... because I just do," Marcos stammered with an answer. "She's Lyla."

"I actually understand better than you realize." Sam thought about his own answer to the same question. Why does he want Leanne? Because she's Leanne. "I'll go find Lyla right now. How soon will you be here?"

"The limo is pulling out of the airport, so in about twenty minutes."

"On it." Sam hung up the phone as he strode from the restaurant, Liam in tow, and headed for the lobby.

Sam was almost creeped out by how quickly the front desk staff were able to locate one of their guests, almost as if they kept tabs on everyone in the resort. He wondered how closely they kept tabs on him, and if they would give up personal information to anyone or just because he was the owner's son. Something to investigate. For now, he was just glad to locate Lyla Donovan.

He didn't have to wait in the lobby for long before a small but distinguished limousine pulled up and Prince Marcos emerged along with his advisor, Collins. They didn't even wait for the driver to come around and open the door for them.

Without preamble, Marcos asked, "Did you find her?"

"Yeah, she's out back at the tiki bar, having drinks with a couple of girlfriends."

"Perfect." Like the confident prince he was, Marcos strode through the lobby, without asking any of them to follow. They all did. Collins hurried to stay at his right shoulder.

Sam and Liam—who had finally pocketed his phone—hung back and waited near the entrance to the back patio as Marcos and Collins approached the table where Lyla and her friends sat.

Marcos swung an empty chair around from the next table and straddled it, leaning against the back directly across from Lyla. Collins also pulled up a chair but sat in a more conventional manner.

The shocked expression on Lyla's face was a combination of anger and wonder. Sam wished he were close enough to hear their conversation but didn't want to eavesdrop or intrude.

Collins lifted his hand to wave over a waitress just as Marcos left his chair and circled the table to take Lyla's hand. With very little coaxing, she slipped her hand in his and allowed him to help her to her feet. He backed away from the table, the entranced girl practically in his arms already.

"Dang, he's good. What the heck?" Liam said.

"He says he's gonna marry her," Sam told his brother. "Come on, let's go see what he does."

Sam and Liam approached the table where Collins now sat alone with Lyla's two friends. None of them even glanced their way.

All eyes in the poolside tiki bar were trained on the prince and his new girlfriend walking in the garden. Some guests in the bar even had cell phones raised, no doubt taking photos and videos that would go live on social media.

Within a few minutes, Marcos stopped Lyla and lifted her hand to his lips, then pulled her close. She didn't seem to resist. Marcos pulled back just slightly and cocked his head to the side, asking her a question none of them could hear.

Marcos pulled her closer and Sam expected him to kiss Lyla. Instead, he leaned down and kissed her neck, just below her earlobe and then moved to the other side and kissed her there as well.

One of Lyla's friends at the table whimpered and said, "Swoon."

"Gee, is that all it takes?" Sam muttered. "Gonna have to remember that."

Marcos whispered something to Lyla, his lips close to hers again and waited, a feather's width apart, allowing her the choice to complete the kiss... or not.

Suddenly, Lyla reached into Marcos's hair, and she pulled him to herself, kissing him with wild passion and abandon. He forgot, or ignored, all the people watching, and kissed her solidly, holding nothing back.

Several patrons at the outdoor bar whistled or catcalled, cheering on the prince for his conquest. People applauded and cheered.

When they finally came up for air, Marcos closed his eyes and pressed his forehead to hers, breathing heavy enough for Sam to see from twenty feet away.

Lyla whispered something to him, and Marcos pumped his fist into the air, calling out, "Yes!" Lyla placed her hand on his chest and spoke to him again, too quiet for any of them to hear. They spoke to each other for a few more minutes before Lyla leaned her head back and laughed.

Marcos picked up both her hands in his and kissed them before lowering himself to the ground and speaking passionately up to her. Sam didn't need to read lips or have hypersensitive ears to know Marcos was asking Lyla to marry him.

"Yes! You silly man!" Lyla called out. "Get up here and give me another kiss!"

Marcos stood and lifted her into his arms, swinging her around as they both smiled and laughed and the people in the bar clapped and cheered. He stopped spinning, rested her back on her feet, and they spoke quietly to one another again.

Marcos eventually cradled her face, and Lyla closed her eyes, surrendering to one more sweet, soft kiss. He pulled away after just a few short seconds, and they both opened their eyes, staring into one another's souls.

"I'm taking notes," Sam said. "I gotta get me some of those skills."

"I think every guy in this bar is taking notes," Liam acknowledged.

"Gee, I wonder if her boyfriend will see the video of that passionate proposal on social media," one of her friends said. They both snickered.

"Do you think he'll box up her stuff and send it back to her parents' house or make her come into the city and pack it up right in front of him?"

"He might just skip all that and throw it all in the dumpster."

"He's too nice of a guy for that."

"Maybe he'll need a shoulder to cry on," the one girl said.

"Rebound relationship?" The other girl wiggled her eyebrows.

"Heck yeah." She reached out to her friend for a high five.

Sam chuckled at their banter.

Eventually Lyla slipped from Marcos's arms and held his hand in hers until the last possible second as she backed away from him, leaving him standing alone in the garden as she glided back to her friends.

Sam watched as they gathered their purses and phones and beach towels and sweatshirts and other belongings and started toward the elevator to head back up to their suites.

Before entering the elevator, Lyla turned one more time and waved lightly to Marcos. His answering expression was that of cheesy, blissful happiness as she stepped into the elevator and disappeared.

"Lucky son of a prince," Sam grumbled. If only convincing Leanne would be that easy. Sam had serious doubts. Instead of dwelling on his own pain, Sam headed over to congratulate Marcos on his engagement.

Chapter Twenty-Seven

Quid Pro Quo

"Nick! How's married life?" Sam was excited to see his younger brother's name on the caller-ID. He pushed away from his desk and stretched, then turned to glance out his window at the Dubai skyline.

"I'm great, Sam. Adele and I have decided to remain on our honeymoon forever."

"That's fine. I'll just continue to run your businesses without you here. That or turn your accounts over to Liam, and he can destroy your future."

"Don't you dare." Nick laughed. "We'll be home eventually. What's everyone up to?"

"Well, let's see, Mom is very pregnant. Dad's busy getting his affairs in order so he can take time off when little Joseph arrives."

"They've named him? That's so sweet." Nick sounded nostalgic. "What about Miriam? Do they know if they're having a girl or a boy? How is she feeling?"

"Not good. She had some preterm contractions and wound up on bedrest," Sam told him. "Lyle's still working, but mostly from home. They're having a boy and are naming him Ishmael, but everyone mostly just refers to him as Baby Ishy."

"Ah, that's so adorable. I can't wait to have kids."

"Adele pregnant yet?" Sam asked. "You've been married well over a month now, right?"

"Not for lack of trying." Nick laughed and called out, "Hey!" It was obvious Adele had smacked him on the arm or stomach or something.

"You need to have your wife talk to her sister," Sam said, an idea forming in his thoughts. "Leanne's not speaking to me right now."

"What did you do?" How quickly Nick deduced that the reason Leanne was upset was because Sam had done something wrong.

"I was just excited that her family was moving to Dubai along with our family, but she said she doesn't want to move because she's still in college, and I said she didn't need to go to college because, if she marries me, she'll be rich and won't have to work, and she got all offended and kicked me out of her hotel suite." Sam took a deep breath after saying all that in one sentence.

"Wait, slow down. Back up. Our families are moving to Dubai... permanently?"

"Well, until Father gets this yacht building bug out of his system and drags us somewhere else on whatever superyacht you design for him."

"Wh-what?" Nick stammered.

"Oh, come on, I know you were at the acquisitions meeting when Dad bought Calwell Industries. He wants you to design him a couple of superyachts, you know those really big yachts that only billionaires can afford."

"I know what a superyacht is," Nick said with exasperation. "I told Dad already that I don't know how to design one!"

"Well, time to do some research, I guess. You can't have sex twenty-four-seven, right?"

"You'd be surprised."

"At this rate, I'll never find out since Leanne won't return my calls. While you're researching yacht building, have your wife call my girlfriend, will you?"

"I'll get right on that," Nick grumbled.

"Where are you guys, anyway?" Sam asked.

"Cozumel."

"Hey, you're pretty close to where Prince Marcos and Lyla are honeymooning in Puerto Aventuras. Get this, they found a resort called the Barcelo Maya Palace. Guess he wants his new bride to feel like a princess before he takes her home to meet the king and queen. They probably don't want to come back from their honeymoon either."

"Wait, when did Marcos get married? He didn't even have a girlfriend."

"He met her the night of your wedding. Married her a few weeks later."

"Why didn't he call me?" Nick asked. "I'm his best friend."

"You've been a little busy the past few weeks. He probably didn't want to... uh... disturb you." Sam cleared his throat playfully.

"No excuse. I'm going to call him and give him a hard time."

"You do that. And get your wife to call her sister."

"Dude, you've said that three times now." Nick chuckled.

"Good, maybe my request will register as being important. I'm a good salesman."

"You are a good salesman," Nick said. "Now, go get back to work, because you're doing my job too, right?"

"Oh, come on," Sam teased his brother. "Liam is sober for a few hours a day. He can handle your accounts."

"Quid pro quo, my brother," Nick said. "You take care of my accounts while I'm on my honeymoon; I'll have my wife talk her sister into being your girlfriend again."

"Deal." Sam breathed a sigh of relief, suddenly wanting to get back to work. "Say hello to Adele for me. Love you."

"Love you too," Nick said.

Sam hung up with his brother and immediately dialed the number for Nick's newest acquisition. "Mr. Netanel, this is Sam Cohen, Nick's brother. Did you hear he got married? He wanted me to check and see if there's anything you need from us while he's on his honeymoon. Oh, good. I'm glad things are going well. Can you meet for lunch next week?"

Chapter Twenty-Eight

Blue Balloons

L yle's impassioned group text contained lots of exclamation marks and two demands: "Come to the maternity ward!!! And pray!!!"

"Mom's in labor!" Sam jumped from his chair and called across the common area between his and Liam's offices. Every secretary and receptionist and designer and salesperson between here and there glanced up with expectant smiles.

"Could be Miriam," Liam said with less urgency than Sam felt. Liam was still staring at his phone as he moseyed out of his office, where he'd been holding down his chair and sipping the flask in his top drawer. "Why else would Lyle be the one sending the text?"

"No, it's way too soon for Miriam to be in labor," Sam said. "That's why she's been on bed rest for weeks." He grabbed the file folder on his desk and handed it to his secretary without any instructions. She was competent enough to know what to do.

"That would explain why he said to pray," Liam reasoned. "I mean, yeah, we want Mom to have comfort while in labor, but that doesn't require prayer. Heck, what do I know? If there is a god, I doubt he'd listen to a sinner like me."

"Hey, everybody," Sam called out. "Get some blue balloons and cigars. We're either having a baby brother or a nephew this afternoon!"

There was a general cheer in the office along with well-wishes and congratulations.

"Oh, and apparently pray," Liam added. "If you believe in that crap."

"I'll pray enough for both of us," Liam's secretary said in a flirty voice.

"You do that, babe." Liam winked at her, then cleared his throat. "I mean, Mrs. Shaw."

"Seriously?" Sam rolled his eyes at his brother and then strode over to the elevator and pushed the button to call the lift to their floor. He turned back to his own secretary. "Can you have the doorman get us a limo out front by the time we get down there?"

"Yes, sir, Mr. Cohen." She picked up the phone.

"Come on, Liam," Sam grumbled as Liam whispered something close to his secretary's ear, causing her to giggle. When he and Liam were finally in the elevator and the door closed, Sam chastised his brother. "That's a sexual harassment lawsuit waiting to happen."

"Eh, we're fine." Liam leaned against the side of the elevator wall and folded his arms across his chest. He smirked and raised his eyebrows, challenging Sam to argue.

Sam wasn't giving Liam the satisfaction of a response. He just glared at him for the duration of the sixty-second ride in the high-speed elevator from the top of the high rise to the ground level.

Their limo was waiting at the front door, as requested. At least one of their secretaries was competent at her job. They were both surprisingly calm on the ride to the hospital, considering they'd been asked to pray.

Sam wasn't sure what he believed about prayer and a higher power. Their father had never insisted his sons participate in any religion, although they were surrounded on all sides with a variety of choices. He'd always encouraged them to have good moral values, which apparently wasn't working on several of his sons. Sam committed to living a righteous life and making his father proud and had thus far succeeded.

His older brothers, not so much, Liam especially. Nick and Jacob on the other hand were perfect saints to the point of extreme. Sam marveled how five brothers could be raised the same but grow to have such a dichotomy of values.

Before he could ponder further, the limo pulled up to the hospital, and Sam stepped from the car before the driver could come around to open the door, not waiting for Liam but knowing he'd follow. After another—slower—elevator ride, they emerged into a waiting area on the maternity floor.

The first family member Sam noticed was his mother, still very pregnant and sitting awkwardly in a waiting room chair. That meant Miriam was in labor. Crap. It was too soon. No wonder Lyle asked them to pray. Sam tried to count weeks and months and couldn't remember either of their due dates.

"Mom, we came as soon as we could. No, don't get up. I'll come to you." Sam leaned over to give his mom a hug. He looked around the waiting room. Levi stood and patted Sam on the shoulder and Jacob wrapped his arms around Sam's waist.

Liam followed Sam into the waiting room but kept his hands in his pockets, mumbling something about hating the smell of hospitals.

"How is Miriam?" Sam sat beside his mom and took her hand in his.

"They're probably going to do a cesarean delivery this afternoon. The medicines aren't working. They can't get the contractions to stop. They're afraid Baby Ishy's in distress." Her throat caught, and she lifted a tissue to her face, not far from tears. Her first grandbaby was in that hospital room, and she was probably having a hard time holding herself together.

"I'm sure the nurses and doctors are doing all they can, and Baby Ishy will be just fine," Sam reassured his mom, patting the top of her hand.

The elevator door binged and opened, and out stepped Miriam's oldest sister, Ruth Ashish, followed by her sister Rachel, and finally, their sister Leanne. Just the woman Sam wanted to see.

Leanne's jaw dropped when she noticed Sam sitting there and looked back into the elevator as if considering reentering and making a break for the lobby of the hospital. The elevator door closed, leaving Leanne standing there staring at him.

Sam rose from where he was sitting beside his mother, and a tunnel formed between him and Leanne. She was here.

He forgot the reasons he was in the hospital as his feet carried him forward, and he stood before the woman he loved. He could breathe again.

She was here.

Chapter Twenty-Nine

Study Partners

"Hi," Sam whispered to Leanne, just barely close enough for her to hear him.

"Hey, what's up?" Leanne took a deep sigh and slouched her shoulders. "Sorry I haven't returned your calls." She scuffed the toe of her sneaker against the white tiled floor of the maternity ward.

"You're not finished with your PhD, are you?" Sam offered an olive branch. "I wasn't really expecting to hear from you."

"Yeah, that's why you had all of your brothers tell all of my sisters that you were crying into your pillow every night in misery because I dumped you."

"Not *all* of your sisters," Sam corrected her. "None of my brothers are dating or married to your oldest sister, Ruth."

"True."

"How is school?" Sam wasn't sure what to say to her. The last time they'd seen each other, he'd offended her and promised he wouldn't bother her until after graduation. Dare he hope she chose to leave college after her master's degree and not continue on for a PhD?

"Honestly? Not the same without Adele at home," Leanne said. "She was my study partner. I keep thinking everything will go back to normal when she comes home from her honeymoon, but then I remember that she'll be living down here with you guys. She's never coming home."

Sam wasn't sure how to empathize. Leanne was right. Adele was never coming home. He wondered how he might be able to alleviate some of Leanne's stress without invalidating her concerns. "That's tough."

"Anyway, classes are fine, I guess." Her face brightened. "Hey, you'd get a kick out of one of the classes I'm taking next semester. Natural Resources Management."

"Now that's something I could help you with," Sam said. "I'll be your study partner for that class."

"I'm gonna hold you to that." Leanne pushed his shoulder playfully.

Sam took advantage of her closeness. "I'm gonna hold your hand." He slipped his fingers in between hers and held on. She didn't pull away.

Leanne rested her head on Sam's shoulder, and he pulled her close. "How is my sister?"

"They're probably going to do a cesarean delivery this afternoon," he told her. "They're trying to keep Baby Ishy cooking as long as possible, but if he goes into distress, they're getting him out of there."

"I wish I could see Miriam," Leanne said. "I doubt they'll let me back to her room."

"Probably not."

As they held one another in the hallway, the door to the elevator opened, revealing a surprise. Nick and Adele, back from their honeymoon.

Leanne and Adele squealed and pulled each other close as only sisters can. Nick and Sam clasped each other's hands and hugged.

Others in the family hurried over to give them hugs and welcome them, everyone's worry about Miriam's pregnancy momentarily set on the back burner.

A minute later the elevator opened again, and the girls' parents arrived. There were more hugs around the group and more smiles and more tears.

Tears shifted to panic when Lyle came stumbling out the door of the maternity ward, collapsed into a chair, and lowered his face to his hands, sobbing.

Chapter Thirty

I May Have Yelled at Her

"Lyle, what happened?" Sam rushed forward and dropped to his knees in front of his older brother, trying to pull his hands from his face. "Is Miriam okay? Baby Ishy?"

"I don't know," Lyle said, raising his tear-streaked face. "They kicked me out because I was having a breakdown."

"Why were you having a breakdown?" Sam sat back on his heels, relieved Lyle hadn't said Miriam or Baby Ishy was dying. He brushed his hands across the pant legs of his business suit, having just come from the office. The floor where he'd been crouched was much dirtier than he preferred for a hospital waiting room. The stench of antiseptic cleanser implied the floors had been cleaned recently, but the grime and debris indicated otherwise.

Lyle's words came out in a rush of emotion. "Because of all the beeping monitors and rising and falling numbers, and Miriam's blood pressure is really high, and they're concerned that the baby's heart rate is too low, and no one will tell me what's going on, and so I got angry and..."

"Please don't tell me you yelled at a nurse..."

"Worse," Lyle admitted. His face showed a combination of shame and apprehension, and he cringed as if he was expecting everyone in the room to hate him for what he was about to tell them.

"What did you do, son?" Levi stepped forward, with a commanding voice.

"I may or may not have yelled at Miriam."

"What?" Ruth cried out. "How could you yell at our sister?" That set the rest of her sisters into a frenzy.

"She's in labor, for heaven's sake," Leanne said. "You should be supportive."

"What could she possibly have done to warrant being yelled at?" Adele asked.

"Whatever you think she did wrong was probably *your* fault, not hers." Rachel said.

"That's what she said too. She growled at me and said I did this to her, as if she wasn't partially at fault for getting pregnant."

"You think it was her *fault* that she got pregnant?" Sam asked, incredulous.

"She should have been on the pill," Lyle said. "She should have made sure she was protected before sleeping with me."

"She didn't even have a *boyfriend!* Why would she have been on the pill?" Leanne balled her fists and leaned closer to him. Sam considered pulling her back but decided that would make things worse between him and Leanne. Besides, if Leanne decked Lyle, he deserved it. Sam would just get Leanne some ice for her wrist afterward.

"You should have been the one using protection," Ruth said.

"You shouldn't have even been sleeping with her before marriage," Adele grumbled.

"I don't think there was any sleeping going on that night." Liam chuckled and smirked but cringed and held up his hands in defense when Rachel smacked his arm. "Ah, come on, babe, I was just teasing."

Sam cocked his head at Liam, who was distracted, wrapping his arms around Rachel, placating her and whispering in her ear. Liam called Rachel *babe*, just as he'd called his secretary *babe*. Sam wondered if Liam called all his conquests *babe* so he wouldn't mistakenly call them the wrong name. What a cockroach. Sam pulled his attention back to Lyle, the other cockroach in his family. "What exactly did you say to Miriam?"

"I told her she got pregnant on purpose to trap me into marrying her," Lyle admitted. That caused another uproar and every sister and brother and father and mother in the room fired retorts at Lyle so fast Sam had a hard time separating who said what.

"You jerk."

"She was drunk. How could she have gotten pregnant on purpose?"

"You got her drunk and took her upstairs to your room. Maybe it was you who got her pregnant on purpose."

"No one gets pregnant on purpose."

"Why would she want to marry you? She only married you *because* she was pregnant."

"You're such an idiot."

"No wonder they kicked you out of the delivery room."

"I'm disappointed in you, son."

"How could you have said that to my daughter?"

"Do you realize I have a shotgun in my closet back home with your name written on it?"

"I... can't... believe... you would say that," their mom called out between sobs, holding one hand to her very pregnant belly and, the other, holding a tissue to her eyes.

Just then, a nurse came into the room and called out, "Is there a woman in here named Ruth?"

"Yes, I'm Ruth." Their oldest sister stepped forward and lifted her chin with hope in her eyes.

"Miriam is asking for you," the nurse said. "She wants you in the delivery room with her and we're just about ready to head in there." As Ruth followed the nurse, others in the family called out questions.

"Is Miriam okay?"

"Is she having a C-section?"

"Is Baby Ishy in distress?"

"Someone will be out in a little while to give you an update," the nurse said, then closed the door between the waiting room and the delivery wing.

The room quieted and everyone relaxed into a tense but resolved calm. People were breathing heavy and scowling at Lyle and turning away and crossing arms.

"Jerk," Rachel grumbled.

"Come on, babe, let's go for a walk." Liam led Rachel down the hall away from the waiting room and all its tension.

Leanne huffed away from Lyle and sat on the opposite side of the waiting room, glaring across the room at Lyle. Sam joined her and sat beside her but didn't try to reach out. She had her arms folded across her chest, and Sam wasn't about to unfold them. He leaned his elbows on his knees.

Adele sat on the other side of Leanne, and Nick settled beside her, holding her hand in his.

Their parents gathered around the boys' mom, Sarah, fussing over her to calm her down lest they had another woman in labor, which wasn't out of the realm of possibility.

Only Jacob stayed anywhere close to Lyle, and even he sat two seats away.

Lyle lowered his head into his hands, elbows on his knees, and that's how they all stayed for countless minutes.

Chapter Thirty-One

Passionate Kisses and Other Disgusting Things

"You want to take a walk?" Sam asked Leanne.

She still had her arms folded across her chest and a scowl on her face directed at Lyle. Getting her out of the room and away from the source of her anger might be just what she needed.

Sam knew going for a walk would help *him*. He wanted to be alone with Leanne, to talk things over, see if they could resolve her anger toward him for offending her the day after Nick and Adele's wedding.

"I guess." After standing, she kept her arms crossed as if to imply that he'd better not try to hold her hand. If she wasn't ready for that, he would respect her boundaries.

They walked in companionable silence down the hall past doctors' offices, most of which still had patients coming and going. There were no patient rooms in this direction, and that was more comfortable than walking past people in beds, with blinking and beeping monitors, a variety of unpleasant smells, and the risk of infection.

Sam tucked his hands into the pockets of his slacks.

"How did you girls get down here from Jerusalem so quickly?" Sam asked.

"Miriam called this morning, crying that she was scared and heading to the hospital. Your dad called in some favors and chartered us a private jet to get down here."

"I'm sure Miriam's glad you're here," Sam said, not wanting to come right out and say that he was glad also. Leanne beat him to it.

"You're not disappointed either, are you?" Leanne bumped her shoulder against his, and he took the opportunity to wrap his arm around her back, not pressuring her to offer her hand but wanting to be close.

"I've missed you," Sam said.

"I've missed you too." Leanne sighed. "I didn't want to admit that I missed you, but you and I used to text back and forth all day long. I've watched Rachel text Liam these past few weeks and laugh with him and flirt with him, and every day, I just wanted to ask her if she could ask Liam how you were doing."

"Same here. Liam's insufferable."

"I have a feeling they'll be the next in our families to tie the knot," Leanne said.

"You think?" Sam considered whether to mention Liam's tendency to sleep around, and how he was probably having an affair with his secretary but chose to wait. Nothing good ever came from gossiping about someone else.

Still, he would have to address the situation eventually in order to prevent Rachel from stepping blindly into a marriage with a jerk like Liam. Dang, was he really thinking that way about his own brother? Yep. And Liam deserved the designation. He was a jerk.

"They sure spend a lot of time texting back and forth." Sam avoided the admission for now.

"What about you and me?" Leanne asked with quiet apprehension. "Do you think we'll ever get married?"

They had rounded the corner at the end of the hallway and found themselves completely alone at a stairwell doorway with a red exit sign. With nowhere else to go, Sam took the opportunity to lean against the wall and pull Leanne close. "I'd marry you today if you'd let me."

"Even if that meant moving back to Jerusalem?" She avoided eye contact but allowed herself to be pulled into his arms.

Sam lifted his hand and raised her chin, leaving his hand cradling her cheek. "At this point, I'm ready to ignore everyone else's expectations and follow you anywhere."

"Even if that means defying your father's wishes?" she asked.

"Yeah." Sam didn't even hesitate. "He raised me to become a responsible adult and plan for my future. You're my future."

"What if he disowns you?"

"One, he wouldn't. My father knows we'll all go our separate ways eventually. That's the nature of raising sons. Two, I'm already a millionaire on my own merits, so I don't need his money. And three, I really don't care about the money. I'd rather live in a one room apartment and sleep next to you each night than live in a mansion without you."

"I feel the same way about you," Leanne said. She finally met his eyes.

Dare he hope she'd have him to be her husband even though she hadn't spoken to him for over a month? That's how he perceived this conversation was heading. He didn't want to ruin the moment by forcing her into a commitment. Instead, he gazed into her eyes and glanced down at her lips, considering how this kiss would be different from any others prior.

They'd been kids goofing off, getting drunk together, playing at being adults without actually stepping into a position of responsibility. This was serious all of a sudden. They were ready to make a forever commitment.

Sam grazed his thumb across Leanne's cheek, then moved his hand down so that his thumb grazed her lips. She parted them with a sigh and relaxed into his arms. He didn't hesitate or waste any more time, just pressed his lips to hers with a soft hunger and passionate desire.

Without registering his actions, Sam turned them both around and pushed her gently against the wall, his lips never leaving hers, his hunger for her growing stronger, wishing they could be truly alone and not stuck in the hallway of a hospital. He wished they were already married and this kiss could lead to far more physical connections. The removal of clothing being one of many desires.

Leanne gripped Sam's hair, pulling him even closer. His lips left hers and lowered to her neck, taking a play from Prince Marcos's playbook. She moaned audibly as he trailed kisses along her neck and up under her earlobes. Yeah, this was working as well on her and it had on Lyla.

They were interrupted by the door to the stairwell opening. Liam and Rachel emerged and stopped short. Liam chuckled. "Dang, guess we weren't the only ones who needed to hook up while we had the opportunity."

As Sam pulled away from Leanne, he realized Liam and Rachel were both tucking in their shirts and straightening their clothes. Yeah, they hadn't been just making out.

"Really, Rachel?" Leanne sneered at her sister. "In the stairwell? Gross."

"Where were you gonna do it? In the hallway? Where anyone can walk in on you?"

"Like we just did?" Liam chuckled so hard he snorted.

"We weren't going to *do* anything at all," Sam said, disgusted at his brother.

"Oh, you were heading in that direction from that passionate kiss we just witnessed," Liam said.

"That's so uncouth, man," Sam said to his brother. "We're here to support Lyle and Miriam, not sneak off to do whatever it was you were doing in the stairwell."

"You're one to talk, you hypocrite." Liam stepped closer and got right up in Sam's face. "You were already going almost as far as we did."

"Not even close." Sam stood toe-to-toe with his older brother. "Having sex in the stairwell at a hospital is almost as disgusting as having an affair with your married secretary."

"What?" Rachel and Leanne said at the same time.

Sam and his brother stepped apart and looked over at the girls, both of whom stood with their arms folded across their chests and scowls on their faces. Oops.

Chapter Thirty-Two

Lost Her Again

"How could you?" Rachel shoved Liam and he stumbled backward. "An affair with your secretary? Don't I mean anything to you?" She stormed away, around the corner and down the hall.

"Rachel, stop. It's not what you think." Liam hurried after her.

"It's exactly what she thinks," Sam grumbled, remembering the way Liam had flirted with *Mrs.* Shaw, his secretary. Before they'd left the office, he'd called her *babe* and whispered something in her ear, making her giggle. The whole scene had been disgusting. And not an hour later, he was with Rachel as if nothing was wrong.

"Why didn't you tell me?" Leanne asked, vitriol in her words. "All that talk about my sister marrying your brother and you didn't think to mention that he was having an affair with another woman? A *married* woman? Don't you think that's something my sister should know about?"

"I did consider telling you," Sam said, backpedaling. "I just didn't think that was the right time."

"When would be the right time? When she's walking down the aisle in a white dress?"

"After what they were doing in the stairwell, I don't think she should be wearing a white dress." Sam's snide comment set Leanne off again.

"You judgmental, hypocritical jerk." Leanne stepped closer and sneered at Sam. "That's my sister you're talking about."

"Who you were just criticizing for doing inappropriate things in the stairwell at a hospital." Sam pointed at the door to the stairs as if Leanne needed a reminder.

"Just because I disagree with my sister's actions doesn't mean I think she should be judged about wearing a white dress to her wedding."

"Whatever color her dress, she shouldn't marry my brother," Sam said.

"Maybe I shouldn't marry *you*, either. What is it with you Cohen boys? You're all a bunch of jerks."

"Your sister Adele sure would disagree with you."

"You didn't see her the past five years since high school." Leanne shook her head. "She never got over Nick's betrayal."

"And yet now they're married," Sam said. "Things worked out for them. They can work out for us too."

"I don't think so, Sam. But good try." Leanne started to leave, but Sam reached for her arm.

"Leanne, don't walk away from me again."

"Let go of my arm," Leanne said through a growl.

Sam released her arm and shoved his hands into his pockets, not wanting her to feel threatened in any way. How did they go from making out to arguing again in the space of five minutes?

If only he could reverse time and not call out his brother for having an affair. No one would be the wiser. Liam and Rachel would still be riding the high of having snuck off to do things Sam could only dream about with Leanne, and he and Leanne could be planning their future together. If only. Ugh.

As Sam watched Leanne walk around the corner and hurry off in a huff, he leaned against the wall where he'd just been kissing her. She was finally his girlfriend again for one brief moment, and then he lost her. Again.

Chapter Thirty-Three

Baby Ishy

After what felt like an eternity, Sam made his way back to the hospital waiting room. He had no reason to go back there and several reasons to stay away. Avoiding Leanne and Liam, the two biggest reasons.

Sam took inventory of his family as he approached the open waiting area. His mother looked sick. He wondered if she was heading into labor soon. He met his father's eyes and saw worry there. Sam knew he needed to do a better job of smoothing things over with his brothers if only for the sake of their mother's health.

The two sources of contention, Liam and Lyle, sat beside one another in the chairs closest to the door of the maternity wing. Neither of them glanced his way when Sam walked into the room, but the scowl on Liam's face spoke volumes.

Leanne huddled in the corner with her sisters Adele and Rachel, whispering in angry but hushed tones.

Sam didn't even try to listen. He made a beeline for his brothers Nick and Jacob, and the three of them sat together in silence.

Cassandra Ashish paced near the doors to the maternity wing, chewing nervously on a thumbnail to the point where Sam wished he had nail clippers to offer her. She glanced frequently at the door as if her willing it to open would miraculously help her daughter get through this frightening time.

Finally, the door opened, and a disheveled doctor emerged with a hopeful, albeit tired, expression. Every family member in the room rose to their feet in anticipation, or maybe just the need to stand and stretch.

Lyle hurried to stand before the doctor, remorse and worry evident in his creased brow. "Is my baby...?"

"You have a little boy," the doctor said, placing his hand on Lyle's shoulder. "He's very little, and he's going to need a few weeks in the neonatal intensive care unit, but I think he's going to be fine."

"Oh, thank goodness." Lyle's shoulders slumped with relief. "And Miriam?"

"She was alert during the surgery and is resting in recovery. There's not much you can do for her right now, so you might as well get scrubbed up, and we'll take you back to meet your new son. Have the two of you named him yet?"

Sam had to give the patient, older man credit. He was probably used to dealing with scared, young fathers and spoke more kindly to Lyle than he probably wanted to after what Lyle had said earlier in the delivery room.

A woman blaming her husband for the pain she was in during delivery was common. Turning that blame around and putting it back on the wife rarely happened. Probably not the first time. The doctor had likely heard it all in his years of service.

"Ishy," Lyle said with breathy reverence.

"Ish...Ish-ee?" The doctor raised his eyebrows.

"Ishmael," Lyle clarified, raising his chin with mature confidence. "Our son's name is Ishmael Daniel Cohen."

"That's a fine name," the doctor said. "Now let's take you back there and meet your son. Whoa..."

The doctor looked over Lyle's shoulder to the side of the room where their mother was cringing and breathing heavy, having just stood from the waiting room chair. Her eyes were closed, and her hand rested on top of her very pregnant belly. The doctor pushed past Lyle.

"How long have you been having contractions?"

"A few..." Sarah breathed several times, then continued. "A few hours."

"A few hours?" Their dad hurried to her side. "Why didn't you tell me?"

"Oh, phooey, we had enough to worry about than little ole me."

"Yeah, well, you're done worrying about everyone else," the doctor said. "Time for you to worry about you."

A woman rushed forward with a wheelchair, and Sarah was helped into the seat. Before the whole gravity of the situation could register, their mom was whisked away to deliver baby Joseph.

"Good luck, Mom," Sam called. His brothers and the Ashish family called out similar well wishes. The mood in the room relaxed into subdued excitement after the doors closed, taking their father and Lyle with them.

The sisters gave each other hugs, then Adele stepped over to Nick, and they kissed, then gazed into each other's eyes. Sam wondered if they'd be celebrating the arrival of another baby sometime in the near future.

He hugged Jacob, then rubbed the top of his head. "Not going to be the baby of the family anymore."

"He'll always be the baby of the family," Liam said with a good-natured chuckle, approaching Sam and Jacob, his face a mask of remorse. "He'll just gain the title of Big Brother like the rest of us did. And being a big brother is usually pretty cool."

"Usually," Sam mumbled. "Unless your younger brother rats you out."

"I had it coming," Liam admitted with a shrug. "Rachel will forgive me... eventually."

Sam glanced in the direction where the sisters were huddled together and wondered at the likelihood of Rachel forgiving Liam.

Nick turned from his wife to join his brothers. He smiled as he approached. "Looks like we're all going to be big brothers now, eh?"

"We were just discussing that, actually," Sam said. "We told Jacob he's still the baby in the family even if there's another baby in the family."

"Nah, he's all grown up now, aren't you, buddy?" Nick wrapped his arm around Jacob's shoulders and then reached his other arm around Sam's. "Come on, guys. Group hug."

Sam took a deep breath, then reluctantly wrapped his arm around Liam's shoulders as Liam wrapped his other arm around Jacob's.

"There is one thing we all have in common besides gaining a brother," Liam said. "We all became uncles today too."

"That's right." Nick nodded in recognition.

"Pretty cool that I got to become an uncle and a big brother in the same day," Jacob said with a grin. "I'm the only one who can say that."

"And Lyle became a dad," Sam added. "He's the only one who can say that."

"I love you, guys," Nick said. "I'm proud to call you my brothers."

"Me too!" Jacob said with enthusiasm.

Sam and Liam glanced at one another and offered half-hearted smiles. Sam fought the desire to roll his eyes or to glare at Liam. Love. Pride. Not sure about that, but family was family, and Liam was part of their family. For that reason alone, Sam would choose to be nice to Liam. For now.

Chapter Thirty-Four

Baby Joseph

"Sam?" Through a fog of restless sleep on a hard, waiting room chair, Sam startled awake. His father jostled his shoulder gently. "Dad?" Suddenly more alert, Sam sat up quickly. "Is Mom okay? Baby Joseph?"

"They're both fine," Levi Cohen said with a smile. "Would you like to come meet your baby brother?"

Sam looked around the waiting room. Other people were leaning on their elbows, propped up, barely awake or snoring. Some of his family had their heads in each other's laps. Eighteen-year-old Jacob was sprawled out across three chairs, his lanky teenage body taking up more space than should be physically possible.

Liam and Rachel were together in the far corner, her arms wrapped around him and using his chest as a pillow. Guess she forgave him.

Nick and Adele were leaning toward one another, heads touching, propping each other up. Both of their eyes were closed but Sam got the impression neither of them were truly asleep.

Leanne's head was in Adele's lap, and Adele's hand rested on her sister's upper back in a way that indicated to Sam that she'd been comforting Leanne, almost as if she'd been petting her sister's hair. Man, he wished he could have been the one to comfort Leanne. Someday, m aybe.

Daniel and Cassandra Ashish had their shoulders and heads together in much the same way Adele and Nick did. They were both awake and yawning.

Lyle was nowhere to be seen, and Sam assumed he was back with his wife, Miriam, and their new baby, Ishy.

Nearby, a coffee pot sat with a few inches of burnt coffee available should anyone be that desperate for caffeine. Sam wrinkled his nose at the metallic, bitter smell.

He realized his father had his hand out ready to lift Sam from his chair, and Sam reached up and clasped his hand, thankful for the help as well as the human connection. His dad was such a good man.

As much as Sam wanted to pretend he'd return to Jerusalem to be with Leanne, he knew the truth. He'd follow his father to the ends of the earth. His trust in him was that strong.

Maybe Leanne wasn't the right woman for him if Sam knew in his gut that his place was with his father. And Nick. Weird thought to pop into his head. Nick was his younger brother, but somehow Sam inherently knew that Nick would one day lead their family.

But Leanne. Sam also knew that he was supposed to be with Leanne. How could he do both? Follow his father and brother but remain with her? There was only one solution, and it had been staring at him in the face for months. He just hadn't worded the invitation correctly. She needed to come with him. Period. End of story. No, beginning of story.

Sam didn't need to live in Jerusalem with Leanne. Leanne needed to come with him. To Dubai? No, he realized, there was someplace else they would go. He just didn't know where yet. Maybe his father knew. Or Nick? Wherever they went, Leanne needed to come with him. There was no doubt in his mind.

"Penny for your thoughts, son," Levi asked quietly as they walked toward the door that led to the maternity wing. He pushed a button and the door opened with a soft whoosh, then closed automatically behind them.

"Thinking about the future, Dad. Not sure about my place," Sam admitted.

Levi stopped him and turned Sam's shoulder so they were facing one another. No one was nearby. The hallway in this section had low lighting, as if they'd been dimmed to allow patients a chance to rest. The rooms around them seemed empty, so Sam felt alone with his father. A rare occurrence.

"What is your heart telling you?" Levi asked.

"I will go where you lead me, Father."

Levi glanced back the way they had just come, back toward the door to the quiet waiting room.

"And she needs to come with me." Sam anticipated his father's question before he asked.

"How do you plan to make that happen?" his dad asked.

"I don't know yet."

"I never have to worry about you, Sam."

"You don't?" Why, at the age of twenty-five, did Sam feel vulnerable in the presence of his father? He wanted his approval. He had it. He wanted his love. He had it. So, why?

"You have already chosen the right path," Levi said.

"I have?"

"You already know you have. You, and your younger brothers, and your mother." His father took a deep breath and glanced back toward the waiting room. "But I worry about Liam and Lyle."

"Me too."

Levi continued as if Sam hadn't interrupted. "I fear they're already too far gone. They see the right path. They see me inviting them to join us and be happy as a family. But they turn from me and *choose* to walk away."

"Insightful words, Father," Sam said. "Almost prophetic."

"I'll never claim to be perfect, my son," Levi said. "But I see the writing on the walls, and I'm able to read between the lines." He patted Sam on the cheek.

Sam wrapped his arms around his father, a rare show of emotions between the two of them. As the middle child, Sam had always been a bit forgotten, a bit invisible. But he was quietly learning and growing and carving out his own place in their family. He would probably never take a stand or be a leader, but he would be here in whatever way the family needed him. He was Sam. And that was just who he needed to be.

"You ready to go meet your baby brother?" his father asked.

They stepped apart, and Sam nodded, excitement filling his heart. They walked down the hall in silence until they came to an unassuming door that was opened. A curtain was pulled between the door and the bed.

"Knock, knock," Levi said in a quiet, respectful voice. "Are you awake, sweetheart?"

"Sort of," Sarah's tired voice answered.

As he and his father came around the curtain, Sam smiled peacefully. "Hi, Mom. How you feeling?"

"Oh, my Sam." His mother held out her hand, inviting him forward. "I'm so glad you're here."

"I heard you brought me another little brother to spoil," Sam said. "I just had to get started right away."

"He's right over here." Sarah indicated toward a little rolling bassinet that was just high enough that his mom could see him from the bed.

"Oh, Mom, he's beautiful." Sam gazed down at the most adorable little bundle of swaddled baby boy he'd ever seen. "May I?" Sam looked up at his father and then mother, with raised eyebrows, asking permission to hold Baby Joseph.

"Of course." Levi stepped back to allow Sam to get close.

With careful but sure hands, Sam lifted the tiny bundle from where he rested in the bassinet. Sam had been a young teenager when Jacob was born. Being an adult and welcoming a baby brother was a different experience. He was old enough to become a father himself. His parents were nearly too old to be having another baby. Yet, here he was. Evidence of their love.

Tears sprang to Sam's eyes. This is what he wanted. With Leanne. Now he just needed to convince her. Maybe he could bring her down to meet his little brother and show her the emotional connection of holding a baby.

"Another son," Sam wondered. "Why didn't you choose to have any daughters?"

His mom and dad chuckled. As if they had any control. Levi reached out to hold Sarah's hand. "Daniel had all the daughters. I had all the sons. That's how we planned it."

"*Who* had all the daughters and sons?" Sarah asked playfully.

"Cassandra had all the daughters," Levi admitted. "And my incredible bride gave me all these amazing sons." His parents held each other's gaze as if Sam wasn't in the room, and he almost felt as if he was intruding on their private moment.

Sam cradled his baby brother in his arms and stepped toward the window, gazing down at the perfect little miracle. Someday *he* would be holding a son.

Someday.

Chapter Thirty-Five

Breakfast and a Nap

The waiting room had cleared out by the time Sam returned from seeing little Joseph, and then down the hall to the NICU to see Baby Ishy through the glass walls. Uncles weren't authorized visitors, and that was okay. Sam was exhausted.

He decided to wait to contact Leanne until after he'd gotten cleaned up and fed, and possibly after he'd napped. He almost fell asleep in the limo on the ride back to the resort. A quick conversation with the concierge on the way into the lobby and breakfast was ordered to be delivered to his suite as soon as possible.

A steamy hot shower washed off the grime of spending the night perched on a plastic waiting room chair in the hospital. But the steam and heat also doubled his fatigue. Just as Sam wondered if he'd be able to keep his eyes open long enough to wait for room service, there was a knock at his door.

Not room service.

"Leanne?" Sam held the door open for his on-again-off-again girl-friend who took him on a roller coaster ride only to crash the cars at the bottom of each hill.

As Leanne tucked herself into Sam's arms, he breathed in the heady scent of her freshly washed, damp hair and savored the soft, thin flannel jersey shirt and pants combination that looked like regular clothes but screamed pajamas. Leanne was probably just as tired as he was.

"Have you eaten?" Sam asked as he rubbed his hands up and down her back, suddenly much more awake than he'd been three minutes prior.

"Not yet," she whispered, holding him in her arms as he held her.

"I have room service on the way up."

"Good." Leanne pulled herself away and strode over to his bed. She didn't bother getting under the covers, just climbed on top of the downy comforter near the end of the bed and curled up in the fetal position. "I'll just wait here."

Sam chuckled, missing her presence in his arms but liking the direction this morning was heading. He knew he would never take advantage of her, and he knew she would never encourage him. But snuggling? Yeah, that could be cool.

There was another knock at the door, and Sam ushered in the wait staff, who moved a large cart to the table. The young man lifted lids on several large platters containing a selection of breakfast foods, fruits, eggs, meats, pastries. Sam slipped the kid a hundred dirham note, and he ducked from the room, never even glancing at the half-asleep girl on Sam's bed.

"Come on, Sleeping Beauty." Sam offered his hand. "You need food just as badly as I do."

Leanne allowed Sam to lead her to the table, where they ate heartily in companionable silence, both of their eyes growing heavy.

Almost simultaneously, they were full and stopped eating as quickly as they'd started.

Sam stood and offered Leanne his hand, then led her over to his bed, this time pulling back the covers and tucking her in. He rounded the bed and climbed in next to her, then scooted to the middle. She willingly rolled into his arms, and they both sighed in contentment, causing each other to chuckle.

He pulled back slightly and brushed her damp hair away from her face.

"This is what it will be like to be married," Sam whispered, loving the soft smile in her eyes.

"Not even close," she mumbled, her lids half closed.

"What do you mean by that?" His hopes fell. Maybe he was reading her wrong.

"We wouldn't have this many layers of clothing on." This time her mumbling was so garbled it was nearly unrecognizable. Her eyes closed, and her breathing evened out.

"Dang, you're beautiful," Sam whispered, not sure she would hear him.

Her answering mumble didn't sound like a word. But she rolled over and tucked herself up against him, snuggling into his arms.

As Sam wrapped himself completely around Leanne, he whispered one more request. "Marry me, my love."

"Mmm-kay," she mumbled and sighed, settling into the cocoon of his arms.

When Sam awoke, the shadows were low in the late afternoon, and Leanne was gone.

Chapter Thirty-Six

Diamonds Are a Girl's Best Friend

"You're a hard girl to find," Sam whispered, pulling up a chair beside Leanne.

"How did you find me, then?" She set down her yellow highlighter and turned to him, with annoyance at being interrupted, scraping her chair on the wooden floor. She likely thought the third floor of the library tucked into a back corner was a safe bet to have privacy and a quiet escape from the busy university and the bustling city of Jerusalem.

"I have connections," he said, tucking a lock of her hair behind her ear.

"Do any of those connections happen to be married to any of my sisters?" she asked.

"Maybe." Sam bit his lower lip, gaging her level of annoyance.

"What do you want, Sam? I'm a little busy right now."

"You mentioned a few days ago that you were looking for a new study partner."

"That class is *next* semester," she reminded him.

"That gives me plenty of time to read up on the class materials, so I'll be able to provide the required level of tutelage."

"I'm pretty sure the earth sciences section of the library is on the second floor," Leanne said. "Knock yourself out. I need to study for my anthropology midterm. Go away." She turned back to her book and picked up her yellow highlighter.

"I don't want to move back to Jerusalem," Sam said.

"I don't really care where you live," she answered. "Your residency status doesn't affect me."

"It does if we're married."

"Well, we're not."

"But we're going to be," he said.

"You're being presumptuous again."

"I'm being realistic."

"You're being stupid." Leanne finally turned again to look at him. "You just said you didn't want to live in Jerusalem, so there's no reason we should be having this conversation."

"I feel very strongly that we need to be together."

"Then move to Jerusalem, you idiot." She turned back to her book.

"We need to follow Nick and Adele," Sam told her.

"What?" She turned to him with a gaping mouth. "Follow them where? To Dubai? I told you; I don't want to live in Dubai."

"Not to Dubai. Somewhere else."

"You're not making any sense, Sam. Go away."

"I'm here to be your study partner, remember?"

"I don't need you as my study partner until *next* semester, remember?" She spoke through gritted teeth.

"That's okay. I'll just be your husband between now and then."

"We're not getting married, Sam," Leanne said much louder than is acceptable in a library. That got the attention of students three tables over. "And I'm not moving to Dubai. And I'm not following my sister or your brother or anyone else. I'm finishing my master's degree, and then I'm getting a PhD. Deal with it."

Leanne stood and gathered her books, shoving them into a designer backpack.

"I'll see you after I graduate." With a flip of her hair, she slung the strap of her backpack over one shoulder and stormed away.

A guy at the next table made a noise like a plane crashing and exploding, then laughed with his buddy.

"Thanks, dude. That really helps." Sam took a deep breath and leaned back in the hard, wooden chair.

The girl sitting across from the guys at the next table gave Sam a sympathetic look, then a bit of advice. "Diamonds are a girl's best friend. Just sayin'."

"Diamonds?" Sam whispered, then gazed into space. That's it. That's what he needed. He hopped up from the chair and glanced over at the girl almost as an afterthought. "Thanks. That really *does* help."

Sam hurried from the library, scrolling on his phone to find the nearest jeweler.

Chapter Thirty-Seven

Please Marry Me

"Oh my gosh! What are you *doing* here?" Leanne stood from where she was perched in the front row of a very full lecture hall. Good. Lots of people would witness his rejection... again. "How many times do I have to break up with you?"

"You've never actually broken up with me," Sam said, barely glancing at the confused and startled professor with his gaping mouth and wide eyes. "You've just delayed the inevitable."

She huffed and folded her arms across her chest, looking off into the corner over his shoulder. He didn't mean to cut his timing so close to the start of her class period, but he had to find the perfect ring.

"I'm never going away," Sam said, stepping closer to her. She didn't back up, but she didn't lesson her defensive stance. "Now that I know how good it feels to sleep in your arms."

Some guy a few rows back whistled seductively. Sam ignored him.

"Do you see what this says?" Sam held up his cell phone with the contacts list open, her name listed first and paired with his. "It says Leanne Cohen. The love of my life. The woman who will grow old with me. The woman who will someday gift me the opportunity to become a dad."

That brought a tiny sliver of a smile to Leanne's lips, but she firmed her expression. "I'm not leaving school and moving to Dubai."

"I'm not asking you to move to Dubai."

"Oh, I know. You want me to follow you and Nick and Adele off to who knows where."

"Hear me out, okay?" Sam hurried on with his impassioned speech. "We'll get married now, finish your master's program here, figure out where Nick is leading us, and go *there* for your PhD."

"But that's so uncertain," she pleaded.

"That's what makes it real. That's why I trust it. That's why I'm asking you to give up all that you have to follow a compass that may or may not be pointing north. And if it's not, who cares." He paused and lowered his voice. "As long as I get to sleep next to you every night from now until eternity—with fewer layers of clothing between us—I will treasure every moment of my life with you."

"You only want to marry me because my sisters are married to your brothers and our parents for some reason think all of their children are supposed to marry each other."

"No, that's not the reason I want to marry you," Sam said. "I love you. I love you because of your intelligence and strength and tenacity."

"Sam, why are you doing this to me?" Frustration gave way to exasperation.

"Because you've already said yes to me a million times in your dreams. But maybe this will persuade you to say yes while you're still awake." Sam lowered himself to his knee in front of her whole lecture hall full of classmates, and one very annoyed professor. With a ring box open that contained an enormous diamond ring, Sam whispered passionately. "Please, my love, for the billionth time, will you marry me?"

He waited for what felt like hours but was probably only seconds for her to say no.

"Yes," she whispered.

"Yes?" Dare he hope that he'd heard her correctly?

"Yes! Yes, I'll marry you and sleep next to you, and follow wherever you lead me."

"Wherever Nick leads us," Sam corrected her, hopping to his feet.

"What?" Exasperation filled her voice again.

"Never mind," Sam said. "You follow me, and I'll follow him, and we'll all be going in the correct direction."

"Whatever. Just get over here and kiss me," Leanne demanded.

"Do you want the ring on your hand first?" Sam asked, holding up the little velvet box.

"Yes." She jumped on her toes like a little girl. "Yes, yes, give me that ring."

Sam slipped the ring from the box and onto Leanne's finger. As they finally kissed one another the lecture hall erupted in applause.

Six weeks later...

"I just got a text from my sister Rachel." Leanne set her laptop on the king-sized bed and shoved aside three textbooks and a spiral notebook. Their bed had gradually become a great place to study since they didn't want to get out from under the covers. Instead, they propped themselves up with lots of pillows.

"Hmm?" Sam didn't glance up from the abstract he was reading on geological assessments in mineral deposit variations. Not a topic his bride was likely to encounter in entry level natural resources management, but he'd gotten distracted on the second floor of the library. Sam's attention was suddenly pulled away by an incoming text of his own. "Ooh, I just got one from Liam. Do you think they're all still mad at us for eloping?"

"Don't know, don't care." Leanne said holding up her phone. "Oh... my... gosh."

"What?" Sam swiped open his phone and glanced at the text from his brother. "Uh oh..."

"I'm pregnant," Leanne read Rachel's text out loud. "She added lots of exclamation points and several hearts. One, two, three, four, five hearts. I guess she's excited."

"Liam's text says, uh, almost the same thing." Sam gulped and read out loud. "Rachel's pregnant! With only one exclamation point. What the heck am I supposed to do now? Am I going to have to marry her?"

Sam and Leanne looked at each other and neither could contain a snicker.

"Stairwell?" Sam asked, raising his eyebrows seductively.

"Probably," Leanne said. "What dorks."

"Should we answer their texts?" Sam asked playfully. "Or make them wait?"

Leanne pulled Sam's cell phone from his hand and tossed it onto the floor along with hers and several textbooks. She closed her laptop and set it carefully on the bedside table, then climbed into Sam's lap "Nah, make 'em wait. They need to learn some patience."

Sam rolled Leanne onto the bed and looked down into her deep blue eyes. "I'm glad we waited." He loved the weight of the thick gold band on his left hand reminding him frequently that they no longer needed to wait.

"Me too." Leanne's peaceful smile invited Sam's kiss. They didn't get any more studying done that night.

Part Three: Voyage of the Lady Bountiful

Jacob Cohen

As told by Jacob Cohen, son of Levi and Sarah Cohen, brother of Nicholas Cohen at the time when King Sayid was in his forty-second year as the story begins...

Chapter Thirty-Eight

Something to Look Forward To

"How many weddings can you cram into one year?" Jacob leaned over and spoke quietly to Nick. They both wore black tuxedos and stood at the front of the atrium where they'd watched their older brother Lyle marry his wife, Miriam. Their brother Sam had married Miriam's younger sister Leanne three weeks ago.

"I'm very sorry Daniel has run out of daughters," Nick said, patting Jacob on the back. "You'll have to marry outside the family."

"Pretty sure I'm a little young to be thinking of marriage." Jacob chuckled lightly. He was only nineteen and barely finished with his schooling, if he could call it that.

As much as they'd been traveling the past few years, calling his learning homeschooling was a stretch. More like unschooling. Learning things the hard way, being dragged to work by his father and brothers, letting Mom rely on him to help take care of his baby brother while she attempted to cram English and math lessons into his head alongside Hebrew and Arabic and world history. She'd finally called it good and declared him graduated, for whatever that was worth.

Schooling was a lifelong pursuit anyway, and Jacob kept studying even without her guidance. Being the son of a billionaire, he'd never need to work outside the family to make a living, but there was always the need for scholars. Jacob was good at journaling and storytelling like his brother Nick and more often tagged along to whatever Nick was working on.

"Well, there's still Ruth," Jacob mused. "About ten years too old for me, but still..."

"Hadn't you heard?" Lyle leaned over from his spot on the other side of their brother Sam. "She's marrying Zach."

"Seriously?" Jacob spoke a little too loud and drew the attention of the few friends and family gathered together for Liam's wedding. He shrunk back and hunched his shoulders.

"Do you guys mind?" Liam took a step forward to look at all his brothers at the same time. "You're ruining my wedding."

"Like you ruined mine?" Lyle baited him.

"I ruined your reception," Liam said. "There's a difference."

"Your wedding hasn't actually started yet," Jacob pointed out. The pianist was playing softly in the background as people took their seats and prepared for the simple ceremony. "Technically there's still time to run."

"And have Father and Daniel fight over whose shotgun to use?"

"Well, these tuxes will work just as well for a funeral as for a wedding," Jacob said.

"Very funny," Liam grumbled.

"You know, if you guys would stop having sex before getting married, you could choose when to get married rather than be forced to get married because your girlfriends are pregnant." Nick lifted his chin, then his mouth pulled into a tiny grin. "Like Adele and I did."

"Yep, you're *perfect*, Nick," Liam said. "We've established that over and over."

"Adele pregnant yet?" Lyle asked with a gleam in his eye.

"I dunno..." Nick pinched his lips together, obviously trying to hide a smile.

"Look at that cheesy smile, you sly dog," Lyle teased. "It's been what? Five months? You should be celebrating by now."

"Not for lack of trying," Nick said under his breath.

Their three older brothers started laughing, but Jacob wanted to crawl under one of the pews in embarrassment from the entire conversation. "You guys are hurting my virtuous ears and delicate countenance."

"Eh, you're going to love being married just as much as the rest of us, little brother," Sam said, reaching around Nick's back to shove Jacob's shoulder.

"That would require me to grow up, oh, and meet a girl." Jacob felt a little flutter in his stomach at the thought. All this talk about marriage and what came after, or in Liam and Lyle's case, before, the wedding had gotten Jacob a little more excited about the prospect. Maybe being married wouldn't be so bad. Something to look forward to.

The music shifted into a traditional wedding march, and the brothers straightened into a line, standing at attention like the upstanding young men they *should* emulate.

Within a few moments, Rachel appeared at the other end of the aisle in a soft pink gown with a high waist that almost hid her growing midline.

Jacob peeked over at Liam, noting the grin that spread onto his face at seeing his bride. The circumstances may not be perfect, but at least Liam and Rachel were in love.

Love. Something even more important to look forward to.

Chapter Thirty-Nine

Taking Ownership

"You'd think they'd be back by now," Jacob said, lifting the last of his suitcases onto the cart. He handed a one hundred dirham note to the concierge, grateful for the help.

"They're on their honeymoon," Nick reminded him. "They'll come back when they're good and ready."

"Yeah, but we're leaving Dubai in less than a day," Jacob said. "We're boarding the yacht this afternoon."

"Trust me, they're insufferable to be around. The longer they stay away, the better."

Jacob shuddered. "How are we going to stand being on a boat with them for four weeks?"

"As long as they stay sober, we should be okay," Nick said.

"She's pregnant. Of course, they're going to stay sober," Jacob said. "Well, at least she'll stay sober."

"Let's hope."

"Sir, is there any other way I can be of assistance?" the young man helping with the bags asked. He stood at attention beside the cart.

"I'm sure that will be all for now," Nick answered, also handing the young man a dirham. He nodded with respect and gratitude.

"I will see that these get to the dock." The young man exited Jacob's suite.

Jacob watched as the cart rolled down the hall, piled high with everything he owned. "Do you think I have more stuff than the rest of you combined?"

"Other than Mother, probably. But she's packing for baby Joseph as well."

"I wish Lyle and Miriam were coming with baby Ishy." Jacob sighed. "I'm gonna miss our little nephew."

"They'll be along in a few months when he gets stronger and is able to travel," Nick said. "Besides, there are only six staterooms on board. We'd need a superyacht to fit our whole family."

"Isn't the *Lady Bountiful* large enough to be considered a superyacht?" Jacob asked.

"Yeah, probably, but it's on the low end of them."

"I'm excited to sail on the maiden voyage of the first yacht made by our father."

"Hey, this was my design," Nick said. "And the workers built the boat, not Father."

"Well, it's Father's company," Jacob said.

"Father may have been the financier, but your brothers run the company. You need to start taking ownership of our businesses," Nick said, then poked Jacob on his sternum. "In here. In your heart. We will someday own these companies, and we need to run them as if we already do."

"That makes sense," Jacob said. "You're really smart, Nick."

"Thanks, little brother. Now come on, let's go help my lovely bride gather the rest of her things."

"Will she have twice as many suitcases as me?" Jacob asked.

"Heavens no, Adele is a simple girl." Nick chuckled. "You are the spoiled youngest son of a billionaire. There's no comparison."

"Not anymore," Jacob said. "Baby Joseph will grow up twice as spoiled because all of us older brothers will coddle him all his life."

"I don't know. Some of us will have our own babies to coddle." Nick puffed up his chest. "Might have to let you be the big brother this time."

"Is Adele pregnant?" Jacob grabbed Nick's arm to stop him.

"We don't know yet. We might just be getting excited over nothing. Don't say anything to Mother yet, okay?"

"I won't say anything," Jacob said.

"We'll make an announcement if and when we actually know for sure."

"I'll be praying for you, my brother."

"Thanks." Nick reached over to give Jacob a hug. "Now, enough of this lovey-dovey crap. Let's go meet the crew of our new yacht."

"Sounds like a plan."

Chapter Forty

What a Beautiful Name

The *Lady Bountiful* was a full 200 feet in length, had four decks above the waterline, two decks below, a helipad, two VIP suites in addition to the owner's suite, a pool and Jacuzzi, a movie theater, a massage parlor and beauty salon, a playroom, a bar, and a library.

Jacob had been the son of a billionaire all his life, but this felt like a step above luxury. He fought the pride that tore through his chest. He followed closely at Nick's heels and tried to emulate his presence, confidence without haughtiness, if that were possible. Jacob wasn't sure he'd ever be able to master the art of true humility like Nick, but he'd like to try.

They met up with Adele and their parents, Levi and Sarah, near the dock where their new home at sea would take them on the maiden voyage to Cancun, Mexico. They intended to put down roots there, for how long, he didn't know.

There would be a celebration that evening with a cocktail party and official launch, but this afternoon was for the family to meet the crew and get settled in their staterooms.

Just as they were about to board, Liam called from the deck overlooking the docks something that sounded like, "Wait for us." He and Rachel held hands as they ran like kids through the sand to meet up with the rest of the family.

They were laughing and happy, and everyone reached around the group, giving hugs, Adele patting her sister's growing baby bump, Liam punching his brothers in the arms affectionately, giving hugs to their mother and father, and lifting baby Joseph from their mother's arms to nuzzle him.

"I missed you, little brother," Liam cooed at baby Joseph.

"See, Nick." Jacob elbowed him. "I'm no longer the spoiled little brother."

"Dude, you will always be spoiled," Liam said.

"How was your honeymoon?" Adele asked her sister Rachel.

"Hawaii was incredible," Rachel said. "Oh, and hanging out with this big lug wasn't so bad either." Rachel wrapped her arms around Liam's waist and held him close.

"You made it home just in time to come aboard and meet the crew," Father said, holding out his arm toward the ramp leading up to the yacht. They all followed him.

The lineup of men, and a few women, was impressive, as if staff from a small resort were commissioned to care for this vessel and its owners. A man slightly younger than Father stepped forward and offered his hand.

"Mr. Cohen, I'm Captain Jeffrey Arnold. Welcome aboard the *Lady Bountiful*."

"Thank you, Captain Arnold." Father shook the proffered hand and turned to introduce the family. "This is my wife, Sarah, and she is holding our youngest, baby Joseph."

"The pleasure is mine, Mrs. Cohen." Captain Arnold nodded regally.

"This is our oldest son, Liam; and his wife, Rachel; our son, Nicholas; and his wife, Adele; and our nineteen-year-old son, Jacob."

"Ah, Master Jacob, you are the same age as my daughter, Maryam." Captain Arnold gestured to his right where an elegant young lady stood, with mysterious eyes and chestnut waves of hair so dark brown it was almost black. "Perhaps the two of you can become friends."

"Maryam," Jacob whispered, suddenly lightheaded. "What a beautiful name."

The adults surrounding him laughed, and Maryam lowered her gaze, biting her lower lip, her olive skin deepening in color. Jacob cleared his throat, mortified that his first encounter with the captain and his family was so embarrassing.

"Anyway, this is my wife, Valerie," Captain Arnold continued. "She is matron of the interior staff, with Maryam as her assistant." The captain pointed out the rows of housekeepers, the chef and his staff, the deck crew, the engineers.

Jacob wasn't paying any attention to the remaining introductions. His eyes were locked with Maryam's, whose tiny smirk answered his unspoken question.

How soon do we set sail?

Chapter Forty-One

Staterooms

"This is my stateroom?" Jacob turned in a circle, wondering how he was going to cram himself into this small space.

"Isn't it great?" Maryam asked. "This is probably the nicest yacht I've ever worked on."

Jacob stopped, and his jaw dropped. He realized with a single word he could offend this young lady, and he needed to be careful. "My brother helped design this boat."

"Wow, that's so cool." Maryam tucked a lock of hair behind her ear. "He must be really smart."

Jacob was momentarily distracted by the unique flecks of brown and gold in her aquamarine eyes. They were unlike any he'd ever seen. He shook off his stupor, flopped onto his bed and tucked his hands behind his head. "How long has your father been a captain?"

"Longer than I've been alive," she said, sitting on the chair by the desk.

Jacob noticed his iPad was already plugged in at a port and waiting for him. He sat up and realized many of his things were already in place. "Did you organize my room?"

"Is it not to your liking?" Maryam hopped up and straightened the chair, pushing it back under the desk. "I can move things however you want them."

"No, no, everything's fine, please sit back down."

"Are you sure?" She kept one hand on the chair and didn't return to her seat.

"What do you do for fun around here?" Jacob asked, changing tactics.

"I work here," she said.

"Well, they have to give you a day off now and then, right? I mean, it's like thirty days that we'll be at sea, right? They can't work you twenty-four-seven."

"No, I mean, yes, I'll get some time off," Maryam said. "But not for the first few days. When the family comes aboard, it's our job to make sure everything's perfect for them."

"Well... I'm family." He batted his eyelashes playfully. "You can be tasked with making sure everything's perfect for *me*."

Maryam giggled, and Jacob's heart rate increased. How was he going to be stuck together with this girl for a month without eventually kissing her? He'd already practically asked her out, and they'd known each other less than twenty minutes. He was in trouble.

"Hey, little brother, how do you like your home away from home?" Liam came around the corner but halted in the doorway. "Ooh, I didn't realize I was interrupting anything."

"Oh, no, sir, I was just making sure Master Jacob had everything he needed." Maryam tried to duck past Liam, but he was leaning against the doorframe, essentially blocking her way.

"I'll bet you were." Liam wiggled his eyebrows playfully.

"Liam, leave her alone," Jacob said.

Liam dropped his arm and stepped out of the way, offering Maryam a wink.

"And Maryam?" Jacob called before she could get too far out the door. She turned back with hesitancy. "Please just call me Jacob."

"Yes, sir." She nodded respectfully and slipped down the hall.

"My little brother"—Liam raised his eyebrows playfully—"you are going to have one enjoyable trip across the Atlantic."

"Whatever..." Jacob couldn't help his mouth pulling into a grin, suspecting his oldest brother was right.

Chapter Forty-Two

Farewell Party

J acob wished this party was over so he could find Maryam and hang out with her for a little while after she was officially done working for the day.

The stern of the yacht had a little boat garage and seemed the perfect spot to hide and sit on the deck stargazing. Whether or not she was willing to sneak away with him had yet to be determined. But he liked to think she would.

He was distracted by a conversation between his brother Nick and the esteemed Prince Marcos Sayid of Madain Saleh, who had joined them for the farewell party. Nick and Marcos had been best friends since they'd met in prep school back when Jacob was just a baby.

Nick and Marcos had been the two richest kids at their school, and probably the two shyest kids at their school. Both hiding behind overbearing older brothers, they'd stuck together. Now that Nick and Marcos were confident adults, Jacob could barely remember the timid boy Nick once was.

Jacob didn't mean to be eavesdropping but couldn't help overhearing something about a contested crown and likely civil war in Madain Saleh. When Marcos's brother, Jared, died in a tragic motorcycle accident last year, his five-year-old son wasn't old enough to be named Crown Prince. There was an argument over who should be given that title. It was all very confusing to Jacob.

Why there had to be princes and kings and royalty at all didn't make sense. All people were created equal. When one person tried to rule over another, the outcome was rarely positive.

"Come live in Dubai until your yacht is done, and then come to Cancun," Nick said. "We can dock our yachts side by side, build mansions next door to one another, and raise our children as best friends, just as we were."

"She's a masterpiece, Nick," the prince said with a grin. "I might get a complex docking my little yacht next to yours."

"Thank you, Your Highness," Nick said. They both leaned against the railing. "I'm glad you and Lyla could make it all the way down here to see us off."

"Anxiously awaiting the opportunity to join you on the high seas." Marcos spoke through an obviously fake smile. Jacob wondered what the prince was hiding and who he was hiding from.

"What's holding you back from leaving now?" Nick asked.

"I want my first child to be born in Madain Saleh," Marcos said.

"Is Lyla...?"

"Not that I can tell." Marcos shook his head. "Adele?"

"We suspect," Nick said softly. "But we're not telling anyone yet."

"She's not gonna handle the rough seas very well if she is." Marcos chuckled.

"We realize that." Nick sighed. "But this is the best time to leave, and the trip will only last a month."

"Can't you just fly?"

"And miss the maiden voyage of the *Lady Bountiful?*" Nick asked playfully. "Not a chance."

"Okay, okay." Marcos held up his hands in surrender. "Good luck handling a wife with morning sickness on a yacht for twenty-nine days."

As if on cue, Marcos's own wife Lyla jumped up from the chaise lounge where she was chatting with Adele and ran to the side of the boat right next to Marcos. She hung over the side of the railing and threw up the expensive appetizers they'd enjoyed all afternoon.

"You were saying?" Nick asked, wrinkling his nose. "I'll go get your wife a water bottle and washcloth. Good luck to you as well, Your Highness." Nick patted Marcos on the shoulder as he hurried away.

"Thanks," Marcos said with a grimace, rubbing his wife's back as she heaved over and over. Oddly he didn't look upset that his wife was sick. More like excited.

Jacob had to turn away or he'd be hurling next. He'd leave the married guys with their pregnant wives. He decided now would be a good time to go find Maryam. He hurried down the deck pondering the strange conversation he'd just overheard, wondering what it meant for his brother's best friend and the future of the Sayid Royal Family.

Chapter Forty-Three

Secret Rendezvous

"Maryam," Jacob whispered as loud as he could while trying to keep anyone else from knowing he was there. He'd been discouraged from coming down into the crew deck, but he felt compelled to see her again.

She was leaning against the wall near the crew's galley, talking to a couple other ladies who all seemed to be taking a break or who were done for the night. The staff had been diligently taking care of used plates and glasses and helping as needed. But there probably wasn't much to do until the party was over and they had to clean up the mess.

"Jacob?" Maryam turned to him, not lowering her voice as he'd been. "Come in here. Meet my friends."

"Am I allowed to be down here?" He stepped all the way into the galley and nervously shoved his hands into the pockets of his formal slacks. He felt overdressed away from the party and wished he'd thought to change into some cargo shorts.

"You own this yacht," Maryam said. "I'm pretty sure you can be anywhere you want." She seemed much more confident down here surrounded by her friends than up on deck with the intimidating royals and dignitaries. Jacob had to admit he liked this laid-back environment also.

"In that case, I *want* to go on a little walk with you in the moonlight," Jacob said. "I promise to be a perfect gentleman."

"Ooh, a walk in the moonlight," one of her friends said. "Sounds very romantic. I'm Hannah, by the way." She reached out to shake Jacob's hand, and Maryam seemed to stiffen beside him, as if she was jealous. Interesting.

"And I'm Ivy." The other friend also extended her hand.

Jacob made a point to maneuver himself closer to Maryam in the process of introducing himself to her friends, and slid his arm around her lower back. He almost rested his head on her shoulder when he spoke softly. "What do you say? Want to come with me for a romantic, moonlit walk?"

Maryam turned toward him, inadvertently wrapping herself within his arms and flirting with her mesmerizing eyes. "I'd love to."

"Nice meeting you, ladies," Jacob said as an afterthought, still gazing into Maryam's speckled aquamarine eyes while backing her away from her friends.

"We're going in the wrong direction," Maryam said. "This is the hallway to the crew's quarters." They still had locked gazes and arms intertwined and wrapped around each other's waists.

"Well then, I guess you'll have to show me your stateroom real quick before we go up on deck." Jacob was surprised how fast he was getting caught up in this girl he barely knew. If he wasn't careful, he'd end up kissing her the first day they met and that would not be a good idea. "You already know what my room looks like. Show me yours."

"I don't exactly have a *room*. I have a bunk."

"That could be cozy," Jacob said. "Show me."

Maryam reached under a top bunk and flicked on a light, illuminating a bottom bunk that did indeed look cozy. She had already taken the time to make the little space hers, even though she'd only been on the yacht a few days longer than Jacob.

"I love it," he said.

"What*ever*." She rolled her eyes.

"Now I'll know how to picture you in my dreams tonight."

"Now you're just being silly," she said.

"Tell me you won't be doing the same thing," he challenged.

"I can't tell you that." She bit her lower lip and averted her gaze.

"Let's go for that walk and get to know each other so we'll know what to talk about in our dreams also," Jacob said, taking her hand. "How about if you lead the way since you know this ship better than I do."

She pulled him gently back toward the galley and then up a small set of stairs and out into the night air. "Where would you like to walk?"

"As far away from the party as possible?" He raised his eyebrows playfully. "How about back near the little boat garage on the stern? That seems like the perfect spot to hide from our parents and sit on the deck, looking at the ocean and gazing at the billions of stars overhead."

"Right this way, sir," Maryam said in her most professional tour-guide voice. "Although, since we're still at port, we'll mostly see the lights from the city." They didn't try to hold a conversation while walking to the back of the boat, but they did hold hands.

"Dubai is beautiful, so that's okay." Jacob was right. The spot was secluded and dark and was as far away from the party as they could get and still be on the same boat. They didn't bring a blanket to sit on, and the night was cool, so the deck had a sheen of condensation. Jacob removed his sport coat and spread it out for them to sit on.

"Why thank you, kind sir." She carefully sat on his coat, and he sat next to her. "I don't want to ruin your nice coat."

"It can be replaced," Jacob said.

"You rich people say that a lot." She let her accusation hang in the air, and Jacob wasn't sure how to respond. "Like everything's disposable."

"Well, other than people, everything *is* disposable." He turned and brushed her hair off her shoulder so he could see her face better. "You are more important than a coat."

"True, but you can care for both the coat and the person if you try. And then you can use the money saved to do something good in the world."

"A valid point. I have a feeling I'm going to learn a lot from you," Jacob said.

"And I from you." She nudged his shoulder.

"Tell me about yourself. Where did you grow up?"

"You're looking at it." Maryam spread her arms wide. "I've lived on private yachts all my life."

"Seriously? That sounds glamourous."

"If you like the sea," Maryam said. "I'd kind of like to put down roots one of these days."

"You've been around the world dozens of times. If you could live anywhere, where would you want to live?"

"I want to live in a forest, in a big house that has lots of windows and lots of light and a big kitchen that's at the center of the house where all the family can gather." Her voice had taken on a soft musing dreamlike state.

"How many children do you want to have?" he asked.

"I grew up an only child, so I'd kind of like my children to have siblings. How about you?"

"I grew up with too many siblings. They fight a lot, and they have a variety of different opinions about life." Jacob gazed up at the stars. "If you disagree with a friend, you can walk away and never see them again. But if you disagree with your brother, you can't just walk away, because they're your brother."

"You're an adult now. You can live on your own." Her voice was soft, no doubt thinking something similar to what he was thinking. The time wasn't far off when they'd both want to live on their own... but with someone they loved, like someone they were married to. "What about you? Where do you want to live when you grow up and move away from your parents?"

"As of about three minutes ago, I've decided I'd like to live in a forest, in a big house that has lots of windows and lots of light and a big kitchen that's at the center of the house where all the family can gather."

"Very funny." Maryam giggled.

"We should do some exploring after we dock in Mexico," Jacob suggested. "Travel either into the United States or south into Belize and Guatemala and Honduras and then keep going down through Panama and into South America."

"Have you been to any of those places?" She raised her eyebrows in disbelief.

"No, that's why we would need to go exploring. Have you?"

"Not really," she said. "I've been to some of the ports, and many of the islands. St. Lucia, Barbados, Trinidad and Tobago, Virgin Islands, Puerto Rico."

"I've lived in Jerusalem my entire life," Jacob said. "Until this past year when we moved to Dubai and my dad bought the yacht company. Brought it back from the brink of bankruptcy. He does that; swoops in to buy up businesses that are failing for pennies on the dollar, waves his magic wand, and rakes in millions."

"Is it true your family are billionaires?" she asked.

"Yeah, I think if we divided up our father's wealth, we'd *each* be billionaires."

"Seriously?"

"Maybe I'm exaggerating a little," he admitted. "But close to it. My dad has a gift with businesses. He does great things with the money too. Starts up endowment funds, donates to charitable causes, hires thousands of people to work in good-paying jobs."

"Like a yacht captain and his family."

"Exactly."

"What do you want to do when you grow up?" Maryam asked.

"Well, I'm helping run the family's businesses." Jacob thought for a minute. "I might want to get more involved in government service or something. I've seen how local laws can make or break a company's ability to prosper."

"That's a lot to understand when you're as young as you are," she said.

"I didn't have a traditional education. My mother sent me off with my brothers and father to learn how to run our companies. She encouraged me to learn a myriad of languages and math. Ugh, I hate math."

"Everybody hates math." She chuckled.

"What about you? What do you want to be when you grow up?"

"I want to be a mom, and a wife, of course."

"Wife comes first, mom comes second," Jacob agreed. "I've watched two of my brothers forced to get married because they chose to reverse those. I want to get married because I love my wife, not because I got her pregnant and had to marry her."

"I want that too." Maryam laid her head on Jacob's shoulder, and they sat that way for a long time, watching the giant skyscrapers of the city of Dubai and the waves lapping the shoreline. That night would be their last night at port before heading out into the open ocean for a twenty-nine-day journey.

They sat for a little while longer before helping each other up and peeling the wet sport coat off the deck. Jacob walked Maryam to the entrance of the crew quarters, kissed her on her cheek, and then made his way up to the deck where his state room waited for him.

While drifting off to sleep, Jacob imagined Maryam in her bunk two levels down, crammed into that tiny space when he had this giant bed to himself. His imagination shifted, and he could visualize her right there beside him. He wrapped his arms around one of the extra pillows and fell asleep that way.

Chapter Forty-Four

Private Tour of the Yacht

"Excuse me, miss," Jacob said in a fake, formal cadence. "Would you mind giving me a tour of this fine cruising vessel?" He came up behind Maryam, placed his hands on her hips and rested his chin on her shoulder. He'd spent half the morning trying to locate her and found her in the laundry room, where she was folding linen tablecloths from the previous evening's dinner.

"Didn't you have a tour yesterday, sir, when the family came aboard?" She continued folding but added a flirtatious lilt to her answer.

"Yes, but that was with the *family*. I want a private tour."

"Shall I go find you one of the stewardesses?" Maryam teased.

Jacob released her hips and stepped away from her. His tone lowered to that of a rejected puppy dog. "If that's who you want me to spend my day with."

"I'm kidding." She reached for his wrist and dragged him toward herself, the tablecloth abandoned in a heap on the laundry pile. "Get over here. What parts of the yacht haven't you seen?"

"It's not really parts of the ship I want to see; it's more I want to *know* things." With his free hand, Jacob ran his fingers up her arm all the way to her head and tapped on her skull near her forehead. "For instance, why is one of your crew members using a hose to spray off the deck when it looks perfectly clean to me?"

"Because of the salt in the air and in the sea spray. We have to hose off the salt at least once a day and give it a full cleaning every three or four days."

"That sounds really time consuming." He somehow managed to lower his cadence to make a simple sentence seem seductive.

"It is." Maryam released the grip on his wrist and ran her hand up his arm, similar to how he'd done to her and tapped his skull. "What else do you want to know?"

"When do you take a break? It seems like you work all day, every day. I want to take you on a date."

"We're stuck on a boat in the middle of the ocean," Maryam said. "Exactly where do you think you're going to take me?"

"There's a little movie theater on the lower deck. Can't we pop some popcorn and watch a movie together?" Jacob asked.

"Taking a break would be easier if there were no guests onboard," she said. "We have shorter hours then. Just maintenance and upkeep, cleaning and prepping. Once guests are onboard, it's all about making sure the guests have the best possible experience. There's somebody awake twenty-four-seven, prepping the boat for the next day. It's a very intensive time. Our work hours go up."

"You're too overworked. I need to add some fun into your day."

"My work actually is a lot of fun." Maryam lifted a shoulder. "It's what we're here for. To make the best possible experience that we can for the guests."

"Well, I'm a guest." Jacob leaned his shoulder against the wall. "Can't you put me to work as a deckhand or something? I can help you get your work done faster, then we can take a break and watch a movie."

"You're not a guest, Jacob. You're the *owner*. My mother and father would throw me overboard if I let you work as a deckhand."

"I would jump in after you and rescue you."

"Do you even know how to swim?" She raised an eyebrow.

"No, not really." He chuckled.

Just as Jacob was leaning closer to Maryam, her mother came around the corner and gasped. "Get your hands off my daughter!"

"I wasn't touching her." Jacob raised his hands in the air as if he were at gunpoint and stepped away from Maryam. "We were just discussing her work schedule, and I wondered if I might be able to take her on a date, you know, to the movie theater, with several chaperones, and, and... popcorn." He gulped.

"Owners and guests aren't supposed to be down here. What is it with you Cohen boys?" Valerie Arnold asked with narrowed eyes. "You think just because you're the son of a billionaire that you have the right to take liberties with my daughter?"

"Ma'am, I would never hurt your daughter or any other woman," Jacob said, backing away farther until he ran into the table where the piles of laundry sat. "My father has taught me that."

"Apparently, he didn't teach your oldest brother the same lessons," Valerie grumbled under her breath. "Never mind. Just get back up where you belong, and let my daughter finish her work."

Jacob glanced once more at Maryam, then shimmied past her mother. He chuckled as he bounded back up the stairs to the decks where owners and guests were supposed to remember their place. Jacob wondered what Valerie meant about his brother. He was afraid to ask.

Chapter Forty-Five

Never

"Little brother," Liam spoke from the doorway of Jacob's stateroom. "I bought you a gift before we left Dubai."

Jacob looked up from his iPad where he'd been typing a blog post. He was determined to follow the example of his older brother, Nick, and keep a record of their travels. His infatuation with the captain's lovely daughter was a welcome distraction from the monotony of traveling the open sea, but Maryam worked long hours and could only fit in a few stolen moments here and there.

Plus, after her mother had caught Maryam flirting with Jacob, she kept her daughter working on the opposite end of the yacht, so those stolen moments were few and far between. Jacob needed a distraction from his distraction. Maryam knew where to find him.

"What is your gift?" Jacob was always leery of Liam. He was usually up to some mischief and straddled the line between right and wrong, often leaning more on the side of wrong.

Liam tossed a box that resembled a nondescript box of medical supplies, perhaps latex gloves or gauze, onto Jacob's lap.

When Jacob read the packaging, he gasped and tossed the box onto the bed with disgust, as if just its presence on his lap would taint him.

"I figured a box of fifty would be sufficient for our trip across the ocean." Liam laughed at Jacob's reaction.

"What makes you think I would need even *one* condom, much less a box of fifty?" Jacob croaked out. "Take them back. I will never use them. Ever."

"You'd be surprised how quickly *never* turns into *right now*," Liam said. He walked over to Jacob's bed and picked up the offensive little box. He turned to the bedside table, opened the drawer, and tucked the box inside. "Trust me, you don't want to be forced to get married."

"I will not need them *until* I get married," Jacob said through clenched teeth. "At which time I will no longer need them *because* I will be married. I don't see the logic in even keeping them."

"There is nothing logical about what your body experiences when in the arms of a beautiful woman." Liam patted Jacob on the shoulder as he passed him on the way out the door. "Keep one with you and use it when the time comes. And believe me, the time will come sooner than later. I've seen the way you look at each other when you think no one's watching."

"That's absurd," Jacob called after him.

"Keep one with you," Liam called back.

Jacob hesitated a moment, then, curious, he walked over and sat on the edge of his bed. Against his better judgement, he opened the drawer and stared down at the box.

"I just wanna see what one looks like," Jacob whispered to himself. Almost as an afterthought, he stood and hurried over to the door, closing and locking it.

With trepidation he walked cautiously back over and sat on his bed again. He hesitated, then reached for the box and slid his finger along the edge to break the seal. The box popped open as if by its own free will, revealing dozens of little grey packages hooked together in rows. He pulled one row of five from the box. Ten rows of five. He shoved the row back in the box and tried to close the lid. Now that they'd been released from confinement, they wouldn't fit back in the box.

He pulled a row out again and detached one little grey package. The visible ring slipped around inside as if lubricated. He wrinkled his nose.

Jacob just wanted to see what it looked like inside. Sure, his father had told him years ago about the changes his body would go through during puberty, but the topic of protection was barely mentioned in passing. The message had been clear: wait until marriage. Period. End of story.

So why did two of his brothers wind up getting girls pregnant prior to marriage? Maybe there should have been less insistence and more education? Maybe Liam was right. Maybe Jacob should learn more and not be so afraid of a natural part of being a man and a woman. He was a man now, after all. Nineteen years old was a man.

Jacob ripped open the package and pulled out the slimy ring. He didn't understand how this *thing* could protect him from anything. He tried to unroll it, but it slid through his fingers. Everything about the little ring was offensive and gross. Without further consideration, he tossed the condom in the garbage can beside his bed along with the empty wrapper, closed the box as best he could and shut the drawer to his bedside table. He shuddered as he rose from his bed and hurried over to the bathroom to wash his hands.

"I am never using one of those disgusting things," he vowed to himself as he scrubbed his hands with soap and water. The words Liam had said echoed in his mind. *You'd be surprised how quickly never turns into right now.*

Chapter Forty-Six

Right Now

"How dare you!" Maryam pushed Jacob's chest hard enough that he stumbled backward and almost fell onto one of the deck chairs. The sun shone down on the sparkling white deck of the yacht, but the chair was protected under an awning. Jacob was suddenly hidden from everyone other than Maryam. "Who is she? What's her name? Is she one of the kitchen helpers? One of the housekeepers? Who?"

"Who are you talking about?" Jacob held up both hands in surrender.

"Exactly!" Maryam turned with a flick of her ponytail and stomped away. Jacob wasn't far behind. The Polo shirt and cargo pants combination all the crew wore gave Maryam a classy but relaxed appearance. Jacob had a hard time transitioning from boardroom attire to boat shoes, shorts and short-sleeve shirts. Obviously, there was something else he was still not getting right.

"Please, Maryam, tell me what I did wrong," Jacob pleaded.

"Oh, so you don't think it was *wrong?*" She turned on him and narrowed her eyes. He took a step back; afraid she was going to push him again. She held up a little gray wrapper. "Would you like to explain *this?*"

"Did you go through my trash can?" He wrinkled his nose.

"So, you admit it was yours?" She turned again and started walking away. "That's typical. I thought you were different, that you weren't like other guys."

"How many other guys have there been?" He hurried after her again.

"How many other girls have there been?" She whirled on him again.

"You," Jacob said, trying to reach for her hand, but she pulled away and folded her arms across her chest. "There's never been anyone but you."

"Then who did *this* belong to?" She held up the offensive little wrapper again.

"My brother, Liam," Jacob tried to explain.

"Are you so daft that you think I'll believe your brother walked all the way across the boat to sneak into your stateroom and have sex with someone?" Then she gasped and held her hand to her mouth. "Is he cheating on his wife?"

"I hope not," Jacob said. "I don't know."

"Why else would he be hiding this?"

"He wasn't hiding them. He gave them to me."

"Them?" Maryam raised her eyebrows, still with pursed lips and daggers in her eyes.

"He gave me a whole box of them."

"Why?" Her stance softened a little.

"He thought," Jacob mumbled, barely audible, even to himself. "You and I might want them."

"That's"—Maryam gulped—"presumptuous."

"I agree," Jacob said. "That's why I told him I will never use them."

"Never?"

"Well, I'm not planning to do... *that*... until I'm married, and then once we're married, we won't need them."

"That doesn't explain why one of them is open," Maryam said.

"I wanted to see what one looked like," Jacob explained. "I'd never seen one before."

"I never have either." She looked down and scuffed her shoe on the deck.

"There are forty-nine more where that came from if you'd like to," Jacob mumbled.

"Forty-nine?"

"Yeah, he gave me a box of fifty." Jacob snickered. "I don't know why he thought we'd want that many."

"It's only a four-week trip from Dubai to Cancun." Maryam glanced from side to side. "Do you think that's how often married people..."

"I dunno. I've never been married."

Maryam giggled. "Me neither."

"Good to know." Jacob took a step toward her and reached for her hand. She smiled at him shyly.

"So," Maryam said through clenched teeth. "Can I see one?"

"They're really gross looking," Jacob said.

"I don't care." She squeezed his hand gently. "I still want to see one."

"Right now?"

"Sure, why not."

"Aren't you supposed to be working?" Jacob raised his eyebrows.

She raised hers right back at him with a little smirk. "I was cleaning your stateroom."

"That is true." He raised his shoulders. "And you just happened to have a question for me."

"And so, I sought you out to ask you the question." With a coy smile, Maryam pulled his arm gently, walking calmly in the direction of Jacob's stateroom.

They didn't see a single person, crew or family member, on their way back to Jacob's room. He pulled the door closed behind himself, then stepped over and opened the dresser drawer.

Neither of them reached for the box; they just stared at it for a moment. Finally, Jacob reached down and pulled out one of the rows of five condoms and held them out to her.

"I don't wanna touch them," Maryam whispered. "You open one."

Jacob ripped one off the strip and grasped the little wrapper between his fingers. He found it easier to open the second time, and he wasn't as afraid of the slimy little ring. Until it suddenly slipped out of the wrapper, and they both jumped back, and Maryam yelped.

They both snickered as they stared at the flesh-colored ring sitting on the floor of his stateroom.

"You're right. That's totally gross." Maryam put her hand across her mouth to keep from laughing too loud.

"I warned you." Jacob leaned down and picked it up and placed it on the palm of his hand. "I don't understand how that's supposed to 'protect' anything."

"You have to put it on first, silly." Maryam giggled.

"I'm not putting it on! You put it on!" Jacob took a step back in shock, realizing what he'd just said. Not appropriate. At all. He flung the thing off his hand and into the wastebasket. "I've never even kissed you before, and I'm certainly never doing *that* until we're married."

"Are you saying"—Maryam stopped and cleared her throat—"that you'd like to marry me someday?"

"Yeah, I'd marry you today if I could." Jacob stepped closer to her now that they weren't discussing the mechanics of prophylactics.

"Why?" She rested her hands on his arms as he placed his hands on her hips. "You barely know me."

"We have a connection that's undeniable and unexplainable, and you feel it too. Admit it." He looked down into her speckled aquamarine eyes that captivated him the first time he'd stood in this very spot and gazed into them.

"You are mistaken," she said, stepping closer.

Jacob was confused. If she disagreed about their connection, why was she closing the distance between them? "Wh-what?"

"You said you've never kissed me before," she whispered, lifting her chin and hypnotizing him. "But you kiss me every night in my dreams."

"What a coincidence." Jacob could barely breathe. "You kiss me every night in my dreams too."

"Maybe we should try kissing each other while we're both awake," Maryam said.

"That is a really great idea." He hesitated, inching his face closer to hers. He'd never kissed a girl before, and he didn't care if he ever kissed any other girl for as long as he lived. He whispered her name, "Maryam."

Jacob drew closer and closer to her, his breath increasing and his heart racing. Finally, she lost patience and pulled him to her, connecting what little space had been left between them.

Instinct took over. His hands gripped into the silky waves at the nape of her neck. He pulled her closer even as he pushed her body against the desk where his iPad sat idle. Knocking it to the floor, he lifted her onto his desk, and she wrapped her legs around his waist, gripping tighter, her hands in his hair and down his neck to the collar of his shirt, pulling him closer.

Jacob was reminded of the words his brother had said when he gifted him that offensive little box. *You'd be surprised how fast never becomes right now when you're in the arms of a beautiful woman.*

That was precisely the moment the door to his stateroom opened and Maryam's mother blocked the sunlight, fists on her hips. "Get your hands off my daughter."

Chapter Forty-Seven

Not How it Looks

"**M**other! This isn't how it looks!" Maryam gasped.

Jacob realized it looked even worse than imaginable. Ripped condom wrappers, the dresser drawer open, revealing a whole box of them waiting, his iPad knocked off the desk where Maryam was still sitting with her legs wrapped around Jacob's waist. Yeah, this looked bad.

They disentangled themselves from one another and straightened their clothes. Jacob rushed over to pick up the wrappers and discard them in the trash, closed the dresser drawer and shrunk away from the intimidating woman still standing in the door to his stateroom.

"Do you have anything to say for yourself young man?"

"Um... I'm sorry?"

"How long has this been going on?" she demanded.

"About thirty seconds?"

"That was at least a minute," Maryam mumbled.

"I don't know. I've never kissed a girl before," Jacob said through clenched teeth. "It happened so fast I couldn't think, especially not about the clock."

"That was your first kiss?" Maryam straightened and faced Jacob, an awed smile across her face. "I was your *first* kiss?"

"Yeah..." Jacob smiled at this beautiful girl standing before him, momentarily forgetting her mom was in the room. He laced his fingers through hers. "I kinda hope you'll be my last too."

"You do?" She melted closer to him.

"I'm still standing *right* here." Valerie Arnold, Captain Arnold's wife, Maryam's mother. Forget waiting to ask her father. Jacob leapfrogged right to the woman in charge, turning to her with confidence.

"Can I marry your daughter?" Jacob blurted out.

Her jaw dropped. "What?" Mrs. Arnold asked.

"What?" Maryam whispered, covering her mouth with her hand, eyes wide and sparkling. "When?"

"As soon as possible," Jacob said, pulling Maryam close again. He lifted his hand and brushed his thumb across her lips, remembering how they felt connected to his. "Ever since we started talking about getting married, I haven't been able to think of anything else."

"That was twenty minutes ago," Maryam whispered.

"What a long twenty minutes," Jacob whispered back.

Maryam reached up and placed her palm against his cheek. "Are you sure you're not just thinking with your... feelings?"

"I was thinking about marrying you before I kissed you," he said, leaning closer to her ear. "This isn't physical. Okay, it's not *just* physical."

Maryam giggled.

"On deck," Mrs. Arnold demanded. "Both of you!" She held the door open, waiting for them to leave his stateroom as they clung to each other's hands.

She marched them to the stern of the yacht while calling out to her husband and Jacob's parents in a firm, insistent voice. Her bellowing drew the attention of crew members as well, but one look at her face and they shrunk back into whatever job they could find somewhere else on the boat.

Nick and Adele emerged from their stateroom; Mother sat up from a lounge chair on deck, removed her floppy hat and sunglasses, and set down the paperback novel she'd been reading; Father and Captain Arnold stepped from the control room; Liam came out of his stateroom, holding a beer bottle, but quickly tucked the bottle back into his room and flicked the butt of a strange looking cigarette off the side of the railing into the ocean; and his wife sat up from a lounge chair, wearing a bikini swimsuit that was not flattering on a pregnant woman. Jacob looked away and shuddered.

"What's the matter, Valerie?" Mother asked, a crease in her brow.

"Your son has been doing things with my daughter that are completely inappropriate!"

"Score," Liam said with no apparent remorse. "I knew those babies would come in handy."

"I have never, nor do I intend, to use those!" Jacob insisted.

"Come on, man, please don't tell me you did it without one. Have you learned nothing from your older brothers?"

"I have learned the most important thing from my older brother, Nick," Jacob said with confidence. "To wait until I'm married!"

"What are you two talking about?" Father asked, turning to Liam. "*What* did you do?"

"I gave him some protection, that's all," Liam said. "Which is a heck of a lot more than you gave me."

"Pr—protection?" Mother stammered. "What do you mean by that?"

"Jacob has a whole box of condoms in his stateroom!" Valerie exclaimed. "And one of them was open while they were... well... I don't even want to think about what they were doing."

"We were kissing, Mother! Kissing. Fully clothed," Maryam insisted. "And it was open just because I wanted to see what one looked like."

"Liam," Father interrupted. "Don't you blame your poor choices on my unwillingness to teach you anything short of complete chastity prior to marriage."

"Thanks, Dad, that works *in theory*," Liam said. "That's not the reality of life. Once you're in the heat of the moment, theories fly right out the window."

"Which is why we don't allow ourselves to get in those situations in the first place," Nick said.

"Shut up, you self-righteous jerk," Liam said. "You think you're so much better than the rest of us? How long did it take you to get married once you and Adele got back together? Two weeks? Three? Try waiting a few weeks or months after falling in love, and see how quickly you get into 'situations' like that." Liam actually used air quotes and sneered at their brother.

"When you know you've met the right woman and you want to be together forever, you get married." Nick nodded once definitively. "You don't allow yourself to be tempted by one another."

"Which is exactly why Maryam and I want to get married." Jacob stepped confidently forward, still clutching Maryam's hand.

"You want to *what?*" Captain Arnold asked.

"I'm sorry I didn't ask you first, sir," Jacob said. "But Mrs. Arnold was standing right there, and I figured even if I asked you, you'd need to ask her, so I just skipped a step."

"We have been at sea for ten whole days, and you think you know my daughter well enough to marry her?"

Jacob turned to Maryam and softened his expression. "Of course not. But love grows over time and many things about her I won't learn until we're married anyway, so why wait?"

"Exactly," Maryam agreed in a quiet, contemplative answer. She squeezed his hand and gazed into his eyes.

"You're too young for us to even have this discussion," Mother said.

"I'm not too young," Jacob said. "I'm old enough that if Israel ever called me to serve as a soldier, I'd be compelled to fight on behalf of our country."

"Well, you're too young to get married."

"By whose definition?" Jacob asked. "Would you rather have us sneaking around and getting into trouble? I'd rather do things the moral way and be legally married first."

"That would be difficult since we're on a boat in the middle of the ocean," Nick pointed out.

"Actually," Maryam corrected him. "My father is legally ordained to perform marriages in the United States of America, which applies to all international waters as well."

All eyes turned to Captain Arnold, who shrugged. "Back when I was captain on a cruise ship it made complete sense. I've performed many at-sea nuptials. It was a good idea at the time. Certainly never thought I'd b e officiating at my own daughter's wedding."

"Why not, Daddy?" Maryam asked. "You're the man I've looked up to my whole life. You and Mother have shown me how a true marriage should work, and I hope to someday emulate the relationship you have. You've been my anchor in stormy seas."

Captain Arnold's shoulders relaxed, and he touched Maryam's cheek in a gesture of affection.

"Speaking of stormy seas," Liam's wife Rachel spoke up for the first time in the discussion. "That storm sure looks like it's going to cause rough seas." She pointed behind them at the dark clouds.

Chapter Forty-Eight

Big Storm

"Where the heck did *that* come from?" Captain Arnold asked, as if he wasn't the only person on that yacht paying strict attention to the barometric pressure meters.

"It's just a little squall." Valerie Arnold waved her hand dismissively. "We've sailed in worse."

"Not in an untested vessel." He shook his head and creased his brow.

"What can we do to help?" Levi stepped forward and laid his hand on the captain's forearm.

"Everything needs to be battened down and secured. Any children onboard should be taken to an interior stateroom along with any of the pregnant women. Eventually everyone needs to be indoors. I'd prefer all family to get inside, but if you're going to be helping, follow the directions of the crew as if *they* are the owners of this yacht, *not you*. You got it?"

Captain Arnold looked around at everyone, meaning business. No one argued. Crew members came out of the woodwork as if getting permission to interrupt the argument, and they worked like a team. They all knew exactly what needed to be done and how to do it.

Liam wrapped his arm around his wife, helping Rachel follow where Valerie was leading. She was the only openly pregnant woman, but it didn't surprise Jacob to see Nick leading Adele in the same careful manner.

Jacob couldn't hide a smile and met his mom's gaze. He could tell she knew Adele was expecting. They shared a moment, and then his mom picked up his little brother, Joseph, and followed the pregnant women.

The wind and waves hadn't picked up yet, but an ominous calm hung heavy in the air. The dark sky was still hovering off to the west as if it was just gathering energy and threatening to unleash its wrath on anyone stupid enough to be sailing the ocean.

"What can I do to help?" Jacob asked Maryam. She'd shown him enough of the ship for him to know there were a million moving parts.

"We need to get everything covered." She rushed ahead, and Jacob followed. Together they helped the rest of the crew drape special tarps designed to fit perfectly over the outdoor furniture.

"How bad is this going to get?" Jacob asked, glancing nervously in the direction of the dark skies.

"Not bad compared to a hurricane," Maryam said. "But it's not what this boat was designed to handle. The ship will be fine. It's the stuff that's in the boat that will start breaking, and it will be uncomfortable for guests and for the crew."

As if a wall of sheer water were dragging toward them across the ocean, they could see the storm rushing forward.

"Let's go!" Maryam said, grabbing Jacob's hand. She pulled him toward the stern and down an interior flight of stairs

"Where are we going? Can I watch from the bridge? Do you think your dad would mind?"

"After he recently discovered that you were making out with his daughter?" She turned toward Jacob and raised her eyebrows. "I doubt he's going to want you anywhere near him."

"What you meant to say was now that he's aware I'm going to marry his daughter, he'll want to teach me everything he knows and keep me on a short leash so he can whip me into shape." Jacob placed both hands on her hips and pulled her closer.

"Yeah, I'm sure that's exactly what he's thinking." She lifted onto her toes and stole a kiss.

Jacob took advantage of the secluded location and gripped her in his arms for something a little more passionate. They got lost in that kiss for about a minute and a half, and then the boat pitched to the side as if it were a toy in a wave pool.

"Come on." Maryam grabbed his hand and headed toward the stairs. He tugged against her.

"Please," he begged. "I want to at least try to go watch from the bridge. If your dad kicks me out, then we'll leave."

"Fine, come on." She led him in the opposite direction, toward the bow. They climbed to the bridge deck and entered through the side door, slinking into the back of the room, holding hands and staying out of the way.

The wind had picked up, and the rain was pelting from the side. The captain was calmly barking out orders to people who all seemed to know what they were doing even without his instructions. The commands almost seemed more of a way of keeping record of each step. Calling out readings on the various gauges and dials, barometric pressures, temperatures, wind speed, wave height. There was ordered chaos that was almost a choreographed dance between the captain, his first mate and crew.

Finally, the moment Jacob knew would happen did. Captain Arnold noticed them standing at the back of his control room. He creased his brow in frustration and scowled. Then he did something unexpected.

"Well, are you gonna get up here and learn something from me," the captain asked, "or are you just gonna stand back there gripping my little girl's hand like she's your life vest?"

"Yes, sir, I mean, no sir." Jacob gulped and stepped away from Maryam, dropping her hand reluctantly. This was what he wanted after all. "What can I do to help?" He grabbed hold of a bar in the middle of the room, holding on for dear life.

"All we can do right now is go with the flow," Captain Arnold said. "This is not a hurricane. It's not even a tropical storm. I've piloted in worse conditions. No flat seas ever made a skilled sailor."

Jacob only nodded and clung to the pole, not even sure if the captain saw him nod. Huge, dangerous waves appeared out of nowhere but didn't seem to faze any of the trained crew. The bow rose and fell as the boat crested the waves and fell down the other side, crashing as if the scariest roller coaster on earth came crashing down at the bottom of a hill rather than continuing on a smooth track.

The bow rocked up, and Jacob could see only air. The bow came down, and the waves crashed over the bow, totally covering the deck with foam.

Keeping the boat perpendicular to the waves was nearly impossible when the waves crashed from all sides, not just up down but also side to side. Waves splashed completely over the deck and wind whipped salt water over everything.

"I've never had to surf a thirty-four-meter superyacht down a wave before," Captain Arnold called out. "This boat is no good in the big sea when the waves are coming from behind. We're fishtailing down the waves just trying to prevent a broach. Have you surfed much?"

"I tried once," Jacob called back. "It was a complete disaster. I couldn't stay on my feet and kept tipping over."

"That's exactly what we're trying to avoid." The captain nodded definitively. "The greatest risk of capsizing is when the ship turns broadside to the waves and the rocking of the boat and the movement of the waves sync up. I'm not going to let that happen."

"Have you ever capsized a boat before?"

"Not and lived to tell about it," he joked.

Jacob laughed nervously. "Considering you're still alive, I'm going to take that as a good sign."

"The speed we normally do is about thirteen knots, fourteen max," Captain Arnold explained. "We were doing nineteen knots down the face of that last wave, and the wave was staying pretty much in line with us. Not a fun position to be in."

"How long will this last?" Jacob asked.

"Not sure. The barometer should have dropped over the course of eighteen hours or so. That much variance in atmospheric pressure causes strong winds. It's feeding off the warm waters. The largest waves are dependent on the strength of the wind."

"They look pretty big to me," Jacob said. "You've sailed in worse than this?" The thought of drowning occurred to him, but then he realized he hadn't learned all he'd learned just to drown out in the middle of the ocean.

"Yes, I have," the captain said. "Your dad wouldn't have hired me if I wasn't the best."

"Well, I'm glad he did." Jacob turned to glance at Maryam with a shy smile.

"I trust we're not going to have a repeat of what happened earlier between you and my daughter." Captain Arnold's words were more of a threat than a question.

"No, sir." Jacob tried to keep his voice as respectful and repentant as he could.

"Don't let your teenage hormones get in the way of making lifetime adult decisions."

Jacob gulped. "Yes, sir."

Conversation between Jacob and the captain became less strained as he watched and learned all he could while clinging to the bar in the center of the bridge through the long night of fighting the storm.

When the rain and wind eventually let up a little, and Jacob could barely keep his eyes open, he finally excused himself to go rest. The captain and crew had sea legs and were prepared for these circumstances. Jacob was a writer and scholar and businessman. He knew his physical limitations and didn't care if anyone razzed him for being a lightweight.

Lying down in his bed while the waves were still pitching and rolling after he'd stood on the bridge all night was a mistake. Within a few minutes, he was hanging his head over the toilet in the attached bathroom of his suite.

He spent that day on the floor of his stateroom, a few feet away from the head, miserable. He may be part owner of a yacht company, but this wasn't the way he wanted to live his life. He'd have to find a way to get Maryam to join him on land somewhere, because he wasn't giving her up.

Chapter Forty-Nine

The Top 1%

"Hey, little brother, you still got any of those babies left?" Liam didn't wait for an answer, just strode over to Jacob's bedside table and opened the drawer. "Oh good, tons of 'em."

"Which crew member are you corrupting now?" Jacob asked, setting aside the book he was reading. After the past few days of feeling sick since the storm, he was glad he could read at all. He was just starting to feel better. "Couldn't convince your younger brother to disobey Father's rules, so you've found some other poor schmuck to lead away into darkness."

"You're funny," Liam said. He grabbed one row of five and dropped them back into the drawer and tucked the box under his arm. "No, these are for me."

"I'm pretty sure Rachel can't get any more pregnant than she already is." Jacob was confused.

"Rachel's not the only beautiful woman on this yacht." Liam took the box and started for the door.

"Wait a minute," Jacob called after him. "Are you cheating on your wife?"

"Cheating is in the eye of the beholder," Liam said and left the room.

Jacob scrambled off his bed and followed his brother. "I'm pretty sure 99% of the people in this world would agree with me that cheating is *wrong*."

"Well, I guess I'm in that top 1%." Liam continued walking, and Jacob continued following.

"You're not going to get away with this," Jacob said.

Liam stopped and turned to face him. "I've been *getting away with it* for weeks. What's a few more days?"

"You are a wicked man, Liam Cohen," Jacob rose his voice, tears threatening. "I've known it for a long time. I didn't want to admit it because you're my brother. But you are. You're wicked."

"You have a right to your opinion. I have the right to mine." Liam turned away and kept walking toward his stateroom.

"What's going on, gentlemen?" Levi stood with Nick near the railing, watching the ocean trailing out behind the elegant yacht.

"Liam's cheating on Rachel," Jacob stated in a loud enough voice for his father and brother to hear him. Unfortunately, several other people were within earshot as well, including Rachel.

Liam slipped past his wife and tossed the box onto the bed in their stateroom, then pulled the door shut and faced the family. "You think she doesn't know that, little brother? You think you just ratted me out? Rachel probably even knows her name."

"Not difficult to guess," Rachel grumbled. "What exactly am I supposed to do about it?"

"You could demand that he stops," Jacob said in exasperation.

Liam laughed, standing behind his wife and leaning against the wall next to their stateroom door, arms folded across his chest.

"Have you ever known Liam to do what someone demanded him to do?" Rachel raised her eyebrows at Jacob. "He has needs, and obviously I'm not able to fulfil that role at the moment." She placed her hand on her growing baby bump.

"I'm a man, Jacob," Liam said with a sneer. "When you become a man, you'll understand these things."

"I am man enough to know that a woman's body is sacred and should be treated as such. You are defiling your wife and defiling the poor woman who you're using for your *needs*."

"Maybe she's using me too," Liam said. "You ever thought of that? Maybe I'm giving her exactly what she wants. Women have needs too. Again, you'll learn about that when you're all grown up." Liam's tone took on a note of derogatory condescension, and he glanced over at Maryam, who had approached and stood beside Jacob. Liam looked her up and down, smiling. He even winked at her.

"You stay away from my girl!" Jacob demanded.

"Maybe it's too late for that," Liam said with a sneer. "Maybe I've been taking care of her for weeks. Since you weren't man enough to do it."

"How dare you!" Jacob rushed Liam and pushed him, hard. Liam had a good thirty pounds of muscle on Jacob and came back at him, swinging a fist. Jacob ducked and landed a sucker punch to Liam's gut. Liam rammed his head into Jacob's chest, pushing him just as hard.

Suddenly, Nick had his arms around Jacob from behind, and their father had a hold of Liam. They both struggled to get out of the restraining grips, but they were pushed away from one another.

Jacob finally calmed down and shook free. He glanced over at Maryam, who had tears running down her face. He couldn't tell if they were from guilt, sorrow, or frustration. Jacob just shook his head and stormed away, slamming the door to his stateroom. He threw himself onto his bed and sobbed into his pillow.

Chapter Fifty

My Mother was Right about You!

"**J**acob?" Maryam knocked on his stateroom door. He tried to let her soft voice comfort him. "Can I come in?"

"Do you even want to come in?" Jacob brushed the tears from his cheeks, embarrassed for her to see him cry. "What's the matter? Didn't get enough satisfaction from my brother?"

"How could you even think that about me?" She stopped near the door.

"I see the way Liam looks at you." Jacob sat up and swung his legs over the side of his bed, placing his feet on the floor, and stood to face her. "What else am I supposed to think?"

"He looks at all women that way," Maryam said. "He's a cockroach and a lowlife and a womanizer, and I can't believe you would think that I would ever go after a man like him."

"All the women go after him. They always have."

"Well, I'm not one of them. I am completely offended that you would ever think that about me." Maryam stalked toward Jacob with narrowed eyes. She pushed against his chest with vitriol. "I don't know why I ever gave you a chance. I was starting to fall for you." She pushed him again.

Jacob righted himself. "I'm falling for you too." He heard the shift in his tone. He felt bad for accusing her of doing anything wrong.

"You know what? I think you're as bad as your brother."

"How could you think that?"

"The first time you got me alone, you had your hands all over me, and you made out with me so passionately my mom thought we were having sex."

"My hands were *not* all over you!"

"Are you trying to tell me that if I had locked your stateroom door and pulled you down onto that bed that you wouldn't have opened one of those condoms and had sex with me right then and there?"

"I would *not* have done that!" Jacob held up his hands as if she had him at gunpoint.

"You tried to convince our parents to let us get married that very day," she said. "Why? Because we'd known each other for years and fell in love? No! You wanted to marry me so that we could have sex! Admit it!"

"I do admit it," Jacob said in defense.

"Ha!" She put her finger to his chest, proving her point.

"But only because I respect you and I'd never take advantage of you. I would never have sex with you before we were married."

"If you respected me so much, then why would you think I'd have sex with your brother?" She pushed him again.

"Because he said he was taking care of your *needs*." Jacob sneered, thinking back on how much his brother's words had disgusted him.

"And you were so quick to believe him?"

"Why else would he need that whole box of condoms?" Jacob pointed in the direction of the door. "He's obviously taking care of somebody's needs."

"Yeah... his own." Maryam got right up in Jacob's face, and her quiet, pointed words were more powerful than if she'd shouted in his face. "And just the fact that you thought I'd be involved with him makes you just as bad as he is."

"Maryam, please—"

"You stay away from me, Jacob Cohen. My mother was right. All of you Cohen boys are trouble. I don't want to see you again for the rest of this cruise. I don't want to see you again for the rest of my life." Maryam stormed out the door, slamming it in his face.

Jacob pulled open the door and called after her. "Maryam, wait!"

"I believe my daughter told you she didn't want to see you again." Maryam's father stood near Jacob's stateroom door with his arms folded and narrowed eyes.

"But Captain Arnold, if I could just explain."

"I think you've said enough," the captain said. "Stay away from my daughter."

Chapter Fifty-One

Barcelo Maya Palace

S eeing land wasn't as exciting as Jacob thought it would be. He'd been depressed for the past three days since Maryam stopped speaking to him. He couldn't even look at his brother, or his sister-in-law, or even talk to any of his other family members.

He felt sick and exhausted and just wanted to get off this boat. Yet he couldn't shake the ominous feeling that if he left, he'd never see Maryam again. There was no choice. She wouldn't let him talk. He didn't blame he r.

She'd been nothing but nice to him, and he'd accused her of having sex with his brother. As if she ever would. He had just been hurt and had lashed out at her. But she didn't deserve that. She deserved to be treated like a lady.

What Liam said about her was offensive and obscene. Jacob wasn't sure he'd ever be able to forgive his brother. Now that they were getting off the boat, Jacob intended to stay as far away from Liam as possible.

The Barcelo Maya Palace resort, where the family would be staying indefinitely, didn't have a docking area, so Captain Arnold piloted the *Lady Bountiful* up the canal past dozens of elite homes to the marina. Each home boasted its own boat slip large enough to dock a large sailing yacht or superyacht.

Jacob listened while his father and two older brothers discussed buying up as many of the homes as they could in order to have room for each brother to live with his wife and children. Plus, they knew Daniel Ashish and his son David would have already arrived by private jet together with Lyle and Miriam and baby Ishy. Sam and Leanne would be following after her semester ended. Prince Marcos Sayid would also need to purchase a home when he arrived next spring. Jacob envisioned the entire City of

Puerto Aventuras owned by either a Cohen, Ashish, or a member of the Royal Sayid family.

Several large limousines waited for them in the parking lot at the marina along with a welcoming party. Daniel and his wife Cassandra greeted their daughters, Rachel and Adele, with hugs after they practically ran down the boarding dock to reach their parents. Their older brother David was there with his wife, Shira. He greeted Liam with a clasped hand and a smirk.

All Jacob wanted was to rush back up the boarding dock to grab Maryam's hand to bring her with him to the resort. There was almost a physical pain in his chest as he climbed into the limousine. He knew the captain's family and the entire crew from the yacht had been invited to stay at the resort for a few days before beginning their charter tours.

Maryam would attend the grand reception later that evening, and Jacob was determined to find a time to talk now that they weren't stuck together on a boat in the middle of the ocean, hopefully away from the watchful eyes of her mother and father. Perhaps she'd finally listen to his apology. He could remind her of their plans to travel into North and South America, seeking out the quaint forest where they could build a home together and live happily ever after.

Moving into his large suite of rooms at the resort was unsettling. The floor beneath his feet was too still and the rooms too large. Everyone else had a spouse. All Jacob had was a view of the ocean, no plans for the afternoon, and an extra-large king-sized bed. He curled up in a ball on that bed and cried himself to sleep, wishing to return to the boat and to his Maryam.

Chapter Fifty-Two

Observing from Afar

"Didn't like the flan custard, huh?" Jacob snuck up behind Maryam, where she sat at a table in the corner of the welcoming reception, and startled her as she poked at the dessert with a turned-up nose and a frown. "Why don't you come with me for a stroll on the beach...?"

He didn't wait for Maryam to answer, just lifted her free hand and pulled her gently from the chair. The open courtyard where the resort held the reception was decked out with sparkling lights and hanging lanterns. Once they stepped out of the lighted courtyard, they virtually disappeared from view.

"Jacob, what are you doing?" Maryam glanced over to her parents on the dance floor, who were completely distracted. She stumbled in a pair of sandals so different from her usual boat shoes. Her sundress was simple and understated, feminine and soft. She'd allowed her curls to cascade down her back rather than tying them up in a professional braid or ponytail. Practicality was important while working on a yacht, but here at the resort, she was able to relax.

"This is the first time your parents haven't been glued to your side all evening." Jacob tucked her hand in the crook of his arm and led her down the cobblestone path to the beach.

"Were you spying on me?" Her voice held a subtle suspicion but mostly wonderment and excitement.

"Observing from afar." Jacob pointed to the sky. "Did you see that full moon?"

"Yesterday was the full moon," Maryam said. "Tonight, it's waning."

"Sorry I missed it." Jacob gulped and hoped Maryam understood there was more meaning in his apology than just missing the full moon. "I'm sorry for everything."

"I'm trying to forgive you. I really am. I just don't know if I can."

"I was a jerk," Jacob said.

"Yes, you were."

"How can I make it up to you?" Jacob turned her to face him and took her hands in his.

"I care about you, Jacob, but this is as far as we can go." Maryam wasn't talking about the distance on the beach. She didn't want their relationship to continue. "We lead very different lives. You're the son of a billionaire. I'm a housekeeper on a yacht that is scheduled to leave Puerto Aventuras in less than a week."

"Don't get back on the boat," Jacob pleaded. "Let's travel together like we said we would. Let's explore and experience a life beyond what either of us has lived in the nineteen years we've been on this earth or, in your case, on the ocean. Let's spend time together and see if we can find a common place between being a billionaire and being a housekeeper."

"It would never work." Maryam lowered her gaze. "We're too different."

"Opposites attract," he reasoned. "We complement each other."

"You have your life to lead, and I have mine." Maryam glanced off toward the ocean, where gentle waves lapped at the white, sandy beaches.

"That was a life chosen by your parents. What do *you* want?"

A tear escaped down her cheek, and she whispered, "You know what I want."

"A big house in a forest, with lots of windows where we can raise babies together."

She didn't answer with words but lifted her gaze to meet his. Every dream she'd ever had was reflected in her eyes.

"Stay here with me, and let's explore and find that forest."

"Jacob... I can't."

"Why?"

"Because... I have my life—"

"Your *parents'* life," Jacob interrupted. "Come with me, and live your *own* life. Marry me. Spend forever with me."

She sighed and looked away, considering. "I don't know. Can I think about it for a few days?"

"Of course. I don't want to put any pressure on you." Jacob ran his hands up and down her arms. "Then again, if you haven't made a decision by the time your father pulls anchor and leaves the marina, I may have to swim after you, and you know darn well I can't swim. So, please don't make me wait that long."

Maryam giggled, and Jacob's stomach fluttered.

He lifted his hands to cradle her face, then leaned closer cautiously, not wanting to scare her away.

She met his kiss with a relaxed passion that hinted at more but was content with just this.

Jacob wanted Maryam to know she could trust him, not just with her body but with her heart. They had fallen in love while crossing an ocean together, but now was the time to face the next phase in their lives. Now was the time to grow up, become adults, and figure out together what the future could hold.

Chapter Fifty-Three

Inheritance

"Thank you all for joining us," Levi Cohen said from his position at the head of a large conference room table. He had requested the family and extended family meet together and hadn't told them why. The Barcelo Maya Palace resort had become the family's temporary home and office until they could purchase homes. The resort had been more than accommodating to the multi-billionaire and his family. "I don't just mean 'thank you for joining us for this meeting.' I mean thank you for coming with us to Mexico."

There were mumbles around the table like, "Of course" and "Good to be here." All Jacob could think was *I didn't have a choice.* He wanted this meeting to be over so he could go find Maryam before her family left to move out of the resort and back onto the yacht.

His patience was wearing thin. She still hadn't answered him, and they had less than a day before she would leave port. Today was his last chance. Jacob planned to try one more time to get Maryam to stay with him.

Captain Arnold would launch tomorrow to start the first of many charter tours around the globe for however many years he continued in employ with Cohen Enterprises. He was paid handsomely to live on a luxury yacht and sail around the world over and over. If a person wanted to make his living as the captain of a yacht, there weren't many nicer than the *Lady Bountiful*.

Jacob fought the urge to look at the clock or check his phone again to see if she'd sent him a text. Meeting his father's gaze, Jacob determined to give his full attention to the meeting and worry about Maryam later. Not an easy task, until his father shocked everyone in the room.

"I'm giving away all my money."

Murmurs traveled around the table, some angry, all confused.

"Let me explain." He held out his hands. "Sarah and I have decided to give each of our sons their inheritance now rather than wait until we die."

That started a different kind of chatter, excited rather than disgruntled. Jacob wondered what that meant. An equal distribution between each of Father's six sons? How much would he keep for himself and Mom? How rich would Jacob become at the ripe old age of nineteen? He'd once joked that his father had so much money they could divide the fortune among all the sons and they'd each be billionaires. Could that really be possible?

"Some of you have been a little distracted with weddings and having babies." Father glanced at his son, Lyle, and wife, Miriam, who was holding their first grandson, Ishmael.

Liam was sitting beside Lyle, with David Ashish next to him, their heads close together, whispering. Their wives, Shira and Rachel, were on the other side of David, heads together as well. Something was up with the four of them.

David's mother and father, Cassandra and Daniel Ashish, sat to the left of his best friend, Levi. Jacob's mother sat at his right.

Nick and Adele had a place of honor beside their parents, the implication of which was not lost on Jacob. He could tell Liam and Lyle knew exactly why their father was singling out Nick; he was being groomed to take over Cohen Enterprises, and the older brothers didn't like that.

Sam didn't seem to have a problem standing in his younger brother's shadow. They all had their role in the business and in the family. He sat confidently with his bride Leanne, who looked the part of a studious graduate with an advanced degree. The only way Sam was able to convince her to leave her university in Jerusalem was to encourage her to pursue a PhD at a major university in the United States. They had both been accepted at the University of Houston and planned to head that direction within the next few weeks.

Leanne sat beside their oldest sister, Ruth, who had married Zach before flying to Mexico. They were officially on their honeymoon. Jacob had no idea what their plans were from there.

His father continued. "Some of you may have noticed I've been quietly liquidating assets in Jerusalem and throughout the Middle East. I have started endowment funds at various institutions, mostly in Jerusalem since that's where I lived most of my life. I wanted to leave a legacy there and a good name should any of you choose to move home."

Move home? Jacob thought. Not a chance. He knew what was in the Middle East. A lot of sand and rocks. He wanted fresh water and trees. Lots of trees.

"We are in the process of disbanding Cohen Enterprises." Father shocked the group again. "I don't want any of you to feel beholden to any of our companies. Most of them will be divided into shares, and you will each have the option to use part of your inheritance to purchase those shares, should you choose, or to receive your inheritance as bonds, and go your separate ways."

That got Jacob's heart racing. Go separate ways? Leave his brothers? Never have to deal with Liam again for the rest of his life? No longer have to live in his shadow? No longer have to obey Father's rules in order to keep him happy?

Jacob envisioned taking Maryam by the hand and confidently traveling the world alone together in search of their dream forest where they could build a big house with lots of windows and a kitchen where the family could gather and they could raise babies. A tiny smile pulled at the corner of Jacob's lips.

Over the past week, he'd done some research about the American continents and decided he wanted to head north first. There was a place called the Great Lakes, and they sat regally between the countries of Canada and the United States. Rivers and valleys and waterfalls and more fresh water than there was oil in Saudi Arabia. That's where he wanted to explore. If he couldn't find Maryam's dream forest there, then it didn't exist.

"There is still a lot of work to be done in the estate planning process," Father continued, pulling Jacob again from his fantasies. "But suffice it to say, you will each be very wealthy men when all is divided. What you choose to do with that wealth will be completely your decision."

If Jacob had a hard time holding still at the beginning of this meeting, he now could barely remain seated. He had to go find Maryam.

"At the risk of sounding greedy, Father, how much are we talking here?" Liam did indeed sound greedy, but he said what everyone else was thinking.

"I wouldn't be surprised if each of my sons"—Father gulped—"were billionaires by the time all is divvied up."

Liam sat back with a smirk and tucked his hands behind his head. Lyle whispered something to Miriam, and she giggled. Sam and Leanne spoke quietly to one another in calm, serious undertones.

Nick barely twitched a muscle. *He already knew.* That didn't surprise Jacob. He was Father's right-hand man and had been for years.

"Now for the bad news..." Father glanced around the table at every person but paused longest at each of his sons. "I was not happy about what happened on the yacht."

Not everyone in the room had sailed on the maiden voyage of the *Lady Bountiful* and were privy to details about the argument. Some people murmured or looked around the table.

"I'm disappointed with the impropriety I saw, the arguing, the fighting, the infidelity." Father didn't turn his head toward Liam, but others did, and everyone in that room knew exactly who Father was talking about. "I do not intend to evenly distribute my fortune, and I will not be disclosing to any of you what the others received."

"Oh, that is a bunch of effing garbage!" Liam rose from his seat and threw his pen down, creating a divot in the polished wood. "You're playing favorites? Based on what? Because my little brother's a prude? Because we threw a couple punches?"

"Hmm... I guess *some* of my sons will be billionaires." Father pursed his lips and diverted his gaze.

Liam must have realized his tirade wasn't helping because he leaned against the wall near the door and folded his arms, glaring at their father. No one else spoke.

"I have an announcement to make also." Daniel Ashish cleared his throat. He glanced over at David and then around the table at his daughters. "We don't have as much money as the Cohen's, but we'd like to give each of our daughters, and our son, part of your inheritance. Ruth, David, Rachel, Miriam, Leanne, and Adele, you'll each get $500,000 immediately and divide the rest of our wealth after your mother and I pass away."

"Thank you, Father, that's very generous." Ruth shifted her gaze. "And Mother, also, thank you." All the girls nodded. David's brow furrowed.

"I also have one other gift," Jacob's father said. "Zach, we promised we would help care for you if you came with us. You have been a great friend, and I'd like to offer you $500,000 as well."

"Thank you, Mr. Cohen. That is greatly appreciated." Zach nodded.

"Let me get this straight." David looked around the room. "I'm the only person in this room who didn't just become a millionaire with the stroke of a pen?"

"Sorry," Shira said, folding her arms across her chest. "Levi didn't have any daughters for you to marry. You're stuck with me for a wife."

"That's not what I meant, and you know it," David said. "I'm just frustrated."

"I encourage all of you to take into consideration what you want from this wealth you've been given, and choose to do good in this world." Father stood and glanced around the table. "That's all for today." He helped Mother to her feet, and together they strode past Liam, who still glowered by the door to the boardroom.

Soft conversations resumed around the table after their father left, and Jacob was the first to follow, hurrying through the resort to go find his bride. Maryam would surely accept a marriage proposal now that he was a billionaire.

Chapter Fifty-Four

No More Liam

"Maryam!" Jacob hurried through the open door of Maryam's hotel suite, expecting to find her packing and getting ready to head over to the boat. Instead, he found a housekeeper from the resort stripping the sheets and cleaning the room for incoming guests. "Where's Maryam?"

"I'm sorry, sir," the housekeeper replied. "The captain and his family have already checked out of the hotel."

Jacob would have panicked at that news except he knew exactly where they'd gone; back to the yacht to prepare for tomorrow's departure. He mumbled to the housekeeper a quick recognition of thanks as he brought his cell phone to his ear, requesting his concierge to bring him a car.

The limo seemed to creep down the streets between the resort and the marina, and Jacob's knee bounced as he chewed his thumbnail, excitement and nerves fighting in his stomach, threatening his brunch to wind up on the side of the road.

Finally, they pulled up to the marina, and Jacob pushed open the limo door without even thanking the driver or shutting the door behind himself. He raced across the passerelle joining the dock to the yacht and hurried through the main deck to the door that led downstairs to the crew's quarters. He wound down the staircases and through several hallways until he found Maryam right where he expected her to be, lying in her bunk, curled up with a tissue and red eyes.

"Oh, my darling, were you going to leave without saying goodbye?" Jacob sat on the floor beside her bunk and lowered his face until he was even with hers.

"Goodbyes are too hard," Maryam whispered.

"I know this will be difficult, but we'll have to say goodbye... to your parents."

That brought a tiny smile. "Very funny."

"I'm being completely serious." Jacob sat up all the way and lifted Maryam into a seated position. He took both of her hands in his and gazed up into her eyes. "I sort of inherited just over a billion dollars today."

"What?" She leaned forward, concern creasing her brow. "Were your parents in an accident? Why didn't you tell me? I'm so sorry."

"No, no, they're fine and very much alive."

Maryam relaxed, but confusion clouded her face.

"They decided to give each of us our inheritance early and suggested we all go our separate ways to live our own lives."

"Are you saying what I think you're saying?" she asked.

"No more Liam," they said at the same time, each with a grin.

"See, now *that* makes me want to consider your offer."

"Dang, if I'd known all it would take was getting rid of my brother, I would have ditched the family days ago," he said. "I would have been a pauper, but you would have loved me anyway."

"At least we'd have more in common," she mumbled. "Aren't you supposed to speak to my father before asking me to run away with you?"

"He doesn't like me very much." Jacob cringed. "Do I *have* to ask his permission?"

"That is the tradition."

"But you are a strong, independent woman with a mind of your own. You should be able to make your own decisions about where you want to live and how you want to live your life. Have you told them your dreams of living on land and starting a family? Preferably with me..." He offered her a cheesy grin.

"No... I've never voiced my opinion on the subject."

"Have they ever asked you what you wanted?"

"No." Her shoulders slumped. "What if they tell me I can't leave?"

"You're an adult. They can't tell you what to do."

"But I won't have a job or anywhere to live. This boat is my home."

"Darling, haven't you been listening? I want you to be my *wife*, not just my travel companion. You will be married to a billionaire. You will never have to work outside the home for the rest of your life, unless you want to.

In which case, I will one hundred percent encourage you and support your decision."

"But that's living off your money. I should have to earn my own money."

"Technically you're already living off my money. Your paychecks come from Cohen Enterprises, do they not?"

"But that's working to earn my money."

"How about if I build you a big house and you can clean all the rooms inside every single day if you want?" He couldn't stifle a grin. "Maybe I can do the cooking and you can do the cleaning."

"You know how to cook?" She raised one eyebrow.

"I have absolutely no idea how to cook," Jacob admitted. "But I'd be willing to learn if you're willing to marry me."

"I have a feeling your ability to learn to cook goes as far as your phone to hire a personal chef."

"Okay, then, you cook, and I'll clean?"

"You know how to clean?"

"Can't we just hire someone to do all of that and you and I can stay in bed all day and make love?"

"I'm liking this prospect a little more all the time." She put her finger to her chin in feigned consideration. "Let me get this straight... You'd be willing to leave Puerto Aventuras, and your family, find me the forest of my dreams, build me a big house, hire me a personal chef and a housekeeper, *and* make love to me every day. And all I have to do is marry you?"

"That's it. Just one little thing." Jacob's heart was racing.

"Could I have a sports car too?" she teased. "I've always wanted a sports car."

"Babe, you can have a hundred sports cars if that's what you want. Just, please marry me."

"You haven't exactly asked me yet." She blinked her eyelashes with feigned innocence.

"What?"

"You haven't gotten down on your knee and asked me to marry you."

"I haven't?" Jacob shifted from where he was seated on the floor and knelt beside her bed. He took her hands in his and cleared his throat then spoke confidently. "Maryam Jasmine Arnold, will you do me the honor of becoming my wife?"

"I'll think about it," she teased.

Jacob fell to the floor as if she'd stabbed him in the heart. He groaned in mock torture. "You're trying to kill me, woman."

"Put the poor man out of his misery." Maryam's friend Ivy hung her head off the top bunk. "If you don't want to marry him, I will. And I don't even need a sports car."

"You've been up there this whole time?" Jacob lay on his back on the floor, grinning up at the two women on bunk beds laughing down at him.

"That was the most beautiful proposal I've ever heard," Ivy swooned, completely unapologetic.

"Did you know she was up there?" Jacob asked Maryam, and her giggle gave her away. He scrambled off the floor and pushed her over so that he was lying beside her on her bunk. "This totally deserves a tickle torture."

Maryam squealed as Jacob tickled her and nuzzled her neck and finally captured her mouth with his, kissing her soundly for several long, glorious moments.

He finally pulled away and propped himself on one elbow, gazing down into her beautiful, speckled aquamarine eyes. His whisper was barely audible and meant for her ears only. "Will you marry me, darling?"

"Yes," she whispered back, then pulled him down for another long kiss.

"I thought I told you to keep your hands off my daughter!" A loud voice boomed from above him where he lay on Maryam's bed. Jacob didn't even need to look up to know he was in trouble.

"Oops."

Chapter Fifty-Five

Squirrel

"**M**om! This isn't how it looks!" Maryam scrambled to sit up, untangling herself from Jacob. He felt the absence of her legs entwined with his and considered pulling her back down for another long kiss.

"Mrs. Arnold, this is *exactly* how it looks, and I plan to marry your daughter immediately, so you might want to hire a new assistant." Jacob sat up and swung his legs over the side of Maryam's bed, then pointed to the bunk above him. "I believe Ivy is available. You'll find her up there."

"Hi, Mrs. Arnold." Ivy gave her a light wave.

"Get off my daughter's bed!" The woman was formidable, but Jacob was done beating around the bush. He stood and faced his future mother-in-law.

"That's fine, I have a king-sized bed in my suite over at the resort. Maryam will be more than comfortable—"

The shock of Valerie Arnold's slap across his face came as a surprise but was well deserved.

"Mother! What are you thinking?" Maryam pushed between Jacob and her mother. Maryam lifted her hand to Jacob's cheek. "Are you okay?"

"I'm fine, darling. You would have done the same thing to a man who spoke to our daughter that way, but she didn't let me finish my sentence." Jacob looked over Maryam's shoulder directly at her mother. "What I was about to add was the phrase after we're married."

"My only daughter will not marry one of you Cohen boys! You're all trouble. You think just because you're rich you can do anything you want."

"If I could do anything I *want*, I would wave a magic wand and force my oldest brother to stop being a complete jerk so that you would see the rest of us as the decent men that we are."

"Humph." Mrs. Arnold folded her arms across her chest and scowled.

"Please, I want our families to live harmoniously. Your daughter and I have chosen to marry; therefore, I will soon be your son-in-law. Let's find a way to get along."

"And you plan to live with her in a resort like your nomad parents?"

"No, I plan to explore the world together and build her dream house in a beautiful forest near a port where *her* nomad parents can dock their yacht and come visit."

"Who would want to live in a forest? She's not a squirrel."

"I'm the one who wants to live in a forest, Mother." Maryam turned to her mother, raising her chin with confidence. Jacob rested his hands on her shoulders in support and solidarity. "I may not be a squirrel, but I want to put down roots and live on land and not on the sea. I've loved growing up on boats and ships, but I'm ready to live my own life now. You saw the way Jacob and I connected immediately when we met, and we've grown to care about one another these past few weeks. We've fallen in love, and we want to get married. Please support my decision. Please."

"I'll think about it." Mrs. Arnold's voice faltered, and she turned on her heel to remove herself from the small berth, immediately helping to calm Jacob's claustrophobia. "Good luck convincing your father," she called over her shoulder.

"Thank you," Jacob called after her. "We're going to need it."

Maryam giggled as Jacob turned around to face her.

"That woman is almost as stubborn as her daughter." He smoothed the hair away from Maryam's face and leaned down to place a quick kiss on her lips. "Should I speak to your father alone? Or would you like to come with me?"

"Which would you prefer?"

"I think I'd like to speak to him man to man. He may have some choice words to say to me about how he'd like me to treat his daughter, and he deserves to have his opinions heard."

"I'd love to be a fly on the wall for that conversation." Maryam patted him on the chest, then lifted onto her toes to speak close to his ear. "I'm marrying you no matter what he says."

"Me too," he whispered, then captured her mouth for one more lingering kiss, aware they still had a captive audience on the top bunk.

Chapter Fifty-Six

Who Owns this Boat?

"Captain Arnold, may I speak with you, sir?"

"I'm a little busy right now." Jeffrey Arnold didn't even look up from the logbook he was examining. "Besides, I have nothing to say to you."

"Well, I have some things I'd like to say to you. Mind if I sit down?" Jacob didn't wait for the captain to answer his rhetorical question but pulled up the closest chair.

The cockpit on the yacht was luxurious and high tech. Navigational computers were mounted where traditional dials and gages would have been a few years back. The captain's chairs were finished in fine leather and there were so many windows the pilots had a nearly 360° view. Jacob almost wished he were returning to the boat for the next leg of the adventure just so he could continue to learn and maybe even have the chance to pilot the boat.

"I intend to marry your daughter." There, just state the fact, no mincing words, no building up to the moment Captain Arnold knew was coming. "I'd like your blessing."

"No." He still hadn't looked up.

"I think Maryam would be honored to have you perform the ceremony."

"I said no."

"I'm disappointed to hear that. I hope you'll at least attend our wedding."

Captain Arnold finally glanced up and disdain clouded his features. "I'm not giving you permission to marry my daughter."

"I'm not asking for your permission."

"Then why are you still sitting in my cockpit?"

"I would have liked your acceptance of our decision, but seeing as how I'm *not* confident you'll provide it, I guess we'll go announce our engagement to my parents, and while on land, we'll see about choosing an officiator."

"I told you, you're not marrying my daughter." Captain Arnold stood and towered over Jacob, balling his fists.

"And I told you I *am* marrying your daughter." Jacob stood to his full height but was still a few inches shorter. He didn't allow himself to be intimidated by the brawny man.

"I want you off my boat!" Captain Arnold pointed in the direction of the marina, vitriol in his eyes.

"I *own* this boat." Jacob remained calm but insistent. "And I will come aboard at my leisure."

The captain growled and bared his teeth, reminding Jacob of a menacing wolf.

"That being said, I am planning to go ashore now so we can share the good news with my parents and family. I hope you'll reconsider performing the ceremony."

Jacob turned away from the captain and strode from the cockpit to find his bride.

Chapter Fifty-Seven

Fireball

In the limo ride on the way to the resort, Jacob sent a text to his father asking for an audience. When he and Maryam arrived, the door to his parents' suite was open, and they were waiting with knowing grins.

Walking through the door while holding Maryam's hand, Jacob felt like a prince introducing his intended to the king and queen. He wondered if this was how Prince Marcos Sayid had felt introducing his parents to Lyla the first time.

In a way, his parents had a similar position in society as would a king and queen but without being tied down to an arid chunk of land in the deserts of the Middle East. The world was their kingdom, and they were holding court wherever they traveled.

Soon one-sixth of his parents' wealth would be his. He hoped he could live up to their legacies. He intended to find ways to give back to the land and communities and people in whatever society he settled.

Money didn't buy happiness, but it could be used to feed the hungry, heal the sick, clothe the naked, dig wells in third-world countries, protect and restore wildlife habitats, build new schools, and a million other good c auses.

But tonight, Jacob pushed aside all those thoughts and focused on announcing his engagement to the lovely Maryam Arnold and planning a wedding befitting a princess. He wanted to spend his lifetime showing Maryam that she was his equal, not as someone cooking and cleaning his house but as someone deserving to live the life of a billionaire and all the good things they could achieve together.

Jacob pulled Maryam gently to his side. "Mother, Father, we wish to announce our engagement."

"That's so exciting, my son!" His mother rushed forward, but instead of embracing Jacob, she pulled Maryam into her arms. "Welcome to our family!"

"Thank you, Mrs. Cohen." Maryam sounded almost as choked up as his mom.

"Congratulations, son." His dad came forward to shake Jacob's hand like a man.

Jacob felt like a man, perhaps for the first time, an equal to his father and his older brothers. No longer willing to live in their shadows, Jacob determined to live up to his surname and make his parents proud.

They had dinner brought into their suite, and the four of them sat around, talking and laughing and planning and sharing their dreams for the future.

By the time Jacob escorted Maryam back to the yacht for one last night in her tiny bunk, they both had stars in their eyes and love in their hearts. Convincing her parents that he was worthy of their daughter would have to wait until tomorrow.

Tonight, they snuggled into a corner of one of the outdoor sofas on the main deck near the bow of the yacht, gazing at the stars and kissing and talking and just being together. Tomorrow would come soon enough. Tonight, they focused on each other.

Until their peaceful evening was interrupted by a loud crash of glass and metal, and a fireball lit the night sky.

Chapter Fifty-Eight

Sabotage

J acob could feel the heat from the explosion that shook the yacht. He ran to the railing and looked down to see the dock on fire and collapsing under the mangled remains of what was once a car.

"It missed, you idiot!" The echoing voice from the parking lot at the marina was none other than Jacob's own brother, Liam.

"You were the one driving!" David Ashish accused. "How was it my fault the car hit the dock instead of the boat?"

They were both slurring their words and staggering, far enough away they couldn't see the people on the boat they had just tried to destroy.

Liam tipped a nearly empty bottle back and drank the last swallows, then threw the glass bottle toward the yacht. He was short by at least a hundred feet but the string of obscenities he shouted carried all the way to the upper deck.

"Y'er so drunk you can't even hit the broadside of a boat." David doubled over in laughter.

When sirens sounded in the distance, Liam and David took off running.

"Pull the anchors and get those stern lines unhooked!" Captain Arnold called from the bridge. "We've got to pull the boat away from the dock or she's going to catch fire." He ran into the cockpit and crew members rushed from all corners of the boat, most barefoot, some wearing only boxers and T-shirts.

Jacob felt completely inept to be of any assistance, and in shock that his brother and David had tried to destroy their yacht. Didn't they realize there were people onboard? Were they trying to commit murder? Or just destroy the boat their father loved?

He sat down hard, and his elbows rested on his knees, his hands gripping into his hair as if he could pull the images and sounds from his head. The crash of glass and metal, the boom of the explosion, the heat of the fire that still burned just out of his line of sight, the call of his own brother's voice, and the knowledge that all this destruction was deliberate and vindictive.

Jacob was barely aware of the yacht motoring away from the dock and the night becoming a little darker and colder. Deck crew members scurried around, and sirens sounded closer. New lights flashed, lights that seemed to travel and flicker, appearing and disappearing and reappearing in circles around the fire trucks.

None of the events made any sense. Liam and David. The car. The explosion. The obscenities. The implication. Jacob wondered if he was the only person on deck who recognized the voices and knew the man driving the car had been his brother. They must have jumped out of the car at the last minute, had cruise control set, had some sort of accelerant on the car in order for it to catch fire that quickly and burn so strong.

Liam must not have known there were people aboard. He wasn't a murderer. Was he? Jacob couldn't fathom why his brother would kill someone, but he also couldn't fathom why Liam would destroy their yacht.

"Jacob?" Maryam was there and tried to pry his hands from his hair. "It's over now. We're away from the dock, and the firemen are putting out the fire. The boat took minimal damage."

"It was Liam," Jacob choked out. "And David. How could they?" He didn't realize tears were flowing down his face until sobs racked his chest and Maryam held him.

"I know. I'm sorry." She rocked him in her arms as if he was a scared little boy. Not far from the truth.

"Were we the only ones who saw him?" Jacob lifted his gaze and met Maryam's eyes. "Were we the only two witnesses?"

"I don't know." She shook her head gently.

"I have to be the one to tell my parents," Jacob said. "This is more than just trying to destroy my father's yacht. This is going to rip apart our family."

"I know. I'm so sorry." Maryam pulled him back into her arms

When he finally calmed down enough to stand, Jacob staggered over to the railing to watch the hoses dousing the flames that consumed the wooden dock.

"The only thing that saved us was that bollard." One of the crew members pointed in the direction of the dock.

The singed end of the stern line that had been holding the boat to the dock was a startling reminder how close they'd come to having the car explode after crashing into the boat rather than hitting the post. Two feet in either direction and the *Lady Bountiful* would have been in flames.

Chapter Fifty-Nine

Witness

"**M**other! Father! Something terrible has happened." Jacob rushed through the open door to his parents' suite.

He stopped short when he realized a dozen people filled the large sitting room, including two police officers, Daniel and Cassandra Ashish, all four of his older brothers—Liam in handcuffs, sitting beside David Ashish.

"I guess you're already aware." He wasn't sure what else to say, his emotions in such contrast to the elation of announcing his engagement just a few hours prior.

Liam and David had glassy eyes, and anger shone from within. Anger at being caught, most likely. Their clothes and faces were covered in soot. Jacob wondered how they'd been caught so quickly. Disdain filled his heart as he crept forward.

"Did you know there were people on that boat when you aimed your car toward the yacht?" Jacob couldn't help asking. "I was *on* that boat. Your own *brother*. I was so close to that explosion I could feel the heat. You could have killed dozens of people, including me!"

Liam didn't answer Jacob's accusation and diverted his eyes.

"Were you a witness to the crime, son?" his father asked.

"Yes, Maryam and I were sitting on the main deck near the bow. We heard every word they said."

"We'll need statements from you both," one of the officers said.

"Yes, sir, of course."

The rest of the night was a blur, with Jacob and his brothers alternating between staying with their mother, talking to the police, talking to each other, discussing the future. Finally, Jacob got a few hours of sleep before he was awakened in the late morning to convene for another family council.

The same group of family members sat together around the same conference room table as they had the previous day. But the mood in the room was much more somber.

Liam and David had been released on bail and awaited trial. Their legal troubles were far from over. They may even be deported back to Israel since neither of them were Mexican citizens.

"Liam, I want you to know that your mother and I, together with Rachel's parents, will take care of Rachel and your baby." Although their father's voice was tired and frustrated, Jacob could tell he meant business. "I cannot speak for Daniel and Cassandra as to how they will handle David, but Liam, you will not receive a penny of our inheritance."

"Oh, that is ridiculous!" Liam stood with such force his chair pushed back several feet and nearly tipped over. "We got drunk and made one little mistake and you—"

"Sit down, now!" Father rose from his chair with nearly as much force as his oldest son. "How about we discuss the million dollars I just paid the Mexican government to bail you out of jail? Or the sixty-thousand-dollar Jaguar you blew up last night? Or the two hundred seventy-five-million-dollar yacht you tried to destroy? Not to mention the twenty crew members on board plus your own brother! Was murder your intention? Or were you just being vindictive?"

Liam pulled his chair toward the table again and folded his arms across his chest, a scowl on his face.

"How about if we add up what you cost me in the past 24-hours, and we consider *that* your inheritance." Father glared across the table at his oldest son then turned his attention to Jacob. "While unfortunately overshadowed by his oldest brother's disgraceful behavior, Jacob has an announcement." All eyes shifted to him.

"Thank you, Father." Jacob sat up straight and raised his chin confidently. "Maryam and I are getting married."

The room erupted in excited congratulations, and the mood shifted. The family seemed happy to have a more positive topic of conversation as a distraction.

"How soon are you planning a wedding?" Nick asked. "No shotguns involved, I'm assuming."

Jacob's face heated, and he smiled at his brother. "No shotguns. We're choosing to wait until marriage." He cleared his throat. "Which is why we'd like to get married immediately."

That brought chuckles around the table.

"First I have to convince her father to give us his blessing, and Maryam's still holding out hope that Captain Arnold will officiate." Jacob returned his attention to his father. "Was there anything else you needed from me? I'd like to go drag her off that yacht before her father sets sail and I'm forced to swim after her."

More chuckles and that earned a smile from his father. "You're free to go, son. Go rescue your princess."

"Thank you, Father." Jacob rose from his seat and hurried toward the door, his brothers calling after him.

"Good luck!" "Hope the fish aren't biting... or the captain!" "Wear a life jacket!"

Chapter Sixty

Get Your Helicopter Off My Yacht

J acob didn't need a life jacket. He needed a helicopter.

The *Lady Bountiful* was no longer docked in the marina.

His moment of panic was soon dispelled when he remembered as the owner of the yacht, his father had GPS tracking on the vessel.

One of the perks of being the son of a billionaire was the ability to pick up his cell phone and have his daddy order a private helicopter with the snap of his fingers. Within an hour, Jacob and his brother Nick were in the air on their proverbial white horse on their way to rescue his bride.

After forty-five minutes of flight time, the yacht showed as a speck on the horizon and eventually came to a full stop as the helicopter hovered over the landing pad. The touchdown was smooth, and the blades came to a complete stop before the pilot gave the okay to open the doors. Jacob and Nick hopped down and were greeted by a family of guests they'd never met, plus familiar crew members.

Maryam pushed past all of them and jumped into Jacob's arms, wrapping her legs around his waist and clinging to him with excitement. "I knew you'd come for me!"

"Leave it to a billionaire to find a way to steal my daughter even after we've left port," Captain Arnold grumbled. "Didn't you get my clear message that I'm *not* giving you permission to marry her?"

"Didn't you get my clear message that I don't care what you want?" Jacob raised his eyebrows. "I'm marrying your daughter whether you like it or not. Soon. Within the next few days."

"Days?" Maryam leaned back in confusion. "How about hours?"

"You don't want to plan a real wedding?" Jacob pulled back and smoothed her windblown hair as she clung to him like a monkey. "With a white dress, and cake, and dancing?"

She leaned closer to his ear so only he could hear her whisper. "I don't like cake, the dress will be lying beside our bed within a few minutes after we say our vows, and we can dance horizontally in our king-sized bed."

"Yeah, I like your idea better." His husky voice was close to her ear and he nuzzled her neck. "Are you packed?"

Maryam slid down and lowered her feet to the deck. Jacob missed the weight of her body in his arms but patiently waited for her to step over to her father for one last plea. "Daddy, will you *please* officiate? It would mean the world to me."

"I won't be returning to Puerto Aventuras for several weeks." He crossed his arms and scowled. "You won't want to wait that long."

"So, do it now." Her logic made sense to Jacob even as her words made his heart rate increase. If they got married right now, within an hour they could be... a tiny smile played at the corner of his mouth.

"Don't get too excited yet, little brother," Nick mumbled. "He hasn't agreed to anything."

"Thank you for reading my mind," Jacob grumbled but couldn't hide a smirk.

"Just keeping it real." Nick patted him on the shoulder.

They waited as Maryam unleashed her aquamarine eyes up at her father with a soft pout. "Please, Daddy." Captain Arnold couldn't possibly resist her puppy dog expression.

"Fine," he relented. "Go get your mother. She won't want to miss your... wedding." The captain glared at Jacob.

"I'm right here." Valerie Arnold wove through the crowd of guests and crew members, several of whom were gushing over Maryam or shaking Jacob's hand or patting him on the shoulder. Valerie lifted her chin in his direction. "What about your parents? Won't they want to attend your wedding?"

"We had a nice dinner with them last night. They'll be fine. They're thrilled to have Maryam join our family."

"As you steal her from ours." Valerie's lip curled in a scowl.

"As I explained to your husband yesterday, we intend to find a place to settle down near a port town where you can visit any time you want."

"But we won't see her every day like we usually do." She was either getting choked up or a good actress.

"Would you rather have me move onto the yacht and we spend our honeymoon here with you?"

"Never mind, get your helicopter off my yacht and spend your honeymoon somewhere far away from here." Valerie flicked her wrist, dismissing them.

"Technically, this is *my* yacht, not yours. But with regards to every other word in your statement, I will take your advice." Jacob turned to Maryam and held out his hand. "You ready?"

"Go gather your things while I draw up the paperwork," Captain Arnold told his daughter. Then he turned to Jacob. "*You* come with me."

"Yes, sir." Jacob found it odd that his confident swagger while talking to the captain yesterday had blown away in the wind now that he'd given Jacob permission to marry his daughter.

When Captain Arnold closed the door to his inner office, he turned and towered over Jacob. "You have more power in your little finger than I'll have in my lifetime. But don't think that means I won't hunt you down if you ever hurt my little girl."

"Captain Arnold, I love your daughter, and I will treasure her like a princess."

"I've seen the way royal families treat princesses and that analogy is not helping your case."

"How about this?" Jacob lifted his chin. "I will treat your daughter the way I would want someone treating my daughter, should I ever be so blessed."

"Humph." Captain Arnold sat at his desk and pulled up his computer terminal. "Sit down. I need to ask you some questions." He proceeded to fill in details about when and where Jacob was born, his citizenship status, his identification numbers, most recent address, and current occupation.

Jacob provided answers to his questions but didn't otherwise engage in conversation, just sat there reminding himself that this would be over soon and worth the few minutes spent in interrogation.

Finally, the captain printed some documents and shifted in his chair to look Jacob in the eye. They sat that way for a moment, and Jacob tried not to flinch or squirm. As if satisfied with the amount of torture he'd put Jacob through, his gruff voice was less a threat and more a plea. "Take care of my little girl."

"I promise." Nothing more needed to be said.

They returned to the main deck and found that Maryam had already loaded her things onto the helicopter and stood beside her friend Ivy and Jacob's brother Nick.

With a few words legally joining them as husband and wife, and a couple of signatures, they were official.

Without waiting for his father-in-law's permission, Jacob pulled Maryam forward and dipped her into a passionate kiss. The guests and crew members cheered and applauded.

Even Maryam's parents were smiling when Jacob finished kissing their daughter—okay, briefly paused kissing their daughter. The remaining kisses would wait until later.

They took a few moments to give hugs and handshakes to Maryam's friends and family, and then Jacob helped her up into the helicopter and took his place at her side. His brother Nick politely focused his attention out the window at the blue sky and ocean as Jacob and Maryam kissed all the way back to Puerto Aventuras.

Chapter Sixty-One

The Princess of the Desert

At six weeks old, baby Emanuel was barely old enough to fly from Michigan to Mexico. Jacob and Maryam wouldn't have risked the flight if not for the private jet.

But they couldn't miss the arrival of Prince Marcos Sayid of Madain Saleh on the inaugural sail of his new yacht, *The Princess of the Desert*, piloted by none other than Maryam's father, Captain Arnold. This would be the first time Maryam's parents would see their new grandson.

The prince's arrival marked the beginning of a dynasty. The Cohen family had fled Jerusalem to avoid an accusation of murder, and the Sayid royal family had fled from a civil war and a contested crown. They were joined together in the beautiful community of Puerto Aventuras.

Jacob's brother, Nicholas Cohen, had borrowed their father's magic wand and bought homes and land and businesses up and down the coast between Cancun and Puerto Aventuras and south almost to Tulum. He was heralded as a savior to the impoverished communities. He took everything he'd learned from their father, buying failing businesses and helping the former owners get back on their feet, teaching them skills to help them flourish. He built and improved resorts and other tourist attractions, always a step ahead of the trends.

Prince Marcos Sayid served by his side, pooling resources and connections until their power was unparalleled. His son, Prince Benjamin, was born to Princess Lyla just two months after Nick and Adele had given birth to their baby girl, Alexandria. The two were destined to grow up as best friends.

Jacob's parents, Levi and Sarah, enjoyed a quiet retirement up the hill from their children and grandchildren, side by side with their long-time friends, Daniel and Cassandra Ashish.

Sam and his wife, Leanne, who had recently finished her PhD in geology, flew in from Texas. She had accepted a research position at the Bureau of Economic Geology at The University of Texas, and Sam was putting his experience in petroleum and potash holdings to good use, working in the engineering department at the college.

Zach continued to serve faithfully as Nick's right-hand man, and his wife, Ruth, helped her younger sister, Adele, with baby Alexandria.

Noticeably absent but rarely discussed were the two oldest Cohen brothers, Liam and Lyle, along with their wives and children. David and Shira Ashish had disappeared as well. As if a scourge on the family name, no one actively researched their whereabouts, and Jacob didn't care to know.

After Liam and David had nearly blown up their yacht, with Jacob and Maryam aboard, Jacob hoped he never saw them as long as he lived.

After two weeks of family reunions, he was thankful to take Maryam and baby Emanuel back home to the sprawling haven of trees near the corner of the Thunder Bay State Forest. They'd purchased property inland from the quaint harbor town of Alpena, Michigan, rented a small house, and had already poured the foundation for Maryam's dream home.

Jacob intended to raise his son to hunt and fish and treasure the land and water, to be studious like his father, hard-working like his mother, a businessman like his paternal grandfather and an explorer like his mother's parents. He wanted little Manny to learn languages and study the arts and the sciences, and yes, even math.

Tucking his baby son into his crib after being gone for two weeks, Jacob felt peace in his heart. He wrapped his arm around his wife's shoulders and pulled her gently from the room.

"Come on," he whispered to Maryam. "I know a couple other people who haven't slept in their own bed for two weeks."

"Well, gee, if sleeping was all you were interested in..." Maryam teased with a tiny grin.

"Woman, I promised you a long time ago that I would make love to you every day if you married me, and you know darn well I'm keeping that promise." He picked her up, and she wrapped her arms and legs around him as he kissed her all the way down the hall to their king-sized bed...

Part Four: The Hunter

Emanuel Cohen

As told by Emanuel Cohen, son of Jacob Cohen, grandson of Levi and Sarah Cohen, nephew of Nicholas Cohen at the time when King Sayid was in his sixty-second year as the story begins...

Chapter Sixty-Two

Found Someone

"A ren't you kinda scaring away the deer?" a snarky female voice called up to Emanuel Cohen perched ten feet up the trunk of a tree on the platform of his hunting blind.

As if to prove her wrong, a doe that had been feeding in the fallow corn field nearby raised her head, stilled for a moment, terror in her eyes, then darted into the woods to the north.

Manny hadn't even bothered to lift his top-end Hoyt Turbo compound bow while watching her eat the past ten minutes because he knew the doe's fawn was resting nearby. Besides, he was holding out for the buck he'd seen two weeks ago on his trail cam. The majestic creature sported an eight-point rack that would hang beautifully in his personal study, his favorite room in their stately home built on the outermost wing overlooking the Thunder Bay State Forest.

"My singing doesn't usually bother anyone this far away from the middle of nowhere," Manny called down to her.

"Yeah, well, I'm lost, and I was hoping to find someone who could lead me back to Alpena."

"Found someone, you did," he said in his best Yoda impression as he collected his belongings and prepared to descend the makeshift ladder made of two-by-fours nailed into the side of the giant red oak.

"Thank you, Jedi Master." Her sarcasm was even more adorable since he knew she'd understood the reference.

"Ooh, she's calling me Master, and I don't even know her name yet." Manny hopped off the last rung and onto the soft ground, his waterproof boots sinking slightly in the marshy soil. He clipped his bow onto its shoulder sling and started toward the road.

Even from twenty feet away, he could see her shiver. Her lightweight blouse may have been perfect for the afternoon sun, but the evening was cooling off.

"Don't you have a jacket or sweatshirt?" he asked.

"I wasn't planning on being away from the boat this long," she said. "I just wanted to escape my parent's eagle eyes for a few hours and took one wrong turn after another on the way back until I wound up here, in the middle of a forest." She spread her arms wide, the shimmering fabric of her blouse floating down like butterfly wings.

"Quite literally in the middle of a forest," Manny said. He removed his hunting vest and sling, carefully resting his compound bow—his most prized possession—in the tall grasses beside the gravel road, and unzipped his parka. Slipping it off his shoulders, he tsked and shook his head. "I hate to do this because you look beautiful—probably too old for me—but still."

He draped the lightweight camo jacket over her shoulders as she scoffed. "I'm only twenty. I'm hardly too old. Suenas como mi papá."

"Wow, in all my nineteen years, I've never had a hot older woman compare me to her father. I'm thoroughly insulted."

"What's insulting is that you keep calling me old." She snuggled into his parka and breathed what could only be called a sigh of relief. Then she did something unexpected. She lifted the collar and inhaled a long breath. "Hueles muy bien."

"I have never wanted to be a jacket so badly in my entire life," Manny said.

She stuck out her hand, pulling the sleeve up over her wrist. "I'm Aloise."

He took her hand in his and didn't let go. "Your hands are freezing, Aloise." Manny lifted her other hand and rubbed them between his, moving a step closer. She didn't resist. "Isn't the heater in your car working?"

"I ran out of gas." Her shoulders slumped.

"This is the luckiest day of my life." Manny finally looked more closely at her face, drinking in her deep brown eyes and olive-toned skin. "What are the odds that the not-so-old woman of my dreams would just happen to run out of gas a few feet from my hunting blind in the middle of a forest?"

"And what are the odds that the best-smelling nineteen-year-old guy would just happen to be a few feet off the beaten path, right at the spot where my car ran out of gas, singing loud enough for me to hear him from the road in the middle of a forest in—what state am I stuck in?"

"Michigan." Manny's word was almost a breath.

"Michigan's beautiful," Aloise whispered.

"You're beautiful."

"You flatter me." She stopped and creased her brow. "What's your name?"

"Manny."

"I'm lost, Manny," Aloise whispered.

"I would *love* to help you find yourself."

Chapter Sixty-Three

We've Got to Be Related

"See that trail to my right?" Manny nodded in that direction, and Aloise looked over his shoulder. "At the other end of that trail is my father's home. If you go with me, I will change into something that may or may not smell as good as my camo, but will be far more appropriate to drive you into town, and we will purchase a can of gas for your car."

"You want me to follow you down a dark trail into the woods?" She raised her eyebrows.

"It's not far, I promise," Manny told her. "Do you have a better idea?"

Her shoulders slumped. "No."

"Don't worry, I have my bow." Manny held up his compound. "I can fend off all the scary bucks and does. But you gotta watch out for those fawns. They're vicious."

"Very funny," she said. "I was more worried about following a guy I don't know into the woods when no one in the world has a clue where I'm located and my cell phone gets zero reception out here en medio de la nada."

"You are *not* in the middle of nowhere," Manny said. "You are surrounded by the Thunder Bay State Forest to the south, my neighbor's prime hunting ground to the east, and my father owns pretty much everything else."

"I didn't mean to offend you." She cringed.

"You're fine." He indicated she should follow. "It's easier to keep a low profile this way." She didn't ask what he meant by that, and he didn't offer. She'd find out soon enough when they emerged into the clearing and his father's home came into view.

She followed close enough behind him to grip the back of his vest as she tripped along the uneven path. The trek took less than ten minutes, but she wasn't wearing hiking boots. She stumbled along in elegant sandals that probably cost a fortune.

"What are you doing here, anyway? You mentioned a boat."

"My papá owns a sailing yacht, and he thought it would be fun to sail up through the Great Lakes. Since he controls everything I have, including my unlimited credit limit, I am compelled to come along. Besides, I really like my mamá, even though she refuses to let me marry until my older sister finds a husband first."

"Well, we must provide for her a suitable selection," Manny said. "How old is she? I'll see if I have any friends her age."

"Twenty-two," Aloise said. "Practically an old maid in our culture."

"What is your culture?"

"We are of Middle-Eastern descent but our most recent generation hails from the Yucatan Peninsula in Mexico and Guatemala," she said.

Manny stopped in his tracks, turning and looking into Aloise's eyes, deep brown in the dimming twilight of the forest. "We have *got* to be related."

"Por qué?" She almost ran into him, and he steadied himself by resting his hands on her hips.

"Because that's exactly the same way my dad describes our heritage. Almost word for word."

"What's your last name?"

"Cohen. Yours?"

"Ashish," she said.

"Aloise Ashish?"

"Yeah, I know. Mis parientes son malos." She pushed on ahead of Manny, grumbling as she did. "It's like they wanted me to stand out even more than I already do."

"I mean, ya know, it's a really pretty name." Manny hurried to catch up.

"Oh my gosh." Aloise stopped short, having come into the clearing and seeing her first glimpse of his house. "Your family must be almost as rich as mine."

"Probably more so," he stated matter-of-factly. "I think we're the only billionaires in this region of Michigan."

"Whatever," she huffed. "My family is so rich we sail around the world on a yacht."

"My father used to own a company that built yachts," Manny said, a chill running through him. He tried to blame the evening temperature.

"My father owned stock in a yacht company," Aloise said, her eyes growing animated. "They sold all their shares when my papá's business partner fought with his brothers."

"This cannot be a coincidence," he said.

"I agree."

"Come on." Manny took Aloise's hand and pulled her gently in the direction of the house. "You need to meet my dad."

Chapter Sixty-Four

You Look Like Your Mother

"A fter we find my dad, I need to get out of these hunting clothes, and then I can take you back to your family. Maybe they'll give us some better answers into our obviously connected pasts." Manny led the way into the house.

"Wow..." Aloise followed Manny into the main entrance, her gaze in awe of the incredible home his father had commissioned. Cathedral ceilings supported by walls of old pine logs towered above the great room. Colors reflecting through a wall of sporadically placed panes of stained glass gave the appearance of sunlight shimmering through a canopy of trees. The whole effect captured the feeling of walking through a forest.

"It still has that effect on me sometimes too," Manny said reverently. When his parents had decided to settle here in northern lower Michigan, they'd chosen acres of land surrounded by forests as different as possible from the arid desert where his father, Jacob, had been raised.

They'd also built a home ten times larger than was needed. Jacob was one of six brothers, three of whom had married sisters from the same family. In some epic family feud, the two oldest brothers had splintered from the family, and the three younger brothers had settled in Central and North America. They didn't get together often, but Manny knew he had family near Cancun and in Texas. This house had been built large enough for family to visit, should they ever choose to travel this far north.

Manny had gradually taken over a whole wing of the house, first with hunting equipment and mounted trophies, then moving his game room and computers over there, then creating a soundproof room where he could record himself singing, then eventually moving his bed to that end of the house.

Although he usually had meals with his mom and dad, in his wing, he had a full kitchen, which he mostly used for its refrigerator, although he had started experimenting with wild game recipes. He'd shoot a pheasant or goose, find some exotic recipe, and send one of his father's staff off to find the ingredients. One of the housekeepers always cleaned up after him.

"Father," Manny called out loud enough to be heard from any wing of the stately home. "Where are you?"

"No need to yell, son, I'm right here." Jacob Cohen came around the corner from the kitchen to the foyer, drying his hands on a dishtowel. He stopped and cocked his head to the side. "You have company. I didn't even realize you had a girlfriend." Dad raised his eyebrows at their joined hands.

Manny dropped Aloise's hand and stepped away. No reason to get his hopes up if she was a cousin or something. "I don't."

"I got lost and ran out of gas near his hunting shack, and your son was gracious enough to offer me a ride into town to fill a gas can."

"I raised him to be a gentleman." Jacob came forward to pat Manny on the back, then held out his hand to Aloise. "It's a pleasure to meet you, miss..."

"My name is Aloise Ashish."

Jacob took a step back and his jaw dropped. "You look *just* like your mother."

"How do you know mi madre?" Aloise's eyes lit up in anticipation.

"Shira is married to *David*." Jacob said his name as if it were vinegar in his mouth.

"Sí, they're my parents. But how do you know them?"

"Son"—Jacob turned to Manny—"help this young lady fill her gas tank, show her the way out of our woods, and get as far away from her as you can. I forbid you to see her again."

"But Father..." Manny watched his dad turn on his heels and walk from the room. He turned to Aloise. "Um... what just happened?"

"Obviously your family hates my family." Aloise pulled her thick, long hair into a messy bun and wound a band around it. Manny was momentarily distracted but reminded himself to stay on task. He needed to get changed and take her into town.

His father had given them no details as to why they were forbidden to see each other or how their families were related. He gently took her hand again, hoping they weren't cousins. "Come on, let's go get my clothes changed and maybe we can figure this out."

"What did you say your last name is?" Aloise stumbled along beside him, her sandals no more practical indoors than in the woods. He wondered if there was a surface upon which they would be practical. A photo shoot, maybe, where she didn't have to walk.

"Cohen," Manny said. "Does that sound familiar? Your last name definitely sounds familiar, but I don't know where to place it."

Aloise stopped short. "My dad's former business partner was named Cohen."

"Great, at least we found a connection." Manny glanced down at their intertwined hands. "Hopefully, business partner is as close to a familial relationship as it gets, or I'm going to be really bummed out that I can't date you." His voice lowered, and she giggled.

"Your father just said you were forbidden to see me."

"Do you always do everything your father says?" Manny released her hand and wrapped his arm around her waist, pulling her close enough he could have kissed her if he were brave enough.

She gulped. "If I want access to my credit cards, I do," Aloise whispered.

"Ooh, she's saying 'I do' and I haven't even proposed yet." He could feel her body close against his and knew he needed to stop this line of thinking. Manny had never taken advantage of a woman and didn't intend to start now, but he'd never been in the arms of a woman so tempting. "Come on, after I change, we'll sneak down to my dad's library and see if we can find his genealogy charts. Maybe we can figure something out."

Manny reluctantly dropped his arm from around her waist but took her hand in his again, intertwining her fingers and leading her down the hall to his wing of the house. There was almost a physical difference in the look and feel as the hallway ended and opened into the east wing. Similar to the main entrance, Manny had a great room with cathedral ceilings and random tiles of stained glass, but unlike the main house, this room was decorated in antlers. His trophy room. He watched her reaction as she marveled.

"What do you think?" His reverent voice combined pride with nervousness. Either she was going to hate his passion for hunting or love it.

"¿Mataste tu a todos estos animales ti mismo?" She hated it.

"Are you afraid of me now that you know I'm a murderer?" He pulled her close again and wiggled his eyebrows, hoping to seem dangerous and exciting but realizing his baby face probably gave him away.

"I was already afraid of you, and yet still followed you down a dark path into the unknown woods," she said, her eyes just as smoldering as he hoped his were. The difference between his youthfulness and her elegance almost gave him an inferiority complex. Showing her his hunting prowess was an inadvertent way to prove his manhood. "You could have been leading me to a cabin in the woods where you'd rape and murder me."

"In a manner of speaking, this is a rather large cabin in the woods," he whispered, allowing his eyes to travel down to her toes and slowly caress every curve of her slim frame before meeting her gaze again. He nodded to the side. "On the other side of that door is my bedroom. I could easily overpower you. And I always keep a hunting knife beside my bed."

"And yet the fact that you were singing show tunes from Phantom of the Opera and let that deer run away without shooting her leads me to believe that you're more harmless than you let on." She didn't pull away.

"If I remember the story correctly, the Phantom kidnapped Christine and took her to his dungeon lair where he seduced her." Manny gave her back a gentle squeeze, pulling her even closer.

"And once he realized he loved her, he set her free." She raised her eyebrows, winning the argument.

"Remind me not to fall in love with you," Manny said, squeezing one more time before releasing her from his arms. He stepped away and called over his shoulder as he walked toward his bedroom. "Make yourself comfortable. I'm going to change my clothes. There are cold beverages in the refrigerator." He nodded in the direction of the little kitchen and slipped from the room.

Chapter Sixty-Five

Genealogy

"These should be a good place to start," Manny said, pulling one of his father's many journals from the perfectly organized shelves. The one he'd chosen was clearly labeled Cohen Family Genealogy. He glanced over his shoulder at the open library door, knowing if his dad walked into the great room, he would see them. Manny took Aloise's hand and brought her and the book to the far end of the library, out of sight of the doorway.

Page one had a narrative explaining the various sections and charts. He decided to start with his father and work his way back. Jacob Cohen was the second youngest of Levi Cohen's six sons.

"Es él," Aloise said, pointing to the name of the oldest son. "Liam Cohen. He was my father's business partner."

"And your father's name is not on this chart anywhere?" Manny asked, relieved excitement in his chest.

"Nope." Aloise grinned and lifted her eyebrows seductively. "No estamos relacionados."

"But what happened that caused my father to hate your father so much that he would forbid me to see you?"

"That is a mystery," Aloise said playfully. "I think we need to play amateur detective and see what we can find out. We have successfully found our first clue. ¿Qué sigue?"

"Let's take my Jeep into town, fill a gas can, bring it back to your car, then you can follow me back out of the woods—wouldn't want you getting lost again—and we'll go talk to your dad. Maybe he can shed some light on the situation."

"What if he acts the same way your padre did?"

"Let's hope he doesn't." Manny paused, noting the worry lines on her forehead. "Is he a violent man?"

"No." She waved a hand dismissively. "I mean, not really. More... controlling, old-fashioned, insistent, overbearing."

"Were you kidding about him not letting you date until after your sister marries?" he asked softly.

"Not kidding." Aloise shook her head and widened her eyes. "They control everything we do. And living all together on a yacht, we can't sneak anything past them. That's why I had to leave when we docked. I took one of the rental cars and just drove. Told them I was going shopping and exploring."

"Did you ever make it to the shopping before you got lost?"

"Nah, I didn't really want to shop. I just wanted to get away from them. Plus, I think they wanted to get away from us too."

"Us?"

"Mi hermana, Alondra."

"Right. Your sister. And you all live together on the yacht?"

"Yep!" She popped her *p* with exaggeration. "Tight quarters."

"I would hate that," Manny said, glancing out one of the many windows cut into the walls of the library. Every room in the house had more windows than should physically fit. The effect was the feeling of living in nature.

"I want to be free," Aloise whispered, her eyes drawn in the same direction as his. "Not just free of the tight quarters, but free of my parents' oppressive control, free of the constant traveling, free to start a life, to put down roots."

"You could come live here," Manny said, only half joking. "You could marry me and live happily in this beautiful forest."

"It is a beautiful forest." She didn't argue, but she didn't acknowledge his suggestion either.

"Come on. Let's go rescue your car." On their way out of the library, he slipped the genealogy journal onto the shelf and snuck into the great room. Skirting the kitchen to avoid his father, they took the long way around to the garage.

"*That* is your Jeep?" Aloise stopped short. "I was picturing a little sporty thing with roll bars and open sides."

"This, my dear, is the all-terrain Jeep Gladiator North." Manny proudly opened the passenger door and offered his hand to help her up. "It's designed for slogging through several feet of snow like we have here in Northern Michigan. I live in the middle of a forest, remember? A person could get lost around here if they're not properly equipped."

"Don't I know it," she grumbled, placing one hand in his and reaching up for the assist handle above the door. Manny put his hand on her lower back as she lifted herself into the giant truck.

He waited for her to get settled, then closed the door and walked around back, clicking the remote to open the garage door and smiling at his vanity license plate that read HNTR4LFE. He thought it was clever. He loaded a small gas can into the bed of his truck and opened the driver's side door.

"Comfortable?" he asked when he was seated. As he pulled his seatbelt around and clicked it into place, he noticed she wasn't wearing hers. He unbuckled himself and reached all the way over—his face drawing tantalizingly close to hers—and pulled her belt around. Reaching down beside her leg, he found the latch and clicked her belt into place. He whispered in a husky voice, "Wearing seatbelts is the law in Michigan."

"I never knew seatbelts could be so... caliente." Aloise was breathing heavy.

"I never knew having a woman in my Jeep could be so hot either." His face was still very close to hers.

"Have you had many women in your Jeep?"

"Not unless you count that doe I shot last year, but she stayed in the bed of the truck."

"You had a woman in your bed?" Her whisper was practically a breath. Two inches closer and he could have kissed her.

"Never," Manny said. "Yet..."

"Hmm..."

For another few seconds, he held her gaze, then sat back and reached again to click his belt into place. He started the Jeep, and it roared to life, and he backed out of the garage.

Chapter Sixty-Six

Be but Sworn My Love

"**I** can't believe it was this simple to get back out of the forest," Aloise said. "I was, like, twenty minutes from town."

"Seventeen, actually," Manny said, slowing down to pull into the gas station.

"Huh?"

"It only takes seventeen minutes for me to go from my driveway to downtown Alpena." He parked near a gas pump, hopped down from his Jeep, grabbed the gas can from the bed of the truck, and set it on the pavement. After swiping his credit card at the pump, he had the gas can half full before Aloise even slid down from the cab and made her way around to his side.

"Qué estás haciendo?" She put her hands on her hips, momentarily distracting him. The can reached its fill line and overflowed while he stared at her slim waist and perfectly manicured hands.

"Whoa!" Manny jumped back to avoid getting splashed and hurried to stop the flow from the nozzle. "Apparently, single-handedly destroying the environment. That's what I'm doing."

"I should be paying for that," she said. "It's my car we're filling with gas."

"True, but dare I remind you that I'm far wealthier than you'll ever be unless you agree to marry me?" Manny replaced the nozzle into the holder on the pump and crouched to screw the fuel cap into place.

"You haven't exactly asked me to marry you." Her playful comment sent shivers up his spine.

Without second-guessing his idiocy and because he was already crouched at her feet, Manny lowered to one knee and reached for her hand.

"My dearest Aloise, deny thy father and refuse thy name. But if thou wilt not, be but sworn my love and you will no longer be an Ashish."

"That's Juliet's line," Aloise said. "Besides in all my childhood fantasies about the day my future husband proposed to me, never did I imagine he would propose at a gas station, kneeling in a puddle of gasoline."

"But will you marry me anyway?" Manny squeezed her hand and grinned up at her.

"Quizás," she said, pulling her hand away. "Now, come on, you have to come meet my father before I can decide."

"Ooh, that's right. What was I thinking?" Manny lifted off his knee, which now had a growing ring of unleaded gasoline soaking his knee cap. He'd probably have to throw these jeans away. That stain would never come out. "I have to ask your father's permission before I can propose. Probably should change my clothes first. I'd hate to meet your father covered in gasoline."

"Very funny."

"I think I have a pair of sweats in my gym bag in the back seat of my Jeep." Manny lifted the gas can back into the bed of his truck and brushed his hands on his ruined jeans. "Let's go get your car."

They headed back into the woods, which were now dark and foreboding. Being out here by herself at night would have been terrifying. He was glad Aloise found him when she did. He pulled up behind her car and pointed his headlights so they shone like a spotlight.

After quickly sliding down from the cab, he lifted the gas can from the bed of his truck and hurried over to empty the can into her vehicle before she could protest. He wanted to take care of her. Not that she was a damsel in distress. Okay, she was indeed a damsel in distress, and Manny liked the way he felt rescuing her.

Aloise didn't argue and headed over to her car to start the ignition. With a little encouragement the rental vehicle purred to life. She lowered the window and called out to him, "I'll follow you."

"I gotta change my pants first," Manny said, unbuttoning his jeans while walking back toward his truck.

"Are we heading back to your house?" She looked over her shoulder.

"No, I'm going to change right here by my truck." He smirked and unzipped his jeans, toying with her.

"You're going to take off your pants in the middle of the woods?" She glanced around as if nervous he'd make a spectacle of himself.

"You're the only one out here to see me, babe. You can watch if you want to."

"Muy divertido." She faced forward and pursed her lips, raising her chin in defiance. He walked backward toward his truck, waiting for her to peek out the side-view mirror, which she did. He grinned at her and raised his eyebrows, then turned to finish his short trek.

Without any further teasing, Manny opened his back door and reached for his gym bag. Keeping the door open to provide some privacy, he slipped off his sneakers and removed his gasoline-soaked jeans, then tossed them into the bed of his truck. His jogging pants matched his hooded sweatshirt, so he wouldn't feel uncomfortable heading to town in mismatched clothes.

He climbed into the Jeep and pulled forward so his truck was parallel to her car. He rolled down the passenger side window and leaned over to razz her a little more. "Boxers or briefs?"

"I was not watching you change your pants," she insisted. "Now show me the way out of this terrifying forest before I have a panic attack."

Manny chuckled at her reaction, rolled up his window and let his foot off the brake, leading the way out of the Thunder Bay State Forest.

Chapter Sixty-Seven

Alondra

T he Alpena Yacht Club sat at the mouth of the Thunder Bay River on the shores of Lake Huron. The marina boasted dozens of boat slips and was a popular summer destination for tourists.

Manny pulled to the side of the road on Harbor Drive, letting Aloise lead the way through the parking lot to her parents' boat slip. They parked beside the largest, most elegant sailing yacht in the marina. Aloise wasn't lying that her parents were wealthy. He climbed down from his Jeep and clicked the key fob to lock his truck just as she closed her car door and came around the front. Manny boldly took her hand, and they made their way down the dock.

The sailboat was well-lit and inviting, but Manny had butterflies in his stomach at the prospect of meeting her parents. If his own father had such a negative response meeting Aloise, Manny wondered how her parents would react.

Aloise led Manny up the boarding ladder and along the deck to a set of teakwood doors that opened to the lower deck. "Have you been on a sailing yacht before?"

"My grandparents on my mom's side have a yacht, but it's not a sailboat," Manny said. "This is so... slim."

"Is that your way of saying it's small?" Aloise laughed and poked him in the side.

"Compact?"

"I get it, your yacht's bigger than my yacht, whatever. Grab that handrail, and come down. Let's see if we can find mis parientes."

The steps down to the salon were not as steep as he was expecting, and the galley was spacious with a larger refrigerator than he had in his kitchen back home. He leaned against the stainless-steel monstrosity and folded his arms. "Your refrigerator is bigger than mine. Does that count for anything?"

"What counts more than size is that there are no dead animals living in mi refri," she said with a satisfied grin.

"I don't have any *dead* animals *living* in my refrigerator either." He couldn't help poking fun at her.

"You knew what I meant, Mister Hunter-for-life." Aloise stepped closer and placed her hand on Manny's chest, nearly close enough that he could kiss her. Tempting but not the way he wanted her father to find them the first time they met. "Come on, I'll show you my state room."

She opened another elegantly carved door and displayed a queen-sized bed tucked into a space just large enough... for a queen-sized bed. There were plenty of stowage cabinets, a deck prism to let light in, and a television mounted in one corner.

"Roomy," Manny said, biting his lips and fighting not to make any more comments about the size of her living conditions. He leaned closer and whispered, "When we get married, we're living at my house."

"Deal." She turned off the light in her state room and closed the door. "Over here is el baño I share with mi hermana. Yes, it may be small, but we have vacuflush toilets, a full shower, high end fixtures and Corian countertops."

"I'm not in the market for a yacht, my dear," Manny said. He stepped entirely within the shower and raised his eyebrows. "I don't think we'd both fit in here together."

"Oh my gosh, stop. You are going to get me in so much trouble if mis parientes hear you talking that way." She pulled him by the arm and dragged him back out of the shower. She walked farther toward the front of the boat. "Down there are crew cabins and the engine room." She tapped on a door that looked like any other door but apparently led to a lower d eck.

Ascending a short set of stairs brought them into another spacious salon where a twenty-two-year-old version of Aloise sat with a television remote in one hand and her smart phone in the other. She glanced up and didn't react to her younger sister leading a man up the stairs. She looked bored.

"Alondra, Manny. Manny, Alondra." Aloise continued through the salon, pulling him with her to the master state room which boasted a king-sized bed, more headroom than most of the boat, multiple deck prisms, and another full bathroom. Aloise turned around and called back to her sister. "¿Dónde están mamá y papá?"

"Ya se fueron a un hotel en el centro," Alondra called back.

Aloise kept a hold of Manny's hand and led him back to the salon. "Por qué?"

"Why do you think?" Alondra said, still staring at her phone. "They've been stuck on a boat with two adult daughters for three weeks. You'd get a hotel room too."

Manny squeezed her hand and wiggled his eyebrows at Aloise. They wouldn't need a hotel room. They could just lock the door to his wing of the house. Not that his parents ever ventured down to his rooms anyway. Should he and Aloise choose to get married, they'd have plenty of privacy.

"¿Quién es el guapo?" Alondra asked Aloise, but her gaze rested on Manny. He knew just enough Spanish to understand Alondra thought he was hot. He raised his eyebrows and couldn't hide a grin.

"This is my future husband," Aloise said, wrapping one arm around his back and placing her hand on his chest. "Emanuel Cohen."

Alondra dropped the remote and sat forward, glaring across the table at him. "Uh, no. Papá would never allow you to marry a Cohen."

"How do you know about the Cohen family?" Aloise asked, her face alive with excitement. "Have you ever met any of them?" She scooted into the bench seat across the table from her sister and pulled Manny with her.

Alondra extended her hand to Manny. "Hola, soy Alondra." He met her halfway and shook her hand. Alondra turned to her sister with a smirk. "Now, I have met a Cohen."

"But how do you know of them? Papá's business partner was Liam Cohen, right?"

"Sounds like you know almost as much as I do." Alondra cocked her head to the side. "Don't you remember stories of how the younger Cohen hermanos stole the wealth from the oldest brothers after their father and our grandfather had already promised them an inheritance?"

"Our grandfather knew the Cohen's also?" Aloise asked.

"Yeah, Papá's sisters married the Cohen brothers, and they all got really mad when their parientes dragged them across the world on yachts. Apparently, they wanted to stay in the Middle East."

"Wait, which Cohen brothers married your father's sisters?" Manny scratched his head. "My mother was an only child."

"Yeah, I think the two youngest hermanos married outside la familia."

"Phew, we're not related." Manny held up their adjoined hands and kissed the back of Aloise's hand.

"Good thing too because I'm going to marry you." Aloise turned to her sister with a smug grin. "He proposed earlier this evening."

"True story," Manny said.

"We've been docked less than a day," Alondra said. "Exactly when did you meet?"

Aloise glanced at her phone. "About two hours ago."

"A little less than that, actually." Manny held up his wristwatch.

"And you're already engaged?" Alondra raised her eyebrows.

"Yes, and I've seen him without his clothes on too." Aloise lifted her chin.

Manny coughed to cover up laughter. "Oh please, I only had my pants off for a minute."

"A minute was all I needed," Aloise purred, obviously trying to get a rise out of her sister.

"If it only took you a minute, you're not doing it right." Alondra turned accusing eyes on Manny. "Maybe you need some educación."

"I've known how to change my clothes when I spill something on them since I was in preschool," Manny teased right back. "Believe me, if I wanted to do anything other than change into clean pants, I'm sure I could last longer than a minute."

"Apuesto a que podrías," Alondra said with a deep, husky voice, pursing her lips.

"Okay, I am officially jealous now, and you are *not* stealing my fiancé," Aloise said, pushing Manny out of the booth seat. "Come on, let's get away from mi hermana before she personally tries to remove your clothing for you."

"Nice to meet you, Alondra," Manny said, allowing Aloise to take his hand and lead him away from the salon.

"Come back anytime, Emanuel Cohen," Alondra called. She had the television turned back on before Aloise and Manny got down the stairs.

They headed back to Aloise's state room, where she opened the door and crawled onto her queen-sized bed, patting the bed beside her.

"You do move fast, woman." Manny climbed in beside her and lay down, tucking his hands behind his head and relishing the scent of her pillow. "Engaged and sleeping together within two hours' from meeting?"

"No me acuesto contigo until we're married," Aloise said, laying down next to him but propping herself on one elbow.

"Too bad the county clerk's office isn't open tonight," Manny said. He pulled out his cell phone and noted the time. Ten o'clock. "We have about eleven hours to wait."

"We'd better dormirnos bien tonight because, by tomorrow at this time, we won't want to sleep."

"I don't want to sleep now." Manny's voice lowered to a husky and seductive purr. He held her gaze and could tell she was considering leaning down to kiss him.

Removing both hands from behind his head, Manny gently cradled her face in his hands, drawing her close to himself. He met her halfway, and they pressed their lips to each other's. Best first kiss ever. She lay half on top of him, and he wrapped his arms around her.

"Ahem," Alondra said from the doorway. Manny and Aloise pulled apart sheepishly. "It's time for tu amorcito to go home now."

"Fine." Aloise slumped into Manny's arms, and he held her for a few more seconds before kissing the top of her head and pushing her gently from on top of him.

"I'll text you when I get home," Manny said. "And I'll come see you first thing in the morning. Maybe your parents will be back by then."

"I doubt it," Alondra said, folding her arms across her chest. "They'll probably be in their cuarto at the hotel for two or three days."

"Well good," Aloise said, squeezing Manny's hand. "We can spend all day together mañana."

"Sounds good to me." He planted one more quick kiss on her lips and scooted to the edge of the bed, using one of the many handrails to lift himself to stand beside Alondra, then helped Aloise out of her bunk. "Walk me to my car?"

"Definitivamente." Aloise led him back the way they came in and up the dock to the parking lot.

Manny gently pushed Aloise against his Jeep, lacing his fingers into her hair at the nape of her neck and kissed her for several minutes. When he finally broke away, he whispered, "If I'd known kissing you would feel this amazing, I would have kissed you hours ago."

"I'll see you por la mañana, Romeo," Aloise said.

"Bright and early, Juliet." Manny kissed her one more time, then opened the door to his Jeep and climbed inside. He watched her walk safely back to her yacht, then reversed out of his parking spot and sped from the lot, knowing the faster he got home the faster he could send her a text and continue their flirty conversation late into the night.

Chapter Sixty-Eight

County Clerk's office

Manny had trouble waking up the next morning after staying up half the night texting back and forth with Aloise. As they'd planned, he picked her up in his Jeep at nine o'clock and took her to brunch at his favorite diner in town. The parking lot just happened to share space with the county building. When they left the restaurant, instead of making a beeline for his truck, he led her down the sidewalk.

"Oh look," Manny said, turning around to grin at Aloise. "We're at the county building. We should go inside and apply for a marriage license."

"Ooh, can we?" Aloise probably thought he was teasing, but he led her up the stairs of the building. "That would teach my parents to try to deny me the right to get married until after my lazy sister gets her act together and finds a husband."

"Way to show them who's boss." He opened the main doors, and they held hands as they walked down the hall to the clerk's office. Butterflies leapt in his stomach as he stepped up to the counter, wondering if she'd actually go through with this. He lifted his chin and spoke with false confidence. "We'd like to apply for a marriage license."

"Are you over eighteen?" The lady at the counter raised her eyebrows.

"I know I have a baby face, but yes, I'm nineteen." He knew why the clerk didn't question Aloise. She looked like a woman. Did she ever.

"And you *really* want to get married at nineteen?" This time the lady looked over at Aloise.

"I'm twenty." Aloise shrugged.

The lady glanced back and forth between the two of them, with pursed lips. Manny envisioned his grandma looking down her nose through her spectacles, questioning whether he needed a chocolate chip cookie an hour before dinner. He felt like answering her that yes, he would very much like a chocolate chip cookie... before dinner if possible.

"Is there an application we need to fill out?" he asked.

Without saying another word, but without giving up her disapproving facial expression, she handed them a paper application. Manny hauled out his driver's license and realized they may have a problem.

Manny turned to Aloise and spoke out of the side of his mouth, "Do you have a driver's license?"

"Uh... from Mexico. Plus, my passport, does that count?"

"We need to see a certified copy of both of your birth certificates," the lady said, almost with a satisfied smirk. Manny tucked his wallet back into his pocket, feeling all was lost.

"I'm pretty sure my parents have that in the safe on our yacht." Aloise shrugged.

"Really?" Manny couldn't help his jaw drop. "Your parents keep your birth certificate on your yacht?"

"Where else are they going to keep it?" she asked. "We pretty much live on the yacht."

"Do you want to get it out of the safe?" Manny asked. This was feeling real. Was she really willing to marry him, just like that?

"Sure," Aloise said. "Do we need to go to your house to get yours too?"

"Oh yeah, I hadn't thought of that." Manny turned to the lady at the counter. "We'll be back in a few hours." He grabbed the application in one hand and Aloise's hand in his other and pulled her from the room.

"This is exciting," she said, bouncing along beside him like a little girl at Christmas.

He stopped right there in the hallway in the county building and pulled her close, looking deeply into her eyes. "Are you really serious about this? Would you really marry me?"

"Yeah, I'm serious," she said. "I want to be with you, and if this is the only way for us to be together, I'm willing to do whatever it takes. They can't force me to leave with them if I'm legally married to you, right?"

"They can't force you to leave even if you're not married... right?" He raised his eyebrows.

"You don't know my father," she said, a panic filling her voice. "He would cut me off, tell me I was dead to him, leave me destitute without a job or any money."

"I wouldn't let that happen," Manny said. "You could stay with me and my family. We would take care of you. You wouldn't be alone."

"Then marry me, Emanuel Cohen," she said. "That would be torture to live with you and not be able to, you know, sleep together."

"Yeah, I don't think I'd want that either." Manny slowly pressed his lips to hers, and she wrapped her arms around his neck, holding him to her. They pulled away from each other and his hoarse whisper was barely audible. "Let's go get our birth certificates."

Chapter Sixty-Nine

Jacob Cohen's Son

"I should be able to find the birth certificate pretty easily," Aloise said, entering her parents' master stateroom. Behind the bedroom door, under a nondescript desk, she opened a cabinet that looked as if it would contain file folders. Instead, it contained a safe. She turned a couple of dials to line up the way she wanted them and then pulled the handle, opening the safe. "Our most valuable documents."

"Not having a permanent residence would make me uncomfortable," Manny said, tucking his hands into the pockets of his slacks, watching her sift through files. "I like having a place to come home to."

"I think I'm going to like that too." From where she was crouched on the floor, Aloise looked up at Manny with a thoughtful expression.

"You take my breath away." Manny's heart raced as he gazed into her eyes. "I love your snark and humor and feistiness, but also, you really are beautiful."

"Thank you," she said with sincerity. "I don't think women get told that often enough."

"What do you mean?" Manny leaned against the wall of the stateroom and folded his arms across his chest.

"That we're beautiful. Men are so afraid of offending us or not valuing us for our brains and personality that they forget we also want to be told that we're desirable physically."

"Trust me, I desire you physically." He chuckled. *Did he ever.* "I'll be sure to tell you every day how beautiful you are."

"Good." She turned back to her task, thumbing through files. "We'll have a very happy marriage."

"But... what if I don't know how to be a husband, and you don't know how to be a wife?" Manny asked, vulnerability seeping through his tough exterior. "What if we fail miserably, and you hate me, and your parents sail off into the sunset and you regret staying with me?"

Aloise shrugged. "That's a possibility. There are no guarantees in life."

"And you're okay with that?"

"Tell you what." She looked up at him again. "Let's *plan* to succeed, and we're less likely to fail."

"Okay." He nodded, and she went back to work.

Outside, a car door slammed and then another. A man and a woman were talking, but their voices were muffled. Aloise startled and pawed through the paperwork faster. "Go sit in the salon," she hissed. "If they get in here before I find the certificate, at least you weren't alone with me in their bedroom."

Manny slipped out the bedroom door and lounged on the bench seat, propping up his feet and holding his cell phone, scrolling through social media posts. He tried to appear bored. He willed Aloise to hurry. He didn't want to meet her parents alone. Nor did he want to try to explain why she was in her parents' stateroom.

He forced himself to maintain his composure as her parents traipsed down the stairs into the smaller salon near the galley. They dropped some bags on the table, talked to one another as they unloaded groceries, and didn't seem to notice him. Granted he was up one small flight of steps, but if he could see them, they could probably see him if they glanced his direction.

"Come on, Aloise, hurry up," he mumbled under his breath, bouncing his knee. He forced himself to hold still. The longer they stayed in the galley, the more likely Aloise would be finished and leave their stateroom.

After several minutes, Aloise's mother noticed Manny, and he waved lightly. She said something to her husband and looked nervous as if she thought Manny was an intruder.

Manny stood and slid his hands into his pockets, attempting to look as sweet and innocent as he could. As they came up the stairs, Manny said, "Hello, Mr. and Mrs. Ashish, I'm a friend of your daughter, Aloise. My name's Manny." He reached out his hand, hoping one of them would r eciprocate.

"I'm David, this is my wife, Shira." David shook Manny's hand. "Where is our daughter?"

Manny hesitated. "Uhh…" Just then the toilet flushed in their suite, and Manny took that as his cue. "She needed to use the restroom. She must have eaten something that upset her stomach." He wrinkled his nose, impressed with himself for coming up with that off the cuff.

A few clunks sounded from within the suite, right behind the door, and Manny suspected Aloise was quickly locking the safe. He hoped she'd had enough time to find the birth certificate.

Aloise opened the door to her parents' suite and took a deep breath. "Sorry about that. I don't know what came over me. Papá, I found your spray, but you might want to steer clear of su baño for a little while."

"Are you feeling better?" Her mom came and held the back of her hand to Aloise's forehead.

"Yeah, I think I must have eaten something that disagreed with my belly." Aloise stepped over to Manny and wrapped her arm through his. "I see you met my new boyfriend."

"¿Novio?" David raised his eyebrows. "He told us él era tu amigo. When did you meet? We've been docked less than twenty-four hours."

"He rescued me when I got lost on a back road and my car ran out of gas. It was love at first sight." She exaggerated a sigh and blinked her eyes at Manny playfully.

"You're too young to know what love is," David grumbled.

"You and Mamá have been such great examples of a loving relación." Aloise wrapped her arm around Shira's shoulders. "I know I'm going to make a great wife someday."

Today, Manny thought, coughing lightly.

"No te casarás ante su hermana," David said. "You will have to wait to prove yourself a good wife."

"That's not fair, Papi," Aloise whined. "Alondra's not even looking for a husband. And I've found a maravilloso man who loves me and wants to marry me."

"You've known him for less than a day." David raised his eyebrows.

"Like she said"—Manny reached for Aloise's free hand—"it was love at first sight."

"When is it you think you're going to get married?" Shira asked. "We're only going to be docked a few weeks."

"Today, if possible," Aloise said, smiling over at Manny. He returned her smile.

"Absolutamente not," David said. "¡Lo prohíbo!"

"Padre, I'm an adult," Aloise said, her voice less placating to her daddy and more standing up for herself as the woman she was. Manny was impressed at how quickly she flipped that switch. "You can't force me to do anything."

"As long as you live under my security, you will do as I say."

"Está bien, Padre." She nodded.

"Good, I'm glad we got that settled." David turned and stomped back down the stairs. "I'm going to finish putting the groceries away."

"As of today," Aloise called after him. "I will no longer be living under your security." She raised her chin with confidence.

David turned slowly, a fire brewing behind his eyes. "You will be cut off."

Manny squeezed her hand to give her reassurance that she will never be destitute.

"I am aware of that."

"I will take care of her, Mr. Ashish." Manny tried to keep his voice respectful but confident.

"You are just a little boy yourself." David started back up the stairs, his stance offensive.

Manny gulped and fought the urge to take a step backward, keenly aware that David was in between them and the door leading out of the yacht. He spoke very quietly out of the side of his mouth, hoping only Aloise would hear him. "Did you get what you need?"

"Yes," she said.

Manny sighed in relief. "You ready to leave?"

"Yep."

"Glad to have met you, Mrs. Ashish," Manny said, nodding respectfully to Shira. "I'm sorry we have to leave on such unfortunate terms."

"You are not taking my daughter anywhere," David commanded with a growl.

"You're right, Padre," Aloise said. "I'm leaving on my own accord."

Aloise pushed past her father, dragging Manny by the hand.

David grabbed Manny and shoved him against the wall. "You will *not* be taking my daughter."

"Please remove your hands from me, sir." Manny maintained firm composure, looking David in the eye. "You are on American soil now, and I have rights."

"And I have a shotgun," David said with a sneer.

"Papi! Stop!"

"David, you can't be serious," Shira said. "Let go of that young man."

David cocked his head to the side, finally looking more closely at Manny. "¿Quién eres?" He let up a bit, and Manny shook him off, lifting his chin confidently.

Knowing he was the spitting image of his father, Manny guessed correctly. "I think you already know who I am... don't you?" It wasn't really a question.

"Which of the little *thieves* is your father?"

"You're a smart man, David. You tell me."

David took a step back and looked Manny up and down. "Too old to be Joseph's kid. Too young to be from Sam. Nick? Or Jacob?"

"You have a fifty-fifty chance of getting that right." Manny didn't give in.

"Padre, what do you have against the Cohens anyway? What did they ever do to you?"

David turned to look at his daughter, his hard expression unchanged. "They stole money from my business partner, dragged all of us across the globe because Nick murdered a man, and their holier-than-thou attitude was stifling."

"M-murdered?" Manny faltered. Nicholas Cohen? The man everyone idolized? The philanthropy-minded man who gave to others and helped out the less fortunate? "Uncle Nick could never murder anyone."

"Maybe you should ask your daddy about that."

"Maybe I will," Manny said. "But first we need to deal with a more time-sensitive topic. I'm going to marry your daughter this afternoon."

"Over my dead body," David said.

"I only shoot deer, pheasants, and rabbits." Manny said, pursing his lips. "So that is not an acceptable scenario."

"What are you hoping I'll say right now? No te estoy dando mi permiso!"

"I'm not asking you for your permission."

"What are you asking for?"

"I'd very much like for you to *not* disown your daughter," Manny said. "She loves you, and respects you, and wants you to support her decision."

"I will not condone that!"

"For what reason? Because I'm Jacob Cohen's son? Because her older sister isn't married yet?" Manny shook his head in frustration. "Those are stupid reasons not to support your daughter."

"You met her yesterday." David moved right up into Manny's face again. "You don't even know her. What's her middle name? What's her favorite food? When's her birthday?"

"Those are things I will learn as we get to know each other," Manny reasoned.

"You're not in love with her."

"Love grows over time," Manny said.

"Then get to know her over time," David said, stepping back. "There is no hurry to get married."

"Valid point, sir. But are you, or are you not, planning to sail this boat out of this harbor and leave forever?" Manny pointed his finger in the direction of the vast expanse of water of Lake Huron.

"I could sail out of here today, and you couldn't stop me."

"Which is one of the reasons we need to get married."

"Are you threatening to kidnap my daughter?"

"Are you threatening to kidnap my wife?"

"She is *not* your *wife*. She is most certainly *my* daughter."

"She will be in a few hours," Manny said.

"Young lady"—David turned toward Aloise—"as long as you live under my roof, you will do as I say."

"And as long as she lives under *my* roof, she will be protected."

"Lo siento, Papi, but this is a choice I'm making for myself." Aloise tugged gently on Manny's hand. "Come on. Let's go."

Manny stepped around David and followed Aloise down the stairs. She stopped at her stateroom and reached inside for her phone charger and a small backpack that must have contained everything she thought she was going to need because she didn't even open it to check what was inside.

"I'll come back for the rest of my stuff tomorrow," she said. They ascended the ladder near the galley and walked down the deck and off the boarding ladder. They hurried up the dock to the parking lot and climbed into Manny's Jeep.

"Are you sure you're making the right decision?" Manny asked, lifting her hand and kissing the back.

"I'm positive." She pulled the birth certificate out of her pocket and held it up with a smile. "Let's go find yours."

Chapter Seventy

Birth Control

"Stay in here until I get back, okay?" Manny led Aloise into his trophy room and handed her the television remote control, not thinking to ask if she even liked watching television. It just seemed like the thing to do. "You're welcome to poke around and explore. Shove all the clothes to one side of my closet to make room for yours. Make a list of things you think you'll need, and we'll stop at the Walmart later. You know, bathroom stuff or food or anything. I want you to feel comfortable here."

"What if one of your parents comes down here looking for you?" She bit her lower lip. Manny approached her and ran his hands down her arms, then took her hands in his.

"One, they never come down to my wing of the house, citing that I'm old enough to need privacy. Two, my dad's at work, and I'm going down to the other side of the house to find my mom right now. And three, they're going to find out you're living here eventually, and we're going to have to figure out how to tell them... soon. Preferably not today. I really don't want anyone else to try to talk us out of this."

"Me neither," she said with a sigh. "Hey, can I ask you a kind of serious question?" Aloise glanced toward the open door to Manny's suite, and he walked over to close and lock the door. He took her hands and guided her over to the couch to sit together.

They turned toward one another so their knees were touching, and they were facing each other as best they could while sitting side by side on the couch. Manny waited for Aloise to gather the courage to ask him whatever she was curious about, but he suspected he already knew.

"Have you ever... you know..." Although she maintained eye contact, she noticeably squirmed in her seat.

"Had sex?" He raised his eyebrows and shook his head. "No. You?"

"Are you kidding? I've never even been allowed to have a boyfriend, remember?"

"We don't have to... do... anything," Manny said. "Until we're ready. I'm not going to put any pressure on you. That's not why I'm marrying you."

"Why *are* you marrying me?"

"Because it feels like the right thing to do." Manny shrugged. "I don't know how else to describe the way I'm feeling."

"Me too." Her face lit up as though she were relieved that he understood how she felt. "I feel so drawn to you, like we were..."

"Meant to be together," they said at the same time.

"Yeah." She nodded.

"Okay, can I ask *you* a serious question?"

"If we're going to be married in a few hours, we should probably feel comfortable asking each other anything we want, right?"

"How do you feel about... children?" Manny was uncomfortable asking this, but the topic was kind of important. "Should we, you know, get some sort of protection when we go to Walmart?"

"We probably should." She nodded. "Not that I don't want to have kids someday, but we are *really* young. And we're going to get a lot of flak for getting married without telling anyone."

"True," Manny said. "Okay, so that will be the number one thing on the top of our grocery list."

Aloise giggled. "Have you ever bought any of them before?"

"Heck no!"

"Is that going to be weird?"

"Probably." Manny laughed. "Maybe we should buy one of each kind and try them all out to see which kind we like best."

"We can only buy twelve different kinds because we are totally going through the self-checkout lane."

"Agreed!" Manny offered Aloise a high five and then pushed himself off the couch. "Let me find my birth certificate, or we won't have any need to shop at all."

"Go," she said. "I'm going to paw through your underwear drawer and try on some of your T-shirts."

"I don't think that's a good idea," Manny said.

"Why? Do you have holes in your underwear?" She reached for his waistband, as if she was going to look down his pants.

"No, you can look through my underwear drawer all you want." He pulled her into his arms and nuzzled her neck. "But if I see you in *just* my T-shirt, we're not going to make it to the county clerk's office before closing."

"You know what I just realized?" She cocked her head to the side, and Manny waited for her to answer her own rhetorical question. "We've never made out. We've kissed, like a couple of times, but that's it."

"We made out by my Jeep last night," Manny reminded her.

"For a couple of minutes." She shrugged.

"I'm going to refer back to my comment about you not trying on my T-shirts," he said. "Let's wait until we have a marriage license in our hands, and then we can make out all night if you want."

"Okay, go talk to your mom." She gently shoved him away, and he smiled at her as he exited the room and closed the door behind himself.

Chapter Seventy-One

Birth Certificate

"**M**om?" Manny called from the kitchen, listening for her to answer from somewhere in their expansive home.

"In my office," she answered from down one hall. Manny headed in that direction.

The kitchen sat in the middle of the main house like the hub of a wheel. Hallways traveling out like spokes seemed to reach into the forest, ending in a suite of rooms, each with three or four sides of windows, plus windows along the hallways.

"Mom, where do you keep my birth certificate?" Manny asked without preamble or explanation.

She barely glanced up from her desk. "In the fireproof lockbox in the mudroom off the garage." There was no hesitation in her voice until suddenly there was, and she narrowed her eyes. "Why?"

"I need it for something." Manny turned to walk away, then hesitated. "Is there a key or combination?"

"Emanuel, why do you need your birth certificate?" She swiveled in her office chair and folded her arms across her chest.

"Would it be okay if I answered that question in a couple of days?" He bit his lip and held his breath, turning to meet his mom's gaze with a confidence he was trying to pull from his nervous stomach.

"What are you hiding from your mother?"

"Mom, I'm a nineteen-year-old guy. Sometimes nineteen-year-old guys need to do things that they're not comfortable telling their mom about ahead of time. Please, just, give me a day or two, okay?"

"Which branch?"

"What?"

"Which branch of the military are you enlisting?"

"What makes you think I'm going into the military?" He wasn't sure if she'd be more upset about him enlisting, or if she found out the truth.

"There are only a few reasons why a person needs their birth certificate at your age, and since you don't have a girlfriend, I assume you're not getting married."

Manny coughed, more like choked, and covered his mouth with his fist. After calming his coughing fit, he said, "That's a reasonable assumption."

"So which branch?"

"Please can we save this conversation for a couple of days? I promise I'll tell you everything. But please don't force me to explain my decision right now."

"The key is on a blue keychain in the top drawer of your father's desk."

"Thank you for understanding." Manny turned to walk away from his mom.

"I don't understand," his mom mumbled. "But I respect your privacy."

Manny stopped but didn't turn around. "I appreciate that, mom." He hesitated a second more, then continued down the hall to the kitchen and common room. He turned down the hallway to his father's office, where he strode to his desk and opened the top drawer. A false bottom lay under a stack of file folders, and he lifted them off and found the blue keychain. He replaced the files, closed the drawer, and retraced his steps.

The entrance to the garage was adjacent to the kitchen in the center of the house, and Manny paused, panic crushing his chest and his hopes. How would he discreetly sneak Aloise back out of his suite and into his Jeep? He'd think of something. First, he had to find his birth certificate.

The key fit easily in the lock and within seconds he found the file folder that was labeled, "Birth Certificates." Much simpler than what Aloise had to do sneaking behind her parents' backs and searching for ten minutes.

"Are you in some sort of trouble?" His mom stood by the entrance to the mud room, and Manny jumped, dropping the keys and the most valuable document in his world.

"You startled me." He pressed his hand to his chest and leaned down and grabbed the items he'd dropped. He stood and turned to face his mom. "No, I'm not in any trouble. Please trust me."

"Okay," she whispered.

"Would you do me a huge favor?" Manny handed his mom the blue keychain. "Would you return this to dad's desk for me?"

She opened her hand without a word, and her lips shook with unshed tears in her eyes.

"Mom." Manny pulled her into a quick hug. "Trust me." Before she could say anything else, he grabbed the extra set of keys to his Jeep from the hook by the door and strode to his truck.

He backed out of the garage, not looking at the door to the mudroom, and pulled onto the grass, driving carefully around to his wing of the house. He parked in a way that his mom would be able to see the back end of the truck through the living room windows but not the passenger side door to the cab.

After coming around the car, he knocked lightly on the outside door and called softly, "Aloise, it's Manny, let me in."

Aloise opened the door, and Manny grabbed his compound bow from just inside.

"Come sneak into the Jeep while I load some hunting equipment into the back end of the truck."

"Why are you going hunting?" Aloise asked, grabbing her small backpack purse and walking out the door.

"My mom's suspicious. I just need her to *think* I'm going hunting."

"Oh, gotcha."

Manny lowered the tailgate and loaded the compound bow into the bed of his truck, then went inside and grabbed a few other random hunting items and loaded them in as well. Checking to make sure the back door to his suite was unlocked, he made his way around to the driver's side and climbed into the Jeep. "You ready?"

"Ready as I'll ever be, I guess." She giggled.

"Alright, crouch down in your seat while I drive past the house. I'd lay wagers my mom is watching from the window."

Aloise crouched so as not to be seen, and Manny waved lightly toward the house to say goodbye to his mom, just in case she was watching.

Chapter Seventy-Two

Witnesses

I n the amount of time they took digging up the required paperwork, the lunch hour had come and gone. But the same clerk was at the counter. She pursed her lips and looked pointedly down her nose. "You again."

Aloise and Manny both laid their birth certificates on the counter, along with their driver's licenses and Aloise's passport.

"Are you trying to get a green card?" the clerk asked. "Is that what this is about?"

"Ma'am," Manny said with as much respect as he could muster. "There is a very specific reason why we need to get married *today*, and I'm really not at liberty to say what that reason is. Please could you just process our paperwork?"

"There's a three-day waiting period to get your license back." She folded her arms across her chest.

"There's no way to expedite the process?"

"Not unless you want to pay an extra $50 in addition to the licensing fee of $20."

Manny pulled a twenty and a fifty from his wallet and slapped them on the counter.

"It's $45 if you want us to perform the ceremony," she said.

Manny calmly pulled another two twenties and a five from his wallet and placed them on his growing pile of cash.

"You need two witnesses." She still hadn't unfolded her arms.

"Hmm..." Manny glanced around the empty office then pulled his cell phone from his pocket. Scrolling through names on his contact list, he found the number for his best friend, Evan. He picked up on the second ring. "Hey, man, are you at home? Can you and your brother come help me with something real quick?"

"I guess," Evan said. "What do you need?"

"I need two witnesses for a document I'm signing at the county clerk's office."

"What? Are you getting married?" Evan laughed.

"Yeah," Manny said, wondering if Evan would believe him.

"Very funny," Evan said. "No seriously, what are you signing?"

"Just get over here to the county clerk's office, please. As soon as possible."

"We're leaving right now, man. Chill."

Manny could hear Evan's keys in his hands. "See ya in five." He touched the screen of his phone to end the call and smiled at the clerk. He gently pushed the completed application, essential documents, and stack of cash across the counter. "They're on their way."

By the time the clerk processed the paperwork, Evan and his older brother strolled into the clerk's office and stopped short.

"Dude, seriously?" Evan raised his eyebrows, staring at Manny and Aloise's joined hands.

"I tried to tell you." Manny turned and placed his hand on Aloise's lower back, presenting his bride to his best friend. "Aloise, I'd like you to meet my friend Evan and his older brother..." Manny hesitated, blanking on his brother's name.

"Warren." He shook Aloise's hand. "Do you by any chance have an older sister?"

"Yes, I do, actually," Aloise answered. "Why?"

"Because you are quite possibly the most beautiful woman I've ever seen in my life, and I would very much like to be introduced to your sister."

"The largest sailing yacht at the marina." Aloise pointed toward the lake. "Her name is Alondra. *Por favor*, take her off my hands."

The guys both chuckled, and Manny didn't doubt for a second that the next place Evan and Warren would be heading was to the yacht club at the end of the pier.

Shaking his head and grinning, Manny turned back to the clerk. "Our witnesses have arrived."

Chapter Seventy-Three

Walmart

If Aloise was nervous about standing in a grocery store aisle in front of rows and rows of prophylactics, she didn't let on. Manny was nervous but knew this was necessary. He let her take the lead.

"Ooh! Glow-in-the-dark." She picked up a package, and Manny fought to keep a straight face. "Those could be fun." She tossed them in the empty grocery cart and turned back to the wall of condoms.

Manny tried to make a sincere attempt to study the choices, but his face heated just reading the labels. Lubricated, ultra-thin, *flavored?* He had to turn around and nearly choked out the words, "Just choose whatever you want, and we'll try them all."

Just as he said that, and while Aloise held three different packages, jockeying to not drop any of them, Manny's former high school principal, Mrs. Laker, came around the corner.

"Well, hello, Emanuel," Mrs. Laker said with a smile, not having noticed what aisle they were standing in. When she glanced down and saw what Aloise was holding, her mouth gaped open. Aloise quickly threw the boxes into the grocery cart, which now contained at least half a dozen.

"Mrs. Laker"—Manny cleared his throat and then gently pulled Aloise closer—"I'd like to introduce my *wife*, Aloise. Mrs. Laker was my high school principal... four months ago."

"Wife?" Mrs. Laker's eyes darted back and forth between them, then glanced down at their left hands, which clearly did not display wedding rings.

Manny leaned closer to Aloise. "We should buy wedding rings. Nobody's going to believe we're married."

"I hadn't thought about that." She looked down at her left hand. "Is there a jewelry store in your town?"

"This is your town now too, babe." His voice lowered. Aloise giggled as they stared into each other's eyes.

"I hadn't heard that you were getting married..." Mrs. Laker drew their attention back to her. "Your mother must be, um, thrilled."

"She doesn't exactly know yet," Manny said.

"We just got married this afternoon," Aloise said.

"Oh, you've eloped. How romantic." Mrs. Laker glanced at the grocery cart full of condoms. "I guess that would explain your desire for, um, well..."

"We don't want to get pregnant," Manny said, dropping his voice lower.

"That's a wise choice," she said. "As *young* as you are."

"Yeah, I bet you wish Tommy and Amy had made that choice over homecoming weekend, huh?"

Mrs. Laker shifted uncomfortably. "Their adorable little girl is... a blessing... in disguise."

"Her water broke during our graduation ceremony," Manny said, leaning close to Aloise and keeping his voice low. "In front of about nine hundred people."

"Oh!" Aloise covered her mouth with her hand, then dropped her hands to her sides. "That must have been... a blessing... to have so many people around to make sure she got to the hospital in time."

"Yes," Mrs. Laker said, nodding slowly. "A blessing."

"Anyway, we have some more shopping to do before we... go home." Manny gulped. "It was very nice to run into you this afternoon, Mrs. Laker."

"You as well, Emanuel. And nice to meet you, Louise."

"Aloise," Manny corrected her, and Mrs. Laker cocked her head to the side in confusion. "My wife's name is Aloise. With an A."

"Oh, well, I hope you have a lovely day." She stepped away from them, backing up her grocery cart.

"We intend to have a lovely day," Manny said, pulling Aloise a little closer and gazing into her eyes. "Gracias."

Mrs. Laker was gone by the time Manny was done kissing his wife while standing in the grocery store aisle across from a wall of prophylactics.

After a brief tender moment and then a lighthearted chuckle about running into Mrs. Laker, they strode over to the aisle where beach towels were sold and placed one on top of their other selections. Then had fun goofing off, picking out different items that they might possibly need, commenting on their necessities.

A candle, bubble bath, massage oil, a box of Kleenex, various energy restorative snacks, sports drinks for electrolyte replenishment, matching silky pajamas, a negligée, and a romance novel with a half-naked couple on the front. Everything they could think of for a *lovely day*, as Mrs. Laker had pointed out.

By the time they got to the checkout lane, their selections weren't any less suggestive than if they'd filled their cart to the brim with condoms. They also forgot they'd planned to use the self-check-out lane until they'd unloaded most of the groceries onto the conveyor belt.

The little old lady who was their cashier probably would laugh off their collection of paraphernalia. As Manny turned to the row of chocolate bars, a girl approached the little old lady and said she could take a break and the girl would take over for her.

Manny could have picked her voice out in a crowded room the size of a gymnasium. He gritted his teeth and closed his eyes. "This can't be happening."

"What's the matter?" Aloise stepped closer and touched Manny's face, trying to comfort him.

"The girl who is our new cashier. Does she have red hair?"

Aloise slowly said, "Yyess."

He spoke through clenched teeth. "She's my ex-girlfriend." Manny opened his eyes and met her gaze.

"If we can get through discussing family planning with your high school principal, I'm sure we can handle having your ex-girlfriend for our cashier."

"Sure, we'll go with that."

Aloise pushed past Manny and strode right up to the girl, extending her hand. "Hi, I'm Aloise. I understand you're friends with my *husband*."

Lexi paused from scanning eight packages of condoms and glanced up to realize Manny was standing next to Aloise, one arm around her waist. She lowered her gaze to the box in her hand that read Glow-in-the-Dark, then scanned it and placed it in the grocery bag beside her. Lexi slowly lifted her hand and shook Aloise's.

"Manny must have... *changed his mind...* about certain things he claimed he *wasn't ready for* a few months ago." She scanned the next box, and the next.

"Amazing what happens when you meet the right girl, huh?" Aloise didn't wait for an answer to her rhetorical question, just turned back to Manny. "Did you pick out which candy bar you'd like?"

Manny held up his selection. "Snickers."

"Fitting for the day we've had." Aloise stepped closer and winked. Manny placed his hands on her hips and fought the urge to press his lips to hers again but changed his mind at the last minute.

"Let's pay for these groceries so we can go home," Manny said.

"I would like that very much," Aloise answered in a voice that was almost a purr.

By the time they were done gazing into each other's eyes with longing and fire, most of the groceries were scanned and in bags. As Aloise loaded the bags from the carousel back into the cart, Manny swiped his debit card and smiled at his ex-girlfriend. "Nice to see you again, Lexi."

"Have a nice day, Manny," Lexi said in her most professional voice.

"I'm sure we will." Manny turned and walked away, ready to take his wife home so they could put into practice all the exciting things they'd discussed since that morning when they'd decided to get married.

Chapter Seventy-Four

You Know What I Was Doing Last Night

Manny pulled up to the side of the house, right next to the door of his suite. He checked that his living room was empty, then Aloise snuck into the bedroom. Before risking his parents walking in, he strode over to the door leading to the hallway and locked it.

As soon as he had unloaded all the groceries, he lowered the gate at the back of his truck, and unloaded his hunting equipment.

Most of the items they bought belonged in the bedroom and bathroom, so he quickly refrigerated the beverages and carried the rest of the bags into his bedroom, locking the bedroom door also.

When he turned around, he was startled to see Aloise had already changed into the negligée and was laying on his bed, propped up on one elbow. The sound that escaped his throat was almost a whimper.

Both his ex-girlfriend and his wife had been correct when facing off at the grocery counter. He hadn't been ready for this a few months ago, and meeting the right girl made all the difference. Although he'd never done this before, Manny got the impression his body would know instinctively what to do with his bride.

"I'm really glad we got married," Manny said, climbing onto the bed and lying next to her.

"I wouldn't be in bed with you if we hadn't," Aloise answered with a resigned expression.

"Me neither."

"I'm really glad you weren't ready a few months ago with what's-her-name," she whispered.

"Me too."

"I'm really glad I ran out of gas in the middle of a forest in this beautiful state that I can't remember the name of."

"Michigan," Manny said.

"Michigan is beautiful," Aloise said.

"You're beautiful," Manny whispered.

"Can we make out now?" she asked.

"I have a legally binding document that says we can."

Aloise leaned forward, and Manny met her halfway, pulling her closer so their bodies were flush and he could feel every inch of her body.

When their lips finally met, they didn't part for a very long time.

Manny awoke the next morning to his wife's insistent whisper.

"Manny, someone's knocking at your door," Aloise said. "Wake up. They've knocked a bunch of times. I think it's your mother because she's texted a bunch of times too."

He groaned and accepted the cell phone she handed him. Among several other texts, one was written in all caps. *I KNOW YOU'RE IN THERE. COME OPEN THIS DOOR.*

The text he sent back was two letters. *OK.*

Manny kissed Aloise on the forehead then reluctantly rolled out of bed and rummaged in his drawer for a pair of sweats, not bothering with a shirt. He pulled the door to their bedroom closed and padded in bare feet over to the main door, opening it halfway. He stood with one hand on the door and the other on the door frame.

"Is it true you got married yesterday?" his mom demanded.

"Would you really rather have had me join the Navy?"

"I would have liked to have known what you were doing."

"I'm pretty sure, having been married for twenty-two years, you know what I was doing last night."

She shuddered. "You know what I meant." Her voice cracked. "Don't you think your mother would have liked to attend your wedding?"

"We needed to do things our way," Manny said. "Because Father forbade me to see Aloise ever again, and that wasn't an option."

"Why?"

"He didn't tell you?"

"No, what was he supposed to tell me?"

"Her last name is Ashish, well, *was* Ashish."

"As in... David and Shira Ashish?"

"Her parents." Manny nodded. "They are *not* happy about this either."

"Can I meet her?" Mom's voice cracked again.

"When I left her lying in our bed a moment ago, she was without apparel. I would really prefer we have this conversation later today... or tomorrow even."

The bedroom door behind him creaked open, and the most beautiful woman in the world stepped into the living room, wearing her brand-new silky pajamas, her long brown hair draped over her shoulders in soft snarls and her dark eyes apprehensive. Manny fought the urge to take her in his arms and carry her back to their bed, kicking the door closed in his mother's face.

"Good morning, Mrs. Cohen," Aloise said, tucking herself under Manny's arm and wrapping herself around his waist.

"I guess I could say the same to you... Mrs. Cohen."

"Mom, this is my wife, Aloise." Manny looked down at her with a smile and in a near whisper said, "This is my mother, Maryam Cohen."

Chapter Seventy-Five

Interrogation

"Why did your father forbid you to see Aloise?" Manny's mother asked.

"You probably know more than I do?" Manny answered. "What happened that split our family in half?"

Mom glanced nervously at Aloise, as if calculating how much to share with her. "Maybe we should sit down." She sat at one corner of the sofa, and Aloise boldly sat near the middle, facing her new mother-in-law.

Manny pulled up a chair from the little kitchen table and sat facing them so that they formed a triangle and were able to communicate without craning their necks. Although still half-dressed and counting the minutes for his mother to leave so he could be alone with his bride, this conversation needed to happen.

"Well, um, your father and his oldest brother never had a great relationship to begin with." Mother twisted her hands in her lap, pulling at the bottom hem of her shirt. "Uncle Liam did and said a few things that were very offensive and started a heated argument they never fully recovered from.

"When Grandpa Levi started divvying up the inheritance, the brothers fought over the family's fortune, and they didn't all get the same amount. David Ashish sided with Uncle Liam, and they"—she glanced at Aloise—"weren't very nice to the rest of the family."

"What do you mean by 'weren't very nice'?" Aloise asked.

"Uh... they kind of... made death threats," Mom answered. "And tried to blow up my father's yacht. Well, the yacht Cohen Enterprises owned, but my father was the captain. And Daddy and I were on the yacht at the time.

"Your father testified to the police against his own brother, Liam; and David. They were furious. Heated words were exchanged, sides were chosen, more threats were made. They accused us of stealing. We accused them of sabotage and attempted murder. Things got very ugly."

"So, what happened?" Manny asked, leaning forward, engaged in the story.

"They finally dissolved Cohen Enterprises, liquidated all the assets, and went their separate ways." Mom shrugged. "But everyone left angry with each other. That was the year your father and I moved as far away from Cancun as possible. Apparently, we didn't move far enough." She glanced at Aloise.

Manny took his wife's hand and offered her a soft smile. Although he couldn't take his eyes off Aloise, he spoke to his mother. "I promised I'd explain why I needed my birth certificate."

"I kind of figured it out when I started getting phone calls this morning from friends saying they heard it from someone else who heard it from someone else that you got married yesterday."

"Yeah, we probably should have driven up to Rogers City or something before shopping. *Everybody* knows me in this town."

"And no one knows *her*," Mom said. "You should realize an out-of-towner stands out like a sore thumb. Especially such a beautiful woman."

"Thank you." Aloise ducked her head and bit her lower lip.

"I agree with her beauty." Manny winked and then turned back to his mom. "Mom, I want you to know that her beauty is not what made me want to marry her. I'm not that shallow."

"Why *did* you marry her?"

"We both felt *compelled* to get married," Manny said. "Like it was the most important thing we needed to do for some reason we didn't understand."

"I'm not sure I believe in love at first sight," Aloise said. "I'm pretty sure we're not actually in love yet. We just had this magnetic attraction we couldn't explain, like we were meant to be together. And it seemed imperative that we get married immediately."

"I understand the attraction at first sight thing," his mom said, relaxing a little. "Your father saw me from twenty feet away, and he made a fool of himself drooling over me."

"He's still a fool for you, Mom." Manny loved his parents, and their relationship was inspiring.

"By the way"—Mom turned to Aloise—"you look so much like your mother. She was the most beautiful woman any of us had ever seen. I truly wish we could have met under better circumstances because I would have loved to meet the woman she is deep down."

"Maybe you'll have that chance now that your son is married to her daughter," Aloise said with a soft smile.

"I'd like that." Mom returned her smile.

Manny had a peaceful feeling in his heart that his wife and his mother were going to be fast friends. Now to convince his father.

Chapter Seventy-Six

A Courageous Man

Manny pulled his Jeep into the marina parking lot and parked beside the largest sailing yacht at the docks, where he knew his wife's parents were likely seething with anger. He didn't care. This needed to be done in order for Aloise to be free of their control.

He climbed from the Jeep and walked around the front to help her down, pulling her into his arms. Her beautiful, brown eyes pleaded with him for reassurance.

"I won't let them hurt you," Manny said, leaning down to place a kiss on her lips, which were slightly swollen from the previous night when they had barely paused for breath.

"I'm not worried about them hurting me," she said. "I'm worried they're going to try to take me away from you."

"I won't let that happen." He leaned down so he could look her directly in the eye. "As soon as we get your belongings off this boat, we will spend tonight in each other's arms, and every night for the rest of our lives."

"Is that a promise, Mr. Cohen?" Her flirty eyes nearly made him lift her back inside the Jeep and kiss her until he couldn't see straight.

"Yes, that is a promise, *Mrs.* Cohen." In the privacy of the open door to his Jeep, they shared one very long kiss before closing the door and walking hand in hand toward her parents' sailing yacht. After only a few feet toward the dock, Manny stopped short. "Did they turn the boat around? Or am I imagining that the bow was facing west yesterday?"

"Yeah... they did. Weird." She shrugged, and they continued down the planks of the dock to where the mounting ladder sat ready.

Nothing seemed out of place, yet Manny had an eerie feeling. They started down the stairs to the galley salon.

"Mamá? Papá? Alondra?" Although she called to her family, Aloise headed straight for her stateroom and climbed up onto her bed, opening the furthest stowage cabinet. "Can you hand me that box?"

Manny shoved the box they'd brought from his house closer to her and waited by her door, wondering how soon her father would come around the corner with his shotgun. Manny refused to lift a weapon against another human, even in self-defense. All he could do was hope.

"You have a lot of nerve showing up here," David Ashish's gruff voice spoke as he descended the stairs.

"Thank you, sir." Manny nodded. "I like to think of myself as a courageous man."

From inside her stateroom Aloise snickered, and Manny fought to maintain his composure.

"You are just a little *boy*." David stepped closer but Manny held his ground.

"My hope is that my youthful appearance will continue into old age," Manny said without flinching.

"You will regret the decisions you made these past two days," David said.

"There are many things in my life that I regret," Manny answered. "But marrying your daughter will never be one of them."

"We'll see about that." David turned and stormed up the stairs, temporarily blocking the sunlight streaming in from above.

"Is that true?" Shira Ashish said from the stairwell coming down from the larger salon. When she came into view, Manny noticed her swollen eyes from crying. "Did the two of you get married?"

"Yes, ma'am." Manny nodded respectfully. "Yesterday."

"She wasn't of marrying age yet," Shira said. "She needed to wait for her sister to find a husband first."

"Twenty is legally old enough in the United States," Manny said.

"We are from Mexico, not United States," she said. "You have disrespected our values and *ruined* our daughter."

"Your daughter is the most incredible woman I've ever met, and I will treasure her until the day I die." Manny was impressed with himself for modulating his tone. "I wish you luck finding a husband for Alondra. I'm sure she's looking forward to getting out from under your oppressive rules as well."

"Manny, can you take this box to the Jeep and bring me that other box we brought?" Aloise interrupted their argument. "I guess I have more stuff than I thought I did."

"I'm glad we decided to bring two." Manny leaned down to lift the heavy box from her bed and turned toward the steps leading outside. The box was awkward and lopsided and carrying it along the side plank of the sailboat was a feat.

He stumbled down the boarding ladder onto the dock and looked up to realize his new father-in-law was beside him. Startled, Manny wondered why David hadn't offered a hand if he was right there watching him struggle to get down the ladder.

The two men regarded one another, but no words were said. Manny turned and stumbled along the dock and up the concrete steps to the parking lot. His keys were in his jeans pocket, so he set the heavy box on the ground and fumbled to unlock the Jeep.

"What the heck does that girl have in here?" he mumbled, lifting the box and placing it on the back seat. He opened the box. "Books?"

Classics. He lifted them to check the bindings. *A Tale of Two Cities*, *Gone with the Wind*, *Pride & Prejudice*, *Twilight*. Really? On top was a Bible. A small smile lit Manny's face as he closed the box of his wife's treasures, feeling he learned almost as much about Aloise from peeking into this box as he had during an entire night of lovemaking.

A different kind of smile shifted on his face, and he hurried to grab the other box before heading back to the boat.

The boat that had been docked directly in front of his Jeep.

The boat that was now exiting the marina and rounding the corner into the Thunder Bay River, nearly to the mouth of where the river flowed into Lake Huron.

The boat where his wife had been packing the last of her belongings to come home with him forever.

No.

"No!" Manny screamed. There were no other patrons in the parking lot.

Dropping the box, Manny ran toward the marina, where the harbor master stood behind the counter.

"Call for the Coast Guard!" Manny yelled to the man, who immediately lifted the receiver of the phone beside him. "We have to stop that boat! They're kidnapping my wife!"

Not waiting to hear the man's conversation, Manny ran back out to the parking lot and watched David Ashish yank the rigging to release the sails. Wind lifted the giant white sails, pushing his slim racing yacht farther out into Lake Huron.

"If they reach the international boundary into Canadian waters..." Manny whispered to an empty parking lot. "I'll never get her back."

Chapter Seventy-Seven

Release My Son

"I'm sorry, son, that boat was registered to a Mexican citizen. They are not under our jurisdiction." Petty Officer Haskins from the Coast Guard wasn't making sense, and more important, wasn't launching a fleet to go rescue Aloise.

"But they've kidnapped my wife." Manny pointed in the direction where they'd disappeared over the horizon.

"Is your wife a United States citizen?"

"N-no... we got married yesterday." Panic crushed Manny's chest.

"How many months had she been in the U.S.?"

"M-months?" Manny stammered. "Two days. She'd been in the U.S. two days."

"You married a woman you'd known for two days?"

Less than 24 hours, Manny thought but didn't tell him that. "I have a marriage license that says her parents can't kidnap her."

"I'm sorry, son, that's not how it works. You're asking the Coast Guard to spend thousands of dollars to rescue a noncitizen. There's nothing I can do, son." The man rested a hand on Manny's shoulder, but he shrugged it off.

Son... he keeps calling me son. *I'm not a little boy!* he wanted to scream. He ground his hands into fists.

Son...

Father! City Hall, where his father worked, was walking distance from the marina.

Manny took off at a full sprint, arriving at City Hall faster than he could have maneuvered his Jeep out of the parking lot and down the street.

After throwing open the door to the building and skidding around the corner into his father's outer office, Manny cried out to his receptionist, "I need to speak with my father."

"I'm sorry, he's in a meeting. You'll have to wait." Her calming voice only served to snap his last semblance of temper.

Manny shoved past the receptionist and barreled through the office to a closed conference room. He threw open the door to where a dozen men and women sat around an oval table, with papers and laptops and presentation folders and cups of coffee and bagels strewn across the table. "Father, they've kidnapped Aloise!"

"Emanuel, I'm in a meeting." Mayor Jacob Cohen stood and offered Manny a disappointed and angry glare.

"David Ashish *stole* Aloise, and they are barreling toward international waters as we speak, and you *have* to get the Coast Guard to rescue her."

"I thought I told you to stay away from that girl," Jacob growled.

"I'm sorry I disobeyed you," Manny said in a calmer voice. "Now please, you *have* to help me get her back."

"I don't *have* to do anything for that family. Now if you'll kindly close the door on your way out, we can talk about this when I get home tonight."

"But she's my wife." Manny's voice cracked as he fought to maintain composure.

"Your *what?*" Jacob's eyes narrowed.

"We got married yesterday."

"What were you *thinking*, Emanuel? I told you to stay away from that family."

"David and Shira Ashish are *not* our enemies. What he and your brother Liam did was wrong, but it's time you forgave them."

Jacob pounded his fist on the table. "Don't you presume to know *anything* about what my brother and David did to our family."

"Father, don't you understand? This is why Aloise and I were brought together. She and I were meant to bring a reconciliation between our families."

A feeling of peace washed over Manny, and he understood how all the pieces fit together. How else could their experience be explained otherwise?

"Why else would she have run out of gas at exactly the spot in the middle of a forest where my hunting blind happened to be built?" Manny pleaded with passion. "Why else would I have been singing loud enough from the top of that hunting blind that she could hear me all the way from the road? Why else would she and I have been drawn to each other like a moth to a flame? Why else would we have gotten married less than twenty-four hours after meeting?" Manny sighed, and his eyes softened.

"Your youthful fantasies and teenage hormones have just gotten you into the biggest mess of your life, Emanuel. Now you can live with the consequences." Jacob pointed out into the office. "Now, pull that door shut so I can continue my meeting."

A city police officer appeared at Manny's shoulder and pulled his arm. "Let's go, sir. You've been asked to leave."

"No! Wait! You don't understand!"

The officer pulled Manny's arm behind him and took handcuffs from his belt.

"Father!" Manny called over his shoulder. "If it were Mother on that boat, what would you do?"

His father had told him the stories of how Grandpa Arnold had gotten angry and forced his daughter, Maryam, onto their yacht, leaving Puerto Aventuras and Jacob, behind. Captain Arnold had told Jacob in no uncertain terms that he was not to speak to her again.

Jacob chartered a helicopter that very day and flew thousands of nautical miles to plead forgiveness and beg for Maryam's hand in marriage. Twenty-two years later, their families joined in happiness, it was hard to remember what the original argument had been about.

The officer slapped a cuff on one of Manny's wrists just as the mayor appeared in the doorway.

"Wait," Jacob called to the officer. "Release my son. We need to go rescue his wife."

Chapter Seventy-Eight

I'd Never Let You Go

P etty Officer Haskins, the Officer of the Day, at the Alpena Coast Guard station was much more responsive to the billionaire mayor than he had been to his son. The officer had a helicopter ready to launch before he'd gathered everyone onto the rescue boat.

"My guess is they're heading due east," Manny said. "He's probably trying to get to international waters before we can stop him."

"We won't let that happen, son." The same aggravating petty officer who had dismissed him earlier had a much nicer tone. Manny wanted to snap at him for his earlier behavior but still needed the man's full cooperation if they were going to reach Aloise in time.

As the helicopter lifted into the sky and the captain made ready to launch the rescue boat, a man's voice called from behind him.

"Manny! Wait!"

"Evan?" Manny watched as Evan and his brother, Warren, came running up the dock.

"We're coming with you," Evan said.

"Alondra's on that boat too, you know," Warren said with a smirk. "She called me the minute they took off, and we high-tailed it down here."

"So... you and her..." I raised my eyebrows.

"We're talking." Warren shrugged, and his face flushed.

"Come on, gentlemen," Manny's father said. "Do you want to rescue these girls? Or discuss relationship status? Get on the boat."

"Yes, sir," Warren said, the first to hop onto the boat. Evan and Manny quickly followed.

Smooth as silk, the coast guard cutter motored away from the dock and out of the marina. Within seconds, they were at top speed, bouncing over and through low waves, heading due east.

None of them spoke over the noise of the boat motor and rushing wind, but Manny's eyes scanned the horizon. He guessed that the helicopter pilots would find David's sailing yacht before they would, but it didn't stop him from searching.

Forty-five minutes passed. The chance of catching up to the yacht before reaching international waters was dwindling. The racer could probably top speeds of 15 knots. The Coast Guard helicopter could top 150. If David stayed on course, the helicopter would find him. If David veered north or south, the Coast Guard would be searching for a needle in a haystack.

"Relax, son." His dad wrapped his arm around Manny's shoulder and spoke over the noise of the motor and rushing wind. "These guys are professionals. They know what they're doing. Trust them."

"It's been too long," Manny answered. "We should have caught up to them by now."

"You don't know that. The Coast Guard has a search and rescue system and protocols to follow. They've probably practiced these rescue missions thousands of times in training. They'll find her. I promise."

"Don't make promises you can't keep, Dad." Even as he lost hope, he leaned against his father for support. Manny might be a man in the legal sense, but he still needed his mom and dad to comfort him.

"There!" The helicopter had come into view, and Manny wondered if that meant they'd found David's yacht. The horizon was below their line of sight, but the helicopter was clearly hovering rather than sweeping back and forth.

One of the coast guard officers with binoculars turned back to make eye contact with Manny. "They've stopped the sailboat."

Manny almost fell over with relief. Step one of getting his wife back. Now the hard part—convincing David Ashish to hand over his daughter.

His knee bouncing faster than the pounding of the waves reminded Manny how nervous he was.

Within minutes, they had reached the yacht, and from the stern of the cutter, a fast response boat made ready to deploy.

"I want to come with you," Manny said.

"I don't think that's a good idea, son," Petty Officer Haskins said. "We're trained professionals."

"I've seen you take reporters out with you who were just as untrained as me," Manny said. "That's my *wife* on that yacht. I *need* to come with you."

The petty officer looked to Manny's dad for direction, and Jacob nodded. Manny decided he needed to run for a political office someday. The mayor received more respect, and people followed his direction. Not that Manny was vain, but the level of respect his father received was notable.

"Let him come along," Jacob said.

Manny didn't wait for them to argue. He scrambled into the little fast response boat, and when everyone was seated and ready, they slid off the back of the cutter and deployed. In less than a minute, the little boat pulled alongside David Ashish's sailing yacht, and two coastguardsmen boarded the vehicle, then helped Manny onto the sailboat. The fast response boat pulled away and trolled around, staying within proximity of the boat.

Without waiting for instructions or permission, Manny hurried down the side deck and around the front to where the stairs descended to the galley lounge. When he saw Aloise crouched in a ball, lying in her stateroom with her father standing between him and her, Manny breathed a sigh of relief.

Aloise scrambled off the bed and pushed past her father, racing into Manny's arms. Fresh tears streaked down her already tear-stained face, and she cried over and over between kisses, "You came for me. You came for me."

"I promised I'd never let you go. I promised." Manny couldn't stop the tears from falling down his own face. "I promised."

"If you think for one minute that I'm going to let my daughter leave this boat with you, you are sadly mistaken," David said, his arms folded across his chest. "As soon as your Coast Guard is done infringing on my civil rights, *you* need to leave with them, and I never want to see your face again."

"I'm sorry, sir, but I'm not leaving without my wife." Manny's voice was firm and confident.

"I do not recognize your sham of a marriage." David stuck his nose in the air. "You have violated my daughter."

"Mr. Ashish, I'm Petty Officer Haskins. We're here because we received a distress call from one of your adult daughters who claims she is being held on this boat against her will."

"Es ridículo! We are Mexican citizens and do not recognize your rights to board our yacht."

"You are sailing in waters of the United States of America," the petty officer said. "We have jurisdiction here and intend to conduct our investigation without interference from you. Sir, if you would step aside please, I'd like to have a word with your adult daughters."

"I took her phone away," David said. "There's no way she could have called you. This man is the person who called for help, not my daughter." David pointed at Manny with disdain.

"I called them, Padre," Alondra said from the top of the stairs leading up into the larger salon. Her gaze drifted over to the guardsman. "Petty Officer Haskins, my sister and I are being held against our will and wish to leave this boat immediately."

"¡Cómo te atreves!" David turned on Alondra. "You had no right to call these Americans and ask them to rescue you. You are *my* daughter."

"Sir, please step aside so that I can have a word with your daughters," the petty officer said. "I do not wish to restrain you, but I will if that is necessary."

David took a step back and glared at Manny.

"Miss, for the record, could you state your name, age, citizenship and the reason for your complaint?" The petty officer spoke directly to Alondra.

"My name is Alondra Ashish, I am twenty-two years old, a Mexican citizen, and my sister and I are being held on this boat against our will by our father, David Ashish." Alondra pointed to her father definitively.

The petty officer turned to Aloise. "Miss, could you also state your name, age, and citizenship as well, and respond to your sister's allegation?"

"My name is *Mrs*. Aloise Ashish-Cohen." Aloise lifted her chin with confidence. "I am twenty-years-old, a Mexican citizen legally married to an American citizen, and I concur with my sister's allegation. She and I are being held on this boat against our wills. We both wish to seek asylum in the United States until at which time we are able to obtain temporary residency or return to our home country of our own free will."

"Oh, esto es ridículo!" David shook his head. "I am not holding my daughters hostage. Esta es su casa."

"Mrs. Cohen and Miss Ashish, do you each have identification?" Petty Officer Haskins asked. Each girl reached for her purse and wallet. Alondra handed her ID to the petty officer.

Aloise stepped forward with two items. "This is my driver's license, and this is my marriage license." She unfolded the document and handed them both to the petty officer.

Manny smiled down at her and sighed. She bit her lower lip, gazing up at him, and he winked at her.

Shira Ashish cried from the top of the stairs leading up to the salon. "You can't take my daughters. They need to be with their madre." Shira hurried down the stairs and threw herself into Alondra's arms.

"Mamá, I don't want to be away from you either, but we need to be free to live our own lives," Alondra said. "We're adults now. Please try to understand."

"Mr. and Mrs. Ashish"—Manny stepped forward—"come back to Alpena. We don't want to break up your family. We want our two families to reconcile. To find common ground. My father and mother are willing to forgive you and ask for your forgiveness in return. I want you to have the chance to see your grandchildren someday."

"Did you get my daughter pregnant?" David took a step toward Manny with hands balled into fists. Petty Officer Haskins stepped in between them and placed a hand on David's chest.

"No, sir, of course not!" Manny took a step back. "I mean, you know, nothing's guaranteed to be 100% protection." Manny's face heated in embarrassment, remembering with fondness the sanctity of the previous night. He didn't wish to speak of such things with his new father-in-law, or anyone for that matter.

"Por favor, David." Shira rushed from her daughter's arms into his. "I don't want to be away from mis hijitas. Please don't punish me, or them, for arguments that happened twenty years ago between you and your business partners."

"Por favor, Padre..." Aloise stepped forward. "Please come back to Michigan and reconcile with my husband's family. I want us to be together."

"It's not that easy," David grumbled.

"It's not that hard, either, Papi," Alondra said. "Por favor."

"Mr. Ashish, once your daughters leave this vessel, you are free to sail away or return to port. Unless your daughters wish to press charges, you are not under arrest."

David glared between his daughters, his wife, and Manny, a scowl disfiguring his face. "I'll think about it."

"Gracias, Papá." Aloise rushed forward and threw her arms around her father and mother, and Alondra joined them. They held each other in a touching family hug, then pulled apart, and Aloise returned to Manny's s ide.

"Are you ready to go?" Manny asked, searching her eyes. "Do you want to bring anything?"

"I have my backpack already," Aloise said, tears filling her eyes. She looked longingly in the direction of her stateroom. "There are other things I wanted to bring, but they will have to be left behind."

"Maybe we'll have a chance to pack up the rest of your things if your parents ever return to visit." Manny kissed the top of her head and fought the emotions pulling at his throat.

"I packed a bag too," Alondra said. She grabbed her backpack and glanced inside her stateroom. "I hope they come back," she mumbled.

"Adiós, Mamá," Aloise said, reaching for one more hug from her mom.

"Adiós, hija mía," Shira said, tears running down her face. Alondra also gave their mom a hug, and both daughters climbed the stairs along with Manny and Petty Officer Haskins.

They made their way down the side deck to the ladder and the fast response boat pulled alongside the yacht. Several officers helped the girls down first, Manny next, and then Petty Officer Haskins.

Not until they were all safely aboard the cutter and Aloise gathered herself into Manny's arms was he able to breathe normally again. The ordeal was over. They were together again.

Manny decided this must be how love feels—setting aside one's own life to rescue another. In the past two days, Manny had met his soul mate, married her, and fell in love. A strange turn of events from hunting alone in his forest without a care in the world to rescuing the love of his life.

"Look, they're turning!" Alondra, tucked into Warren's arms, pointed to the east.

David had raised the sails and turned his yacht toward the west, heading back in the direction he'd come, back toward Alpena.

Aloise and Alondra had convinced their father to reconcile with Manny's parents.

Manny gathered his wife closer, ignoring everyone around him, and pressed his lips to hers with a passion barely contained enough for mixed company.

Epilogue—Reconciliation

After the Coast Guard deposited the families back at the marina, took statements from each of them, and recorded the necessary documentation of the day's events, they left everyone and returned to their regular duty station.

Maryam had arrived and gathered Alondra and Aloise into her arms, as if they were the daughters she'd never had. She insisted the Cohen family had plenty of room and both girls could stay as long as needed while obtaining the necessary legal documentation to become permanent residents or return home to Mexico.

Manny had every intention to jump through whatever hoops were necessary to keep his wife by his side, even if they had to return to Mexico and wait in the proverbial line to obtain permanent status. He vowed never to be apart.

They waited almost an hour before the Ashish's sailing yacht came into view. The sisters broke into sobs of relief and held each other as they watched their parents lower the sails and motor slowly into the marina, parking in the same boat slip they still had rented.

Without even assisting to secure the vessel, Shira Ashish rushed off the boat and into her daughters' arms.

Manny and his father instinctively hurried over to help David secure his yacht, along with assistance from Evan and Warren. Within ten minutes, they had the boat docked and settled and Jacob stood before David with his hand extended.

"Ahalan, baruka ha-shav," Jacob said.

Manny was startled to hear his father speak in Hebrew to this man who had been his enemy for many years, welcoming him like a long-lost friend or brother.

Jacob and Maryam had taught their son many languages, saying he needed to remember how far their families had come in three generations since they'd left Israel. Since moving to Dubai, they'd spoken mostly English and some Arabic, and the many years they'd spent in Mexico had the family fluent in Spanish.

Very few people standing near the dock at the marina in Alpena, Michigan, would understand the phrase and even fewer would understand the significance. Jacob was extending a message of peace and reconciliation dating back to when both men lived in a simpler time in their lives, before the fighting and violence.

"Harbe zman lo hitraenu," David returned the greeting, acknowledging that they'd been apart for too many years.

The exchange nearly brought tears to Manny's eyes, and *did* bring tears to Shira's.

Maryam pulled Shira into her arms like a long-lost sister even though they'd barely known one another, and they had a fifteen-year age difference.

"Um... what are they saying to each other?" Aloise asked, probably echoing the thoughts of her sister and Evan and Warren.

"They're welcoming one another after many years apart," Manny said, pulling his wife into his arms. "Our families are together now. Everything will be okay." Manny kissed the top of her head, barely taking his eyes off their parents.

Yeah, everything would be fine now. A peace entered his heart, and he couldn't help taking a tiny bit of credit for what he and Aloise had done by choosing to get married. He pulled away slightly and looked down into the most beautiful, brown eyes he'd ever seen. He leaned forward to whisper in her ear.

"What do you say we go home... and come back for your things tomorrow?"

"I would like that very much," she said.

With barely a word of goodbye to the others, Manny helped Aloise up into his Jeep, backed out of the parking lot, and held his wife's hand the entire seventeen-minute drive home.

<u>Turn the page for a bonus chapter of Emanuel's story or continue reading the Royal Family Saga: Honorary Prince.</u>

Bonus Chapter

A few hours later, Manny and Aloise were awakened from their afternoon nap by insistent knocking at their outer door. Manny pulled on a pair of boxers and shut the bedroom door as he called out, "Hang on, I'm coming. I'm coming."

"Why is this locked?" Manny's father, Jacob, complained as Manny pulled open the door. "And why aren't you dressed?" His father looked him up and down.

"We're newlyweds, Dad," Manny said. "Use your imagination."

"Married... right. That's going to take some getting used to." His father pushed his way into the sitting room, holding up what looked like a formal wedding invitation. "We've been invited to Prince Benjamin's wedding!"

"Who?" Manny wanted to complain that he wasn't in the mood for company right that moment but decided now was not the time.

"Your Uncle Nick's best friend's son!"

Manny's jaw dropped. Whoever the heck was this son of his uncle's best friend was not important enough to pull him from his bed, but he just stood there.

"We've been invited to a royal wedding," his father said, as if that should just explain the intrusion. "Prince Marcos himself will be there."

"Who?" Manny was trying to maintain his temper while standing there in his boxers, wishing for a shirt and a pair of sweats, or better yet for his father to leave him alone.

"The crown prince of Madain Saleh. He's your uncle Nick's best friend. His son Benjamin is a year older than you; I think. Uncle Nick's kids will all be at the wedding. Your cousins."

"I don't even know my cousins, Dad."

"Exactly." His dad started pacing back and forth with excitement. "This is the perfect chance for you to meet them. The wedding is going to be in Cancun."

"If the prince is from Madain Saleh, why is the wedding in Cancun?"

"Well... there's still a lot of fighting going on in Madain Saleh. We shouldn't question it. We should just be thankful that we don't have to fly to the Middle East right now."

"Right. So, I'm going to fly back to my bed right now," Manny said, pulling his dad gently by the shoulder toward the outer door to his sitting room. "Thank you for telling me about this royal wedding, but if you'll kindly stay out of this wing of the house for the next several days, well, weeks, I'd greatly appreciate it."

"You're too young to be married," his dad grumbled on his way out.

"I'm the same age you were when you married mom," Manny reminded him, ushering him into the hall.

"I was more mature."

"Goodbye, Dad." Manny shut the door with a shake of his head and clicked the lock into place. Heading toward the bedroom, he whispered, "Hello, Aloise."

Continue reading the Royal Family Saga: Honorary Prince.

Would you rather read something completely new? Check out Senator's Son, a spinoff story featuring Hazel Cohen-Sayid's twin brother, Mateo Cohen, son of Senator Alejandro Cohen!

Love Letter

Author Julie L. Spencer

O h, my friends, I love these characters. They are so special to me. Have you figured out the secret yet? If you haven't, you may never figure it out. If you understood the references, you wouldn't have gotten past page one of this book without at least suspecting the truth.

I have a confession to make. Billionaire's Sons was originally written as Book One of the Royal Family Saga. The reason I moved this to the end of the series was because of how obvious the secret was revealed.

Did you notice how this final book in the series took you back in time to the beginning. You finally heard the story from the perspective of the illusive and distinguished gentleman known as Nicholas Cohen. Now you know what caused him to flee his homeland. Now you know that he did actually kill someone, but that it wasn't murder. Now you know what happened with his brothers that tore the family apart.

By the way, I'm cracking up that *Billionaire's Sons* is currently touted as the final book in the series because I've now started several more stories! The first to be available is *Honorary Prince*.

Remember Alex, Jr. from *Billionaire Crown Prince*? *Honorary Prince* is a little side story about the summer after high school when he and Ellen were pushing through the challenges of falling in love. They work through his spinal cord injury, the devasting effects from PTSD, guilt for his past sins, and the new knowledge he has that there is a God and remembering things from his near-death-experience.

Below is a link for you to check out Honorary Prince. I'm going back to writing.

God bless you, my friends. Stay safe! -*Julie L. Spencer*

<u>Continue reading the Royal Family Saga: Honorary Prince.</u>

<u>Would you rather read something completely new? Check out Senator's Son, a spinoff story featuring Hazel Cohen-Sayid's twin brother, Mateo Cohen, son of Senator Alejandro Cohen!</u>

Honorary Prince

Continue reading the Royal Family Saga: Honorary Prince.

An hour ago, God didn't exist. And now, God had always exist-ed. Alex had merely forgotten.

As quickly as he had this perfect recollection, all his past sins were placed before him for every peaceful being to observe. For God to observe.

Follow Alex, Jr.'s journey from a rebellious playboy through his tragic car accident when he has a near-death experience, which he calls a journey to paradise, and claims to have been in the presence of God.

Witness his transformation dedicating his life to God and speaking out against teen drinking.

Watch him fall in love with Ellen, struggle to maintain the standards God expects of him, and attempt to heal his body and heart.

Note: Honorary Prince includes teen drinking, extensive discussions about prayer, God, and repentance after committing teenage promiscuity, and brief partial nudity without descriptions. The first half of the book includes multiple bonus chapters from other books in the series.

Continue reading the Royal Family Saga: Honorary Prince.

<u>Would you rather read something completely new? Check out Senator's Son, a spinoff story featuring Hazel Cohen-Sayid's twin brother, Mateo Cohen, son of Senator Alejandro Cohen!</u>

About Author Julie Spencer

Julie is a bestselling multi-genre author who writes under three pen names. Her young adult sports romance have a little less spice and little more sweet-n-innocent. As Julie Spencer and Julie L. Spencer, she writes books with more serious subjects and maybe some religion thrown in.

Her more controversial books can be found under the new pen name J.L. Spencer. These books come with a content warning and may contain a little more heat, spice, and perhaps a few discussions about or trips to the main characters' bedrooms.

All of her stories include snarky, flawed characters, and romantic twists and turns. Julie believes we can change the world one story at a time.

www.AuthorJulieSpencer.com

All's Fair in Love and Sports Series

Take Me to the Winter Games

Meet Me at the Summer Games

Ride the Halfpipe with Me

Pass Me the Ball

Catching Waves with You

Strike Three, You're Mine

Meet Me at Half Court

Cheer for Me

Basketballs and Mistletoe

Running to You

Matching You with Love
(with co-author Audi Lynn Anderson)

All's Fair in Love and Sports Collection

Prince of Israel Series on Kindle Vella

First Prince of Israel

(Prequel to the Prince of Israel Series)

Royal Family Saga Series

Billionaire Crown Prince

Billionaire Hero

Billionaire Professors (The Geek Twins)

Billionaire's Brother

Billionaire's Sons

Honorary Prince

Royal Family Saga Special Editions

Royal Family Saga Volume I

Royal Family Saga Volume II

Royal Family Saga Volume III

Love Letters Series

Who Wants to Marry a Mormon Girl?

Who Wants to Marry a Billionaire Gamer?

Christian Romance

The Cove

The Farmer's Daughter

The Man in the Yellow Jaguar

The Refusal

Rock Star Redemption Series

Almost a Rock Star

Billionaire Rock Star

International Rock Star

Fallen Rock Star

Forever a Rock Star

Rock Star Redemption Series – Complete Collection

Opening Act: Buxton Peak Meets Infusion Deep

Opening Act: Infusion Deep Meets Buxton Peak
(with co-author Lara Wynter)

Julie writes some more controversial books under the pen name J.L. Spencer
These books may contain heat, spice, and perhaps a few discussions about or trips to the main characters' bedrooms.
Here is a list if you'd like to check them out:

Road Trip

Combustion

A Million Bucks

Hidden Swan

She's Not My Sister

Nonfiction

Writing Romance Is Not About Sex... or Is It? How Far Is Too Far in Clean Romance?

How to Outline a Romance Novel – Fiction Writing Skills for Romance Authors

How to Write a Romantic Subplot – How to Add Romance to Other Plot Structures

Listen to audiobooks by Julie L. Spencer

All's Fair in Love and Sports Series

<u>Running to You</u>

<u>Meet Me at Half Court</u>

<u>Pass Me the Ball</u>

<u>Basketballs and Mistletoe</u>

<u>Strike Three, You're Mine</u>

Social Issues

<u>Combustion</u>

Royal Family Saga

<u>Billionaire Crown Prince</u>

Billionaire Hero

Love Letters Series

Who Wants to Marry a Mormon Girl?

Who Wants to Marry a Billionaire Gamer?

Rock Star Redemption Series

Almost a Rock Star

Billionaire Rock Star

International Rock Star

Fallen Rock Star

Forever a Rock Star

Rock Star Redemption Series Complete Collection

Christian Romance

<u>The Cove</u>

<u>The Man in the Yellow Jaguar</u>

www.ingramcontent.com/pod-product-compliance
Lightning Source LLC
Chambersburg PA
CBHW071103250626
47159CB00002B/572